It Started with a Glance

Cover Illustration: Blue Water Books

Interior Design: Mountain Heights Publishing

Author website: www.megeaston.com

Nestled Hollow Romance

Coming Home to the Top of Main Street

Second Chance on the Corner of Main Street

Christmas at the End of Main Street

More than Friends in the Middle of Main Street

Love Again at the Heart of Main Street

More than Enemies on the Bridge of Main Street

The Royal Palm Resort

A Kiss at Midsummer

A Kiss at Christmas

How to Not Fall

How to Not Fall for the Guy Next Door

How to Not Fall for the Wrong Guy

How to Not Fall for Your Best Friend

How to Not Fall for Your Ex

A Mountain Springs Christmas

The Christmas Pact

The Christmas Bet

Love Started

It Started with a Sunset

It Started with a Note

It Started with a Glance

Coming Home to Silver Leaf Falls

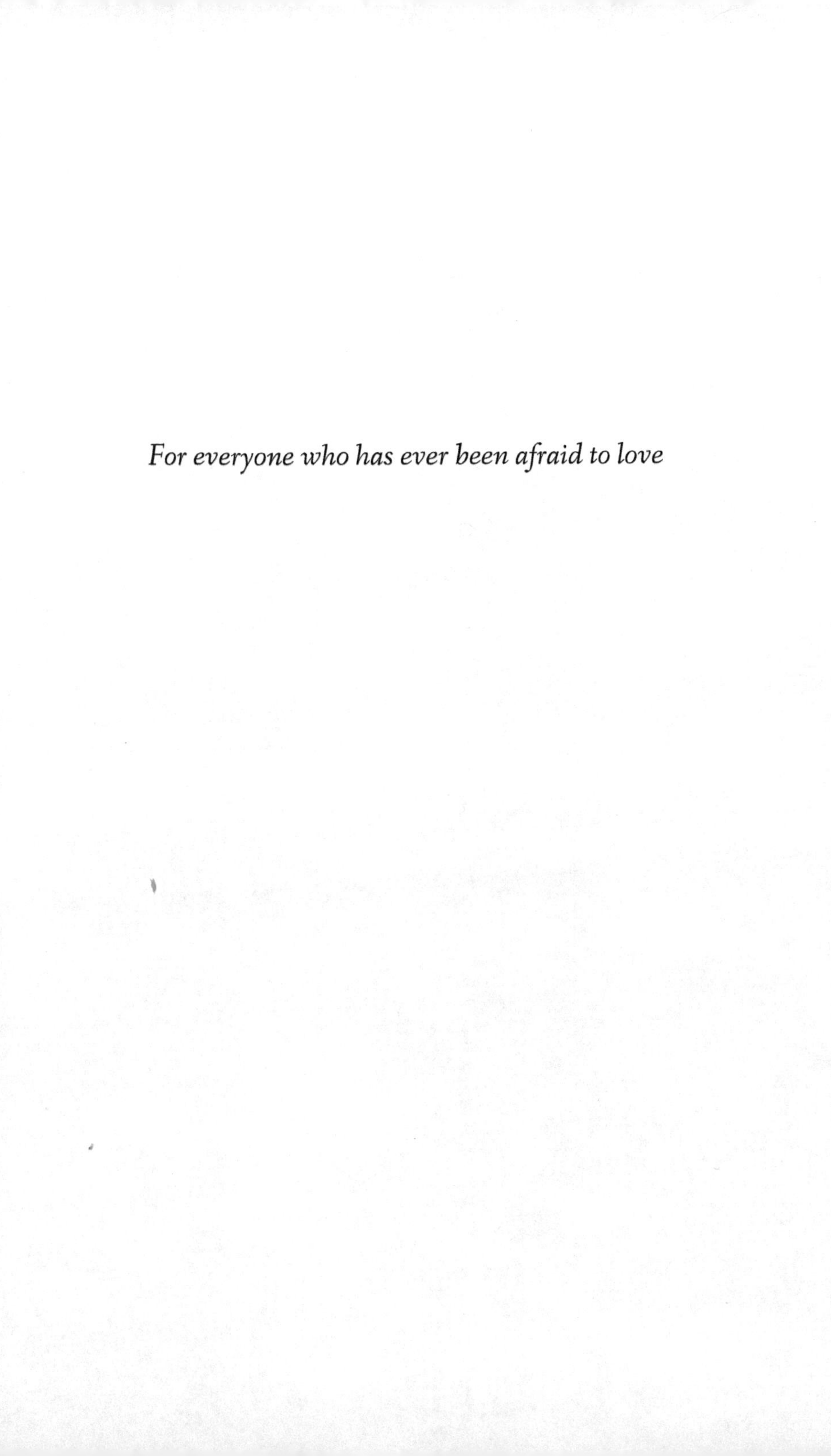

For everyone who has ever been afraid to love

It Started with a Glance

It Started with a Glance

MEG EASTON

IT STARTED WITH A GLANCE

Chapter One

ELLE

Elle's mom had slept with Elle's rock star dad in the hopes that Elle would inherit his magical voice.

Elle hadn't.

Normally, she didn't care. Right now, though, as she stood on stage in front of a group of high school students, microphone in its stand, the karaoke screen staring at her, it felt kind of unfortunate that she hadn't.

Her mom had also slept with the rock star because of his great business sense (genes she'd also hoped Elle would get) and his "buns of steel." All Elle could claim of his at that moment was his ability to make bad decisions. Like this one.

She turned to her friend and coworker, Summer Graham, who stood next to her on the stage and looked much happier to be on the verge of performing a currently unbeknownst song to them than she was. "I can't believe I let you talk me into this."

Summer laughed. "Remember last year when we were running this event and you said, and I quote, 'Karaoke is more fun to watch when the people *aren't* good singers.'"

"That didn't mean that I wanted to be the 'not good' singer." Elle's dad's voice was like the thrumming of a harp. Elle's was more like a hippo playing the violin for the first time.

Elle ran three big events at Lake Baldwin State University each year. The Ambassadors Weekend in the spring, the Ambassadors Retreat later in the summer, and the one she was currently at—the State Leadership Academy.

This one was a full nine days long—the biggest event all year—and tonight was their final night. This group of seventy kids, all seventeen-year-olds who just finished their junior year of high school and would start their final year in the fall, were always amazing teens with bright futures. They had to be to even get selected to attend.

There were quite a few in every group who were very musical, but even more so this year. She'd known it from hearing them sing together all week at every chance they got. They'd riff off one another, or someone would pull out a guitar, or they'd find a piano in a random room in the student center and start playing.

And now she was going to be singing in front of them. Sixty-six of them hooted in the audience, trying to hype up Elle and her coworkers for their performance, while the remaining four of the seventy students spent an excruciating amount of time huddled around the karaoke songbook. Deciding her fate, essentially.

"It'll be fine," Summer said. "We've all got each other's back."

Elle turned to look at the four coworkers on stage with her. She was glad that they always joined her each year for the final night of this event because it was definitely better that they were in this together. She knew Everett could sing pretty well because he'd hopped up on stage with a group of kids last year and belted out *Livin' on a Prayer*. "Pavani, Brock, do either of you sing?"

"Only in the shower," Brock said, looking as uncomfortable with someone else choosing a karaoke song for them as she was.

Pavani, whose baby bump was finally looking unquestionably like a baby bump, shook her head. "I mean, sometimes. But even my dog starts complaining when I try."

That actually made Elle feel better. Maybe their discordant voices would somehow come together in a way that wouldn't sound like a train crashing into a building during a lightning storm.

"I've got it!" called out Tucker, one of the first kids whose name she had memorized at their opening event eight and a half days ago. "*I Want to Show the World What We're Made of.*"

Summer let out a laugh that was half-snort until she put a fist up to her mouth to cover it. Summer knew who Elle's father was and that this was one of his songs; Tucker did not. Regardless, Elle thought it was a good choice. That was exactly what she was trying to do at this event—bring the best leaders in the state together to teach these kids how to be leaders and show them what they were made of.

"Let's do this," she said as she stepped up to her microphone and pulled it out of the stand. She grinned at her coworkers as each followed her lead.

The music started and the words appeared on the screen. Somehow, though, all of them except Summer managed to miss the first line. Summer was no professional, but she had the voice of birds chirping when she spoke, so her singing voice was rather beautiful. Elle joined her on the second line, but she was the only one. So there was Summer's beautiful voice and Elle's scratchy and hoarse one from having to speak loud enough to be heard by seventy teenagers at once for days on end.

It was okay. Elle had spent twelve to fifteen hours a day with these kids for eight days straight. They'd bonded, so the teens wouldn't be harsh judges. Besides, they would enjoy their leaders singing comically bad more than they would enjoy the adults nailing it, right?

Somehow, Summer and Elle starting on different lines gave the unspoken message to her other coworkers to join in one at a time. Brock's voice was hesitant but nice. Like a stream tumbling over rocks. Then Everett joined. His was rough in a good way. Like fingers scratching beard stubble. Pavani started singing on the fifth line, and Elle now understood Pavani's dog's reaction. Which was funny because Pavani's speaking voice was more like a bell choir.

Then they started singing the chorus. All five of them together. The first line, "You're good at this" was hilariously ironic, because they clearly were not. "You've got the skills, the drive, the ability to thrive" was bad, but tolerable. But by the time they got to "It'll be tough but you're tougher. You can shine, it's your time, this is your sign," they sounded like a pack of monkeys playing drums made of overturned pots and pans. And her voice wasn't helping matters.

She missed the next line, she was laughing so hard. Yeah, she really hadn't gotten her dad's voice. And since this event was the biggest, most involved event she ran all year, it came with a lot of stress over the previous few weeks. Which meant far too many donuts consumed and far too few trips to the gym lately, so she couldn't exactly claim the "buns of steel" part, either.

Her laughter must've been contagious because the others were struggling to continue singing over their own laughing. So Elle held the microphone out toward the crowd of cheering teenagers, who took over the singing as she just bobbed her head to the music. Clearly, the audience was all living on the high of coming to the last night of an intensive leadership conference with all the people they'd gotten so close to.

Then Elle brought the mike back to her mouth and she, her coworkers, and all seventy kids sang the last line together. "Together we'll shine; together we're strong, together we'll sing our victory song," and it sounded great. Or maybe it was just so much enthusiasm in one place that was so ear-pleasing.

It must've been for everyone else, too, because as the last notes of the song faded away, the cheer from the group sounded like it came from a group four times its size. Elle breathed heavily as she grinned right along with the other four she shared the stage with.

As they stepped aside for a trio of kids eager to sing and made their way to their seats, the image of Declan Davenport standing on stage popped into Elle's mind. Probably because Declan's assistant had emailed her earlier in the day to ask a couple of questions about her upcoming interview with Declan.

From seeing his YouTube science videos, Elle knew Declan had a speaking voice like chocolate poured over strawberries. Whether he could sing or not, the man could've just gotten up on stage and spoken the words of the song with no tune at all and slayed karaoke while this crowd went wild.

But then one of the girls in the audience would've gone up to him with stars in her eyes, her hands clasped over her heart, and bravely shared something personal. And Declan would walk away, dismissing her and breaking her heart. Because that was how celebrities were.

She was going to have to steel herself for this interview. And pray that it'd be short. For the other alumni interviews she had conducted for the college's magazine to help attract new students to their school, she'd gotten fairly personal about her own life. And then they would open up about themselves.

But she would have to do Declan Davenport's interview differently. She planned to be closed off and not share anything personal at all. In her experience, celebrities didn't care about personal stuff anyway, so sharing meant awkwardness at best, heartbreak at worst. And she wasn't looking for anything in that range. She would just have to get whatever she could from him quickly and if she had any additional questions later, she would ask his assistant.

When the last of the groups finished with karaoke, Elle went back up onstage and grabbed the microphone, grateful to have it with her voice protesting its overuse. Despite the exhaustion, she was the only one from the Welcome Center who'd been with these kids through the entirety of the State Leadership Academy, which made her the saddest to see it come to an end.

"Okay, everyone, it's time to head back to the dorms. Now, I know that we've had a whirlwind eight days and you probably want to stay up on your last night here, but don't stay up *too* late. Listen to your advisors when they suggest lights out. You won't want to miss the breakfast buffet we'll have waiting in this room for you at nine a.m., and you definitely won't want to miss the awards ceremony we'll have right after."

She stepped off the stage and met them at the door. As the last of them fist-bumped, high-fived, hugged, and waved to her on their way out, Elle turned to her coworkers. "I'm going to miss this group." Some of them would go to school here in just over a year—they all got scholarships just by attending this event. Some would apply to be ambassadors and she'd see them again at the Ambassador Weekend in March. Some would go their separate ways and she'd never see them again.

Everett nodded. "They were a good group."

The five of them walked out of the building into the twilight and toward the employee parking lot. Brock and Summer were holding hands, Pavani walked with a hand resting lightly on the side of her stomach, and Everett had quite the bounce in his step.

"Everett," Elle said, "you're looking more jaunty than usual."

He grinned and shrugged. "I just might be officially dating someone right now."

"Wow!" Pavani said. "Everett dating someone *exclusively*?"

Summer grabbed his arm. "Is it Rachelle?"

"What? No."

"Jenny?" Brock asked.

Elle shook her head. "Sandra!"

"Stop, guys. You're all so behind the times. It's Paige."

"Oh, Paige!" Pavani said. "Sometimes it's hard to keep track. I take it you're seeing her tonight?"

Everett glanced down at his watch. "Yep—we're meeting for ice cream. I've got to go. Catch you all later!"

"Well, who would've thought," Brock said as he watched Everett walk away. Then he turned back. "Summer and I have to get all our invitations ready to mail tonight, so we're going to head out."

"I am, too," Pavani said. "I told Zane that I was craving Kesar Peda, and he texted to say that he made some tonight. Isn't that the sweetest? My mouth is watering just thinking about it."

As the others dispersed to their cars, Elle waved goodbye and opened her door before climbing in. Maybe it was because everyone else was leaving to be with someone they were either married to, about to be married to, or in a relationship with, but she suddenly felt very alone heading to her place.

Elle didn't even have a roommate anymore. She'd shared her last apartment with Camilla, her roommate of four years, until Camilla's wedding six months ago. Upon the engagement and announcement that Camilla would be moving to Chicago, Elle had taken the wedding date as a countdown to buy her own place.

And she had. She bought the cutest condo on the north side of town that she loved to pieces. She was so freaking proud of herself for buying it all on her own, too. She had officially been an adult for a decade now, but she had never felt more adult than while sitting in the title office half a year ago, signing the billion papers that made the condo hers.

Every night she arrived home, she stepped over the threshold and breathed in deeply, letting herself feel the joy and excitement and sense of accomplishment all over again.

And most of the time, she could even manage to do it while completely ignoring that small bit of her that whispered, *But you're so alone here.* She had good friends— many of whom she worked with. Camilla might be married and living in Illinois now, but they still texted and talked to each other on the phone almost daily. And she had a brother, a stepdad, and a mom who was basically a best friend. She was far from alone.

And she'd just spent eight days connecting with dozens of teenagers, helping them to discover their inner leaders. She also worked with the Sterling Scholars at LBSU. She knew all the staff in the Admissions and Financial Aid departments. She was networking with a lot of people through her monthly alumni articles. Summer helped her manage all fifty of the college's student ambassadors. It wasn't like Elle was lacking connections with people in her life.

She pulled into her empty driveway. Was it that bad if she lacked the one connection in her life that felt most important?

No, she decided. She had plenty of others that more than made up for that deficit.

Chapter Two

DECLAN

*D*eclan Davenport swiveled his chair, twisting from where he had been deep in research at his main desk to the desk behind him. The only thing sitting on it was a box that held an open-topped Plexiglas container of soil and worms, the outer box keeping out the light.

He opened the flap and looked in at the little guys. There were ten worms and because he kept things dark, they were often visible at the edges of the container. He'd been studying them for the past week, and he knew them well enough to name them and recognize them by sight.

"Well, hello, Doug. It's nice to see you again. I see that you were off growing during that two days of hiding." He grabbed his notebook from the desk behind him and started taking notes about everything he was seeing, including the moisture in the soil. He needed to take some samples for more evaluation.

The red lights in all four corners of the room flashed and he sat up straight in surprise. He blinked a few times, feeling like he was coming out of a deep sleep. Could it be five minutes to four o'clock already? He quickly jotted down notes of everything that had been going through his head so he wouldn't forget any of it, hoping he'd be able to pick up tomorrow right where he'd left off.

He glanced at the clock on his desk that sat right between two framed pictures—one of Declan with the group of kids that had been part of his first visit to an elementary school to talk about science three years ago, and one of his mom, stepdad, two younger brothers and him—the last family picture they'd taken before his mom passed away. One minute until four.

Declan's assistant, Mato, had installed the lights shortly after he'd hired the man. Partly because when Declan got deep into research, the real world faded away and clocks and deadlines and responsibilities ceased to exist. And partly because Mato had quickly found out that Declan didn't notice texts while he was working and phone calls and "popping his head in" always jarred Declan to the point that he lost focus.

But the lights? The lights had been a brilliant idea. They were just jarring enough to get him to wrap things up. He finished jotting down the last of his notes, closed the flap to the worms' habitat, and shut his laptop.

Mato had been a godsend. Before him, Declan was always missing things or being late simply because he forgot about the outside world when he was focused. He'd be deep down in a research rabbit hole without realizing any time had passed. His science education business never would've taken off without Mato.

He stood up and walked to the door, mentally leaving all the science in the room behind him, and went out to the main area of the offices he had built right into his home —the area he and his team called the Beehive. He smiled, as he did every time he saw his team. It was because of them that magic happened.

His outreach specialist, Halona, stood at one end of the Ping-Pong table in the main area, her long, dark braid halfway down her back, paddle in hand. She was a no-nonsense mom of three teenagers and fierce enough to stand up to anyone, yet gentle enough to wrap her arms around a crying child.

And she was facing off against his ads manager and merchandising expert, Jen. Jen and her husband were the outdoorsy, sports-playing, always-tanned type. She usually came to work with her blonde hair in a ponytail and wearing athletic clothes, like she wanted to be ready just in case she came across a soccer game that needed her while she grabbed a bite to eat for lunch. Her competitiveness made her the perfect ads manager and her zeal for life made her great at running their social media.

His video editor and tech expert, Sam, a guy in his mid-twenties with curly brown hair, pale skin, and stylish glasses lounged back on the couch, his feet crossed on the coffee table. He tossed a smaller-than-regulation-sized basketball into the air and caught it.

And of course, there was Mato. Instead of playing or relaxing, he sat at the round table in the center of the room, a stack of papers and his tablet on the table in front of him, looking at something on the tablet. Declan was pretty sure that Mato's name meant "bear" in Sioux, and the man had the shoulders, arms, and brown skin reminiscent of a bear. He was clean-shaven, though, and had his hair pulled back nice and neat like usual. His "bear" heart was more teddy than grizzly. The man smiled broadly at Declan.

"Catch," Sam said as he threw the basketball to Declan. He caught it just as Jen shouted, "Yes!" She pumped both arms into the air as Halona missed the ball Jen had sent in her direction. After bumping the tips of their racquets together and setting them down, the two women headed over to join the meeting at the table.

"Okay, so here's the deal," Sam told Declan as he took a seat. "We've all guessed how many baskets you can make in forty-five seconds. Whoever guessed closest gets to start the meeting."

Declan looked down at the basketball in his hands and then glanced over at the arcade-style basketball hoops before looking back at his team. He drummed his fingers on the ball. "Or maybe we should let whoever guessed the highest number—and therefore showed the most faith in my abilities—go first."

"Nice try," Halona said as she gave his shoulder a playful shove. "Now get over there and show us what you're made of!"

So he did. This was the first game he'd bought for their offices and his favorite. He'd worked through quite a few problems while taking a break to shoot baskets. As the ball dropped into the net again and again, all four of his employees counted in unison. And he hit quite the rhythm with some impressive accuracy. Forty-five seconds wasn't that long when doing most things, but he pushed himself hard enough to breathe heavily, grinning, by the time the buzzer sounded.

"Thirty-nine!" they shouted as the last ball swished through the net.

"Yes!" Mato said. "I'm first."

Declan took his seat again at the round table with the others. It was funny that his team had this tradition of coming up with different challenges to decide who went first each week. Declan didn't care who won—they all brought up stuff at this meeting that had to be discussed to keep things running smoothly.

"Okay," Mato said as he looked down at his tablet. "I have two bigger things and one, two, three smaller ones. But the thing I want to discuss most is your interview coming up with your alma mater."

"Oh, that's right," Declan said. He had a very vague recollection of Mato asking him if he would do something for the Lake Baldwin State University magazine a couple of months ago. "When is that, again?"

"Next week. I've been finalizing things with the interviewer, but I want to propose a change."

Declan raised an eyebrow.

"I think we should ask if she'll do a *Twenty-four Hours in the Life of Declan Davenport* kind of gig."

"And I think it should be over the phone." It was almost laughable that Mato thought he'd be down for something like that. "You know I don't like personal things."

"I do, but I think that this will be good. You'll open up in the interview more if it's in person. And if it's a full-day interview, it'll give her a better chance to see what you do here. Much more than talking with her for thirty minutes or an hour will do."

Halona raised a shoulder in a half-shrug. "You've got some die-hard science fans on your channel, but you've also got a lot of people interested in science who wouldn't have been otherwise, and they are interested because of you. I think that the more you can make a connection with them, the more people will be invested in you and what you're saying. They'll want to learn more, and isn't that your goal anyway? To help people get more excited about science? It especially fits with your goals to take your Declan Talks Science Kids Camp nationwide."

Declan understood the concept. He did. Mato was always drilling into him that people watched a single video because of the hook or because they liked his voice. They subscribed and watched them all because they liked *him*.

And he had big plans for his Declan Talks Science Kids Camp. Right now it was based in South Dakota, but to pull off those big plans, it needed to be nationwide. That would take a lot more support and sponsorships to pull off. The fact that he now had his doctorate helped to give him the clout he needed, but Mato and Halona had been trying to convince him that letting viewers know who he really was mattered more. That it was the vehicle to get him the support and partnerships that he needed.

But for Declan, it was only about the science. In theory, he understood the rest, but in reality, he just didn't get it. Why did they have to know him to connect to science? "If the interview is that long, the interviewer will get too personal."

Jen cocked her head to the side and asked, "Is it so bad to open up and let someone in?"

Mato continued as if Jen hadn't said anything, probably because he guessed that Declan didn't want to answer her question, which he didn't. But her question still stuck in his mind as Mato talked. "The interviewer's name is Elle Markle. And if she does push too hard, then don't answer. It's just twenty-four hours. We're not asking her to follow you around for a year and get access to your thoughts."

"Besides, it's a small-town college magazine," Halona added. "They don't have a super large audience, so there won't be a ton of people who'll see it. It might be a great way for you to get more comfortable sharing a bit more about yourself with a small audience rather than a large one."

"So how would this even work? Is she supposed to watch me stare at my computer screen for a good portion of the day? Watch me while I sleep at night?"

Jen chuckled. "A video of you sleeping would probably still get a million vie—"

"No," Mato said, cutting Jen off. "Not of you sleeping." And that was why he paid Mato the big bucks. He never entertained thoughts like that. "People like to see the flashy parts of a celebrity's life. Think of all the reality TV shows out there where they feature celebrities in their own homes."

"I'm not a celebrity."

Sam snort-laughed.

"I'm *not*," he reiterated.

Sam held up his hands. "Okay, you're not."

"To most people, you are," Mato said. "We want to show the real, human stuff, but also the flashy stuff."

"What do I have in my life that's flashy?"

"From what I've seen," Halona said, "when people see someone on a YouTube video, they assume one of two things. Either that it's a one-man show—just a guy with a camera in his garage, filming after he gets home from work in the evenings or on the weekends. Or they think of you as a big-time celebrity and that you have handlers—people who plan everything out for you and you just show up to do your thing, easy peasy, no effort from you."

Mato nodded. "You may have started as that guy filming in your garage, or, actually, at your kitchen table, since you didn't have a garage back then, but it's not how things are now and viewers know it."

"You want to know what's 'flashy?'" Jen asked. "I can tell you from a social media standpoint that it's things like having employees." She ticked off on her fingers. "Having our offices in a section of your home. Having a big fan base."

"Having high-quality editing," Sam said, and Jen ticked off another finger. "Having an area whose sole purpose is filming."

"And having famous people reach out to you to collaborate," Mato added. "Running a business that is solely dependent on the face of one person. Now, obviously, the most flashy parts are probably when you're working with kids or teaming up with other celebrities. But I don't think that would be best for the interview, because events with kids take all day and the collaborations with other celebrities aren't part of your normal schedule. I think we should show the interviewer the more typical parts."

He handed Declan a piece of paper. "Here's a schedule for the day that I'm proposing."

Declan glanced down at it and spotted a few things—filming, research, team meeting.

"Most people don't understand that you're the boss," Halona said, "and you're running your own company. We can show them what it's really like. I think people will find it fascinating. Of course, this isn't a video interview, but if you like how it goes, we could do something similar to post on your channel. A pulling back of the curtains."

"I agree that people will find it interesting," Jen said.

Mato nodded. "And it's on a small scale. It'll give you a chance to see how you feel about opening up a bit."

Declan still didn't like it. He stared down at the paper just to give his eyes a place to land—not that he was seeing any of the words on it. Why did people need to know more about him? His personal life had nothing to do with science.

"I think it fits with your overall goals," Mato said meaningfully.

Declan met his eyes and knew exactly what he meant

—that Declan's mom would approve and this was one way Declan could honor the sacrifices that she'd made for him.

But Mato didn't say the words because he knew Declan well. He understood that it was a big driving force for Declan on its own. That he internalized his responsibility to honor his mom all the time without being reminded of it. And Mato also knew how much it bugged Declan when someone used his mom as a way to get him to agree to something . . . even if it *was* the best way to get him to agree to something.

Not bringing it up or using it as a tool was also why he paid Mato the big bucks.

Declan looked back down at the schedule and a few more words jumped out. *Editing. Social media.* Maybe he could do this. His mom had always seemed to know that he had the potential to reach a lot of people. He liked to think that she was watching him from heaven and that she was proud of him. She would probably also agree that he needed to open up a bit more. To let people connect with him.

He took a deep breath. "I don't love the idea. But I'm willing to do it, as long as it doesn't get super personal." He pointed a finger at Mato and then to everyone. "But I'm not cooking breakfast for the interviewer the morning after she stays over. That's *our* thing—I'm not okay with letting a stranger into that tradition."

A smile spread across Mato's face and he gave a nod.

"Fair enough. I'll reach out to the interviewer to see if she's game for a change in plans, and I'll make sure we have pastries and coffee on hand that morning."

Declan had no problem being decisive in his business. But being decisive didn't mean he was always right, and he hoped that this decision, in particular, wasn't wrong.

Chapter Three

ELLE

*E*lle walked down the hall of the Student Center at LBSU toward the Welcome Center, where she worked, adding some thoughts to her notes app that had occurred to her on the drive there. She'd gotten all seventy of the State Leadership Academy kids off yesterday morning after a fun closing ceremony, so it was time to focus on the next thing.

Summertime might be a slow time of year for most people in the Welcome Center and the Admissions departments, but it wasn't for her. Not that any time of the year was slower for her. Elle was over events, and events happened year-round. Now that she was done with the State Leadership Academy, she needed to turn her focus to the ambassador's retreat. Luckily, it was fun and the planning was not nearly as taxing. She felt the weight of the State Leadership Academy lifted from her shoulders as she crossed the Welcome Center lobby toward the offices.

Elle's coworker, Summer, was walking into her office when she spotted Elle. "Oh, good, you're here." She grabbed her metal water bottle and clinked her rings against it, the Welcome Center's own personal call to gather. Time to head to Aquamoose Crossing, LBSU's convenience store inside the Student Center, to get ice water, soda, or coffee at the start of the day.

Which meant that Elle was the last person to arrive this morning. With as many hours as she'd put in over the past nine days, she didn't feel the teeniest bit bad about that. She chuckled as Brock came out of his office. He used to hate the sound of Summer's rings clanking against the metal, but then he'd fallen in love with her. Based on the look on his face, the sound was more like a heavenly choir of angels now beckoning him to join.

As they walked in a big group to Aquamoose Crossing, Tess, Elle's boss, walked next to her. "I got all the feedback forms from both the students and the business leaders you brought in to speak at SLA." She'd always loved Tess's voice. Powerful but calming. Like the wind through aspen trees.

"Oh, yeah?" Getting those feedback forms was one of Elle's favorite parts. The reward for a job well done.

"We'll go through all of them in our meeting, of course, but what I've seen so far has been glowing."

Elle was pretty sure that she was glowing just hearing that. Everyone in the Welcome Center helped with the event, but it was hers. She was responsible for it. Getting praise from others felt pretty incredible.

Summer was at the front of the group and turned to walk backward so she could face them all. "Do you all have your plus ones for Brock's and my wedding?"

"I've got my plus one-and-a-half!" Pavani said, putting a hand on her baby bump.

Everyone else started saying whether they had dates (or built-in dates, for those who were married or engaged). When Summer's eyes met Elle's, Elle said, "I will by then. Don't worry." But she was a little bit worried. She hadn't gone on a date in a while where she'd liked the guy enough to go out again, let alone a date for a wedding. But she'd find someone.

Just as they were walking back to the offices, Elle felt a text come in and glanced at her watch. It was from Declan Davenport's assistant, Mato, saying that he was driving up from Sioux Falls and wanted to know if he could stop by her house after work to bring over some papers for her to sign. That was weird. This was her fourth interview of LBSU alumni for the university's paper, and it was officially the first to have paperwork to sign.

Maybe it was because she'd agreed to a twenty-four-hour thing. Or maybe it was just because her interviewee was a celebrity this time. The other alumni that she'd interviewed had been a business owner, a historian, and a software developer.

She had agreed to change the interview to a twenty-four-hour deal when Mato had called her to pitch the idea, but she'd been second-guessing her decision ever since. He had explained that Declan didn't open up to people quickly and he thought the interview would be more successful and insightful if it were for a longer period of time than usual.

She understood that. And she knew that her article would be more compelling if the interview was longer. But she didn't understand how twenty-four-hours would be better than just spending the daytime part of the day with him.

When she'd asked Mato, he'd said, "Imagine how much more interesting an article with a title that included the words 'twenty-four-hours in the life of Declan Davenport' is than simply stating it was an interview with him. It would draw in more readers."

That was a good point. Then he'd said that it was easier to catch people more as they truly were when it was a full twenty-four hours. People could act a certain way for a short period, but you really got to know who they were if you spent a full day and night with them. He also pointed out that if she was doing a full-day interview, she wouldn't have to worry about making the forty-five-minute drive back to Lake Baldwin late at night or staying at a hotel in Sioux Falls.

"And," he'd added, "Declan has a huge fan base but doesn't let viewers in. You'd be offering your readers information they've been hungering for."

It had all sounded way too beneficial for her, so she'd asked, "So, what's in it for you? Or for Declan?"

"As much as Declan isn't thrilled about the idea, he's willing to do it, and I think it's exactly what he needs."

He hadn't elaborated and she didn't need him to. The Welcome Center was always looking for ways to reach students and give them a reason to come visit their university to see if it might be the perfect fit. They didn't often get an opportunity like interviewing someone as famous as Declan, and she wanted to make the most of it.

After work, she pulled into her garage and pushed the button to shut the door. Then she got out of her car and breathed in deeply, smiling. Not that her garage smelled much like a garage—the only thing in it was her car. Come to think of it, she didn't know what kinds of things made a garage have a "garage smell." What did people typically keep in them? She'd never had one to know. But she smiled because it smelled like a garage *she owned*.

She passed through the door into the kitchen, hung her keys on the hook, and took a look around. She wanted to believe that she was the type of person who had a clean house all the time, but the evidence today called her out. And she didn't even have a roommate to blame any of the mess on. Or to pick up the slack, sadly.

She'd spent pretty much every waking moment during the nine days of the State Leadership Academy with the teens, so she'd done zero house cleaning. Mato was going to be there soon. She raced to put the dishes that were on the counter and the table into the sink, then glanced at her living room. *Crap.*

Yesterday, after the closing ceremonies of the event ended and she'd finally made it back to her condo, she'd warmed up leftover Thai food, ate dinner on the couch while watching TV, then curled up in a blanket and had fallen asleep right there. Her dishes and the empty box of masaman curry were still on the coffee table and the blanket was still in a heap on the couch. Not to mention evidence of exhausted living everywhere. She raced to the coffee table to grab the dishes but didn't quite make it before a knock sounded at her door.

The man was already there? He must've been in the car right behind her as she pulled onto her street! She grabbed the jacket she'd left on the back of the couch and the pair of socks on the floor and tossed them all into her bedroom, not caring where they landed. Then she pulled that door shut and took a deep breath before opening the front door.

"Hello," the man said, a big smile on his face as he held

out his hand to shake hers. Elle had talked to him on the phone a couple of times, so she immediately recognized the voice. On the smooth-gravelly scale, it leaned toward gravelly but in an ear-pleasing way. Like rocks tumbling down a stream.

But the picture she'd had in her mind to go with the voice and the texts and emails was nothing like the man at her door. She'd known he was a good guy from their interactions, but she'd imagined someone kind of average in height and weight, young but with a slightly receding hairline. Maybe wearing a dress shirt and tie and having the look of someone who was always organized and always stressed.

Mato was probably forty, though, with a full head of hair pulled back into a short braid at the nape of his neck. He had more of a look of someone who was kind and happy. And instead of a white shirt and tie, he wore a western shirt tucked in, dark-wash jeans, and rugged brown leather shoes. Instead of looking like he spent all day at a desk, he had a stocky build with big shoulder and arm muscles. Not showy muscles, though. More like they came from helping his kids build a tree house or the neighbor build a deck. She immediately liked the man.

She invited him in, apologized for the mess, and then led him through the living room to the kitchen.

"Thank you for your willingness to let me come over and for signing these papers. I apologize that I couldn't get here early enough in the day to bring them to your office."

"It's no problem," Elle said, not knowing what she was even supposed to sign, but she sat at the table. It seemed like the place to sign papers. Mato pulled out a chair and sat down too, placing his portfolio on the table. He didn't open it, though—he just met Elle's eyes and told her how excited the entire team was that she agreed to do a twenty-four-hour interview.

It wasn't lost on her that he said the team was excited, not that Declan was.

They chatted for a few minutes. Then he tapped two fingers on the portfolio and said, "There are just a few things we need to discuss." He opened the folder and pulled out a couple of pieces of paper. "Now, obviously, Declan doesn't want his address or other personal information spread across the Internet. So I'll need you to agree not to share it, photos of the outside of his house, street signs near his house, or anything else identifying where he lives."

Okay, that was totally understandable.

"He also doesn't want anything published about his dad or where he grew up."

That was. . . not totally understandable. Out of all the questions she could ask him, why were those an issue for him? She suddenly wondered if maybe his dad was famous too and just as secretive about where he lived. Or maybe Declan was embarrassed about who his dad was? Maybe it hadn't been the wisest move on Mato's part to even bring it up, because she might not have ever wondered about either of those things, but now she *really* wanted to know.

"You are welcome to audio record any part of your interview with Declan, but that recording is for your use only—no parts of the recording can be posted online or sent to anyone else."

Elle nodded. She had no problem with that.

Mato stood and slid the papers just in front of her. "So, I'll just need you to sign this non-disclosure agreement. There are just a few other minor things listed right here, as well."

"You want me to sign an NDA?"

Mato nodded. "Part of my job is to protect Declan, and this is a necessary part."

Her mind suddenly flashed back to when she was a nine-year-old girl, desperately wanting a relationship with her dad and coming home to find her mom sitting at their kitchen table with her dad's lawyer standing next to her. A pen was in her hand and she was signing a different NDA, preventing her from saying anything about Elle's dad being her dad.

Elle stood so quickly that her chair scraped across the floor behind her, her breaths coming fast. Her reaction was immediate and intense and surprised even her.

"Is everything okay, Miss Markle?"

Elle tried to calm her breathing and nodded. The reaction wasn't even logical—the man stood next to the table and she sat with an NDA in front of her, sure, but everything else about this moment was completely different.

But understanding the reaction wasn't logical didn't remove the almost overpowering urge to call everything off. Memories of her dad were a big part of the reason why she hadn't wanted to interview Declan in the first place, and this just added fuel to an already burning fire. *Not. Logical,* she told herself in a firm voice.

"I'm fine," she said and sat back down. "I'm sorry."

Because it was fine. It *was*. This was not the same.

For starters, there was a huge difference between Mato and her father's attorney. The attorney wore a suit. Not that she was against suits—she was very much for a man in a nice suit. But the attorney's suit had been worn to intimidate. Whereas Mato looked like if she said she was cold, he'd take off the shirt he was currently wearing and hand it to her. Her dad's attorney had seemed to purposefully wear an expression that brought the cold.

From everything she had been able to glean from very limited interactions with both Mato and her father's attorney, Mato seemed like a genuinely good guy and the attorney had not. She hadn't met her dad or Declan before meeting the people they had chosen to represent them, but if she had to judge either one by who they'd hired, she judged Declan *much* less harshly.

And the fact that Mato seemed loyal to Declan might have been the only thing keeping her from calling it off. So she let her logical brain take the wheel and signed the NDA.

"On a personal note," Mato said, "I just thought I should pass along that Declan isn't thrilled about being interviewed. If he's a little terse, especially at first, I want you to know that it's not about you. He's just not too keen on sharing personal information."

Elle let out a chuckle in a sharp breath. "Oh, don't worry—I don't have any interest in things getting personal, either. I have limited experience with celebrities, but what I do have... well, let's just say that *getting personal* hasn't had positive results."

Mato studied her for a long moment before giving a single nod. The moment they'd finished and Mato had gathered his papers and left, Elle picked up her phone and called her mom. Even though she'd chosen to act logically, she was still feeling a bit rattled and needed to talk.

"Hi, Elle-belle!"

"Hi, Mom. What are you up to?"

"I just got home from work and *ungh* I'm just trying to get *umph* the dog *oof* into the backseat of the car." She let out a big breath in a huff. "I think he knows we're going to the V-E-T." Elle heard the car door shut and another open. "What's up, sweetie? You sound like... something's up."

Maybe she shouldn't be telling her mom this. But she told her mom everything. "I'm interviewing Declan Davenport for the LBSU magazine, and his assistant just came over to have me sign an NDA. I just had a bit of a flashback and it's... I don't know. It's just left me kind of shaken, I guess."

"Oh, honey," her mom said, and she heard her car door close and Louie's soft whining from the backseat. "Honestly, if I'd have had any idea that signing your dad's NDA back then would've caused you trauma, I never would have. I thought you felt the same way as I did. I should've asked."

"It's totally fine, Mom." Elle shook her head. She wasn't looking to make her mom feel bad about it. "I know you did what you thought was right and always had my best interests at heart, and I love you for it." It wasn't her mom's fault that she'd handled it so wrong. She'd been dealing with her own inner demons.

Besides, it wasn't like she could still be mad at her mom for it—her mom wasn't the same person she'd been back then. She'd grown a lot since Elle had become an adult and moved out, and somewhere along the way, they'd become friends.

"Thanks, sweetie. You know, it's too bad your brother

didn't get the lawyer genes—then he could go over that contract for you and make sure it was on the up-and-up."

For the record, Levi's dad, an actor, hadn't been an actual lawyer. He'd just played one in his most famous role. Levi hadn't gotten his dad's acting skills, either. But her brother was an artist, living in Baltimore, and made a good living at it.

"No, it's fine—it's a pretty straightforward contract. It just served as a good reminder to keep my distance when I go for that interview with Declan next week."

"Then maybe it's a good thing. Because once you hear that scrumptious voice of his with your own ears and be so close to that gorgeous face of his, he could easily catch you, hook, line, and sinker."

"Mom!"

Her mom laughed. "I'm just kidding, honey. You've got so much stronger of a will to resist than I ever had."

Elle hesitated for a moment, then said what had been weighing most heavily on her mind. "Do you think that agreeing to do a twenty-four-hour thing was a bad idea? I mean, it's kind of weird, right?"

"It's definitely weird for a regular interview. But it's not unheard of. In fact, the last time I was in Sioux Falls, I went into a Five Guys restaurant, and you know how they display on their walls magazine articles that mention them? I saw one of Ed Sheeran on the cover of Billboard magazine, eating their fries, as part of *a twenty-four-hour interview.*"

"Mom. I think that was to promote a new album or for when he launched a music label or something. It wasn't for a small-town college magazine."

"Well, Declan's assistant wouldn't have set it up if he didn't think it would be more beneficial than a regular interview."

"Yeah, I guess." She still wasn't sure, though.

"It's going to be fine. The interview will go well, you will write the greatest article LBSU has ever seen, and your boss will give you a big pile of money as a raise. Oh, and your picture on the wall as Employee of the Month. No, year. No, *decade.*"

This time, Elle laughed. And that was why she had called her mom. Her wishes for Elle were seldom within the realm of possibility, but she always dreamed big on Elle's behalf. "Thanks, Mom."

"Anytime, Elle. You keep that heart of yours safe, you hear?"

"I will."

All it was going to take if that voice of his started doing her in was to think back to her mom, sitting at the kitchen table in Elle's childhood home, signing her dad's NDA.

Chapter Four

DECLAN

eclan bent over the table next to Sam, positioning the Plexiglas container so it received optimal lighting. It contained some of the most fertile soil he'd ever seen—soil that came from his backyard. He wanted to get a few video clips taken before their team meeting and filming session. It was tricky to film the worms in such low light, but he didn't want to make them retreat from the edges of the container, either.

Jen scurried around the room, getting the rest of the space ready for filming. Every once in a while he could sense her movement stop, likely because she was taking pictures for social media. Even though he knew she was getting his backside in a lot of the pictures, he'd gotten used to it over the years.

She was setting up something on the laptop when she

picked up her phone and made a high-pitched sound. "Mato texted that he just pulled into the driveway and that the interviewer is pulling in right behind him. I'm taking a peek. Want to come? I know my office doesn't have the best view of the driveway, but I bet we can see her."

Declan shook his head without even looking up from where he and Sam worked. He would meet her soon enough. Jen hurried out of the room, probably grabbing Halona to watch with her.

Why was he nervous for the interviewer to come? He filmed two videos a week and he could guarantee each would get well over a million views. Their social media posts got millions of views on top of that. He could go on camera knowing those stats without any nerves at all.

Yet someone he hadn't met before coming to do an interview gave him a rolling stomach?

Mato said this wasn't going to get too personal, he reminded himself. It was fine. But that didn't mean he was thrilled about having her in his space. He stood up straight and rolled his shoulders, examining their setup.

"I saw Mato bringing her inside," Jen said, starting the sentence before she was even through the doorway, Halona right on her heels. "I don't know what kind of girl is your type since you never talk about it. Do you even date? But if I had to guess what kind would be your type, it's her. She's beautiful." Jen waggled her eyebrows.

Declan shook his head. "It's not going to happen. She's just here for an interview for a single article." He probably should've greeted her at the door, given her a tour of his home, and shown her to the guest room himself. But the point was to keep things impersonal, and the best way to do that was to have Mato do those things, not him.

"Say what you want, spoilsport. I'm going to the Beehive to greet her as they come in. Join me?"

Declan shook his head. "We're still setting up in here."

Halona stayed behind, quiet for a moment before saying, "You know, it'd be good for you to have a partner in life."

"A guy who gets as deep into research as I do would never make a good partner," Declan said as he squinted at the camera screen to see if things were lined up well. That wasn't the only reason he wouldn't be a good partner, but it was enough on its own.

Halona shrugged. "You might surprise yourself." Then she headed out into the Beehive.

Normally he flat-out ignored the "love" parts of his life —or the lack of them—and he intended to keep doing just that. His focus needed to be on work and his goals: to get people more connected to science. Whenever he felt like he needed more of a life than just socializing with his employees, he ignored the feeling and threw himself into more science or focused on the parts where he got to help kids.

Until the weekend, of course. That was when he went to visit his stepdad and brothers. They kept him fully connected to family and feeling grounded all week.

At least, he told himself that it was all the social life he needed. He didn't spend a lot of time thinking about whether it was or not because if he did, he'd start wondering how much fuller his life would be if he had a girlfriend. Or even a wife.

But if he thought about that, he started to worry about how much of his biological dad he might have in his DNA. And that was a subject he never wanted to think about.

"I think this will work," Sam said. "I'll do a couple of test shots and then we can look at the footage."

Mato must've just had the interviewer drop off her bag in her guest quarters because Declan could hear the two of them entering the offices. As soon as Sam got some of the footage shot, Declan stepped between the legs of the tripod to stand behind the camera and pushed the button to watch the playback. "Looks good," he said just as Mato walked into the room.

"Elle, I'd like to introduce you to Declan and Sam. And I'd like you both to meet Elle Markle."

Declan glanced up. Shock at how beautiful she was hit him, and he bumped one—or possibly two—of the legs of the tripod, sending it toppling. He scrambled to catch the camera, fumbling it and then re-catching it just as the tripod clattered to the ground. He made a less-than-graceful chuckling noise as he carefully set the camera down on the table using both hands. Sam righted the tripod, smirking, before slipping out of the room.

Declan rubbed his hand on the back of his neck, which was now on fire, and stepped out from behind the table. He held out his hand and Elle shook it. "It's nice to meet you. Sorry about that."

"Thank you for having me. I was going to tell you to go about your normal day and not make a fuss on my account, but..." She tilted her head toward the tripod.

She had a gleam in her brown eyes as she said it, and it made him smile. "We'll try to make sure fewer things come crashing down for the rest of your visit."

Now that he'd gotten past that initial glance and embarrassing fumble, he was able to take in more of Elle. She wore a stylish blazer over a fitted plum-colored t-shirt, jeans, and tan ankle boots. Her brown hair fell in waves to the middle of her back. It was a casual but nice look. Just what he hadn't realized he had hoped for. He wanted to keep things professional, but he suddenly realized how uncomfortable he would have been if she'd shown up in a suit and a tight bun.

He also realized that he'd assumed the interviewer would either be a student or an older woman. He didn't know why it hadn't occurred to him that it might be someone close to his age. Or someone so... alluring.

Alluring. That was a word he wasn't sure he'd ever

thought before, yet here he was, attracted to a woman he'd met less than two minutes ago. How had Jen guessed that this woman, Elle, was his type? He hadn't even known that he had a type. But now that he'd seen Elle, he knew it was definitely her.

Of course, he didn't actually know anything about Elle other than her looks and the fact that she worked for LBSU. Not that he had any interest in dating anyone, he quickly reminded himself.

"Okay," Mato said as he looked down at his tablet. "Just a quick overview of the schedule today—we're about to have a team meeting, which we almost always do on Monday mornings. Then we're going to film a segment, then lunch, then 'research.' Normally that means this guy closing himself off in his office to stare at a computer screen and think deep thoughts, but today it means interview questions. Then we'll finish it off with some social media. We normally don't fit all of it into a single day, but we wanted you to get a feel for what we do here."

Declan watched Elle as Mato spoke, trying to guess what was going through her mind, but he came up empty.

"We can start, though, with either Declan or me taking you on a tour of the offices and introducing you to the others."

Declan was opening his mouth to volunteer when Elle said, "It looks like Declan is busy, Mato. I can go with you." She gave Declan a polite smile, but he could guess that the fact that he hadn't bothered to stop his work to greet her gave the impression that he couldn't be bothered by her. Which was not the message he'd been trying to send at all.

The message he'd been trying to send was that he didn't want her digging into his non-professional life. Keep it professional. But maybe the impression he had inadvertently given off helped that goal anyway.

"We've got things under control here," Declan said. "I'm happy to show you around too." Apparently, he couldn't manage to keep up that impression for more than two seconds. Instead of solidifying the "can't be bothered" vibe, he was giving off the "golden retriever" vibe. Like he was up for everything.

Not that there was much to show her on this tour. The work section of his home consisted of six offices—his, Mato's, and Halona's, plus the one Jen and Sam shared. Then there was the filming room and another for storage. There were another two rooms down a small hallway that they didn't use and wouldn't until the company grew. All the offices opened into the main area—the Beehive—which was filled with couches, arcade-style games, a table, a kitchenette, and a door to the backyard since they did so much filming there. Elle had already seen most of it walking in.

Which was good, because he, Mato, and Elle didn't make it far on their tour. They arrived at the Beehive to find Jen, Sam, and Halona huddled together, each holding a Ping-Pong paddle and bouncing a ball in quiet concentration while trying to nudge the person next to them in an attempt to disrupt their rhythm.

"Today might have been a good day to draw numbers," Mato said.

"What's the fun in that?" Jen asked as she slowly moved closer to Halona with each bump of the ball on her paddle. After a few bounces, Jen bumped her hip into Halona, whose ball hit the side of her paddle, sending it careening across the room. For a moment, it looked like Halona was going to dive for it before she gave up and let the ball go.

When Sam took his eyes off his ball to see what was going on, Jen took the opportunity to bump into his shoulder, making his ball hit the ground and bounce its way to a stop right at Elle's feet.

"First!" Jen shouted, raising her paddle into the air.

"We, um..." Declan grimaced. "This is how they decide who goes first in our meeting."

Elle's eyebrow rose. "Interesting."

"Well, technically, it's not this *exactly*. They come up with a new method to decide each time."

Before today, Declan's main concern was that the interviewer not make personal things public. He hadn't realized how much he would care about what the interviewer herself thought about it all.

"We should stop letting Jen choose the method," Sam said as he picked up the errant ball and returned it and his paddle to the Ping-Pong table. "I say next time, we should see who can write the most error-free lines of code or edit a section of raw video footage the fastest."

Mato cleared his throat. "Maybe we should just get started with the meeting and finish our tour later."

They all took a seat at the round table. He'd bought a table big enough to fit up to four more employees as the company grew, so adding Elle was no big deal at all. She immediately turned her phone's voice recorder on and set it in the middle of the table. He'd forgotten that Mato had said he was going to grant her permission for that.

Declan cleared his throat and took a deep breath before speaking just to Elle. "We have two team meetings a week. The first one—this one—is at nine on Mondays, and it's where we discuss what's on tap for the week. Everyone shares what they'll be doing and I make any changes or additions to it, based on what our priorities are.

"And then on Fridays at four we each do a report on our week, a kind of post-mortem where we discuss what went better or worse than expected. This is when we do a lot of brainstorming too. Sometimes we'll bring up the beginnings of a plan that goes nowhere. But by our Monday morning meeting, after it's had a chance to percolate on the back burner all weekend long, we'll come up with some of our most brilliant ideas."

Elle gave him a curious look, tilting her head ever-so-slightly to the side, and his curiosity about what she might be thinking intensified.

Mato raised his pen. "We also work with some freelancers for design work on images, proofreading, and things like that. I conduct virtual meetings with them weekly too."

"Jen," Declan said, "I believe you've won the honors of going first."

Jen grinned and started talking about the numbers like she did every Monday morning. The number of new followers on each social media platform, the number of views each video got, how they compared to the week before, how they compared to their projections, how paid ads were going, and how the Declan talks Science merch was selling.

He was always very interested to hear the numbers. He'd always loved statistics, and he loved how clearly it showed the progress they were making toward their goals.

Today, though, he was struggling to focus on them. Probably because he was so focused on Elle's face as Jen read the numbers. They were a direct result of how he ran his business—from the videos he made to the way his carefully-chosen employees filmed them, edited them, and marketed them. His team performed magic every week, yet he was the one who was ultimately responsible if things went south. It surprised him how much Elle's thoughts about them mattered.

He shouldn't care what Elle thought. But in the same way a guy might want to impress the women at his gym with his build, he hoped that Elle was impressed by the numbers representing the company he'd created.

"And speaking of the store," Jen said, "I have some ideas for new products."

It still baffled him that people wanted merch with *Declan Talks Science* on them, let alone any with his quotes. If it hadn't been for Jen pushing the idea two years ago, they never would've had a store. It had been rather successful since then. Plus, as Jen said, it had helped people feel more connected to his channel.

"Do you remember on your video last week about bees," Jen continued, "when Sam went in tight for the shot of you watching the bee buzzing around your hollyhocks and you told it, 'I can't help pollen in love with you'?"

He nodded, then shook his head, already guessing where this was going.

"Well, people went insane in the comments. So I made some mockups of some products I think they'll clamor to get. Especially if we make them a limited-time-only thing."

Jen tapped a few times on her tablet and then held it up for the table to see. The first item was a water bottle with "I can't help pollen in love with you" and *Declan*

Davenport in his usual script font with the *Declan Talks Science* logo underneath. The next one she showed was a tote bag. Then a honey container. Then a set of couples T-shirts and everyone at the table laughed while Jen grinned even wider. All with the quote, his name, and the channel logo.

Declan glanced over at Elle, whose expression was unreadable as she wrote something on her tablet.

Then his eyes went to the voice recorder still sitting in the middle of the table. He'd gotten used to the fact that a lot of people saw him each week. But they only saw the parts that he chose to show on camera. They weren't in his meetings or seeing his process and judging it. It wasn't something he was used to or felt comfortable with. He and his team had figured out what worked for them—they'd gotten to that point after years of working together. Maybe the way they did things wasn't super traditional, but it worked for this particular group of personalities.

But Elle was a newcomer. She didn't understand what had become the way they did things after much trial and error. It made him wonder how critical she would be with this article of hers.

Not that he should be bothered either way, he reminded himself. This was just a small-town college magazine and Elle was someone he had barely met. He had no interest in dating anyone—let alone the interviewer peeking into his life—so it wasn't like he needed to impress her. He probably wouldn't ever see her again after tomorrow morning.

Actually, he didn't care about impressing people in general. He wanted his business, and therefore his YouTube channel, to do well—but for very different reasons, all of which had to do with science and making his mother proud. He didn't care whether people were impressed with him as a person or not.

Except, apparently, for this woman.

Chapter Five

ELLE

"Elle?"

Declan's voice was like sitting on a covered porch wrapped in the softest banket watching thunder rumble across the skies. It was deep and smooth yet somehow still rumbly and... luxurious. She'd known that before today, but hearing it in person was even more glorious than she'd imagined. And hearing that voice say her name sent tingles up her spine.

"Did you have a question?" he prompted.

"What? No." In an attempt to make it look like she was just taking notes, she pushed a little too hard on the tablet pencil and it skidded off the tablet and out of her hand. She hurried to pick it back up. "Just listening." And daydreaming, apparently. A wave of heat washed over her as she realized she had been staring at him enough that he thought she had a question. Or maybe that was just his way of pulling her out of the trance. It worked. She refocused on the meeting even more.

Because there was nothing personal about admiring his voice. It was just a part of him and she wasn't interested in being attracted to any part of him. But a girl could daydream about that voice belonging to someone who wasn't a celebrity because it would be so much more attractive.

She was impressed, though, at how he was running this meeting. He and his team seemed to work well together, which wasn't exactly something that could be faked. She had imagined him the same way she'd imagined every other celebrity—that they were there for the glory and let others do the work. She hadn't expected him to be so hands-on.

And she realized that she hadn't expected him to react well when told that something hadn't worked out as planned or when his team made a suggestion he didn't like or didn't think was a good idea. He'd been gracious and supportive.

Which was more than she could say about how he'd treated her at the beginning. Before arriving, all communications had gone through his assistant—she hadn't talked to him a single time. Which was fine. He probably didn't have time for working out details.

But he hadn't even bothered to greet her at the door of

his house when she and Mato had arrived. It was the smell of waffles and maple syrup that had welcomed her instead, which still made her stomach growl. (And made her wish she hadn't missed breakfast this morning.) Declan hadn't even walked the ten feet to the main area when she'd first entered his offices. Like he wanted to make sure that she knew that she didn't matter at all. A show of superiority.

But she'd definitely noticed his reaction to first seeing her. She had been trying to decide between two different outfits this morning. She smiled, knowing that she'd picked the right one. The game he seemed to want to play was to ignore the other person and she'd won that round. She planned to win the next round, too.

Everyone got their turn in the meeting, and she took notes furiously as they each talked. Their voices were a fascinating blend for one small group. Halona's was slightly hoarse, authoritative, and made her think of freshly-baked crusty bread—a little hard on the outside but warm and soft just underneath. Sam's voice was full, yet had a thinner quality to it, like shouting in a tunnel but without the echo. Jen's was bubbly, like champagne. And Mato's was like a drum beating in the distance.

Everything that might be involved with running a YouTube channel had never occurred to her, and it was kind of fascinating to hear what Sam was editing this week and what shots he wanted to get in their filming today, as well as all the plans Jen had for advertising and marketing, what admin jobs and interviews and promotional things Mato had lined up, and all the outreach stuff that Halona talked about.

The latter was what interested Elle the most because that was what caused the biggest change in Declan's countenance. She kept glancing up from taking notes to glimpse his expression, then just gave up and kept her eyes on him. This was all part of the interview, so it wasn't weird. It was just her doing her job. The recorder could do its job while she stared.

As soon as Halona said, "And they're a very poor school district. Their kids are hungry for science," Declan sat up even straighter, all of his focus on Halona.

"And the district is open to letting us come during the school day?" he asked.

Halona grinned. "For two full days and an evening event with parents. I've even got a few local businesses in that area to help sponsor."

"Excellent!" Declan said, his entire body seeming to light up.

Elle liked that look on him. It was kind of beautiful. She held her pencil up and the motion caught Declan's attention. "Does it make a difference that it's during the school day?" It was the first question she'd asked. Normally, she was full of questions during an interview, but she felt a bit outnumbered in this meeting. The other three people she'd interviewed were alone, and they had met somewhere neutral for the two of them. This was on his home turf—in his offices, which also happened to be in his home. So it was doubly his home turf.

And he was surrounded by his team—people who had a lot of familiarity with each other, which made them a unified front and her an outsider. Plus, there was the whole part about her winning the "who can ignore the other person" round. Which, as an interviewer, probably was about the worst goal of hers she'd ever had.

Declan nodded. "It does make a difference. No matter how much a kid wants to go to an evening or Saturday event, most can't make it. Especially in an area where many parents work a second job to make ends meet—it impacts their ability to get there. And we want to reach as many kids as possible."

He watched her as he spoke as if he cared what she thought about it. She was impressed, sure, but the look on her face was probably more along the lines of conflicted than impressed. Because every time he looked at her like that, it made her forget to breathe. And every time she forgot to breathe, she let the lightheadedness remind her that none of it was real.

She had promised herself when she was a little girl that she was never *ever* going to get involved with a celebrity, and she'd been promising herself that ever since. Her breathing issues and lightheadedness were irrelevant.

ONCE THE MEETING WAS OVER, Halona, Jen, and Mato headed off to their offices. Elle went with Declan and Sam to the room where he'd been setting things up to film when she'd first arrived. The backdrop to filming was mostly white—a long white countertop ran from wall-to-wall along the back with white bookshelves rising up on the sides, both filled with books, beakers of growing plants, some Declan Talks Science merchandise, and a few models of... plant cells, maybe?

She hadn't seen the rest of the room in any of his videos, but the side walls seemed to be covered in some kind of sound-deadening panels. All in all, it was an attractive space for a science lab-themed area.

The two men moved around the room, getting lighting and cameras set up while discussing what to film and in which order. It had a certain chaos to it, but it also felt practiced. Almost like the order they did things ensured that nothing would get forgotten. She couldn't take her eyes off their process. The Welcome Center had filmed plenty of clips to put on social media, but it was nothing like this.

Sam glanced at his laptop. "And then we'll film the part with you talking about the worms to go with the footage that we shot just before the meeting this morning."

Declan nodded. "Do I look presentable?"

Sam's eyes scanned Declan. "Give your shirt a little tug at the right shoulder. Yep. You got it. Looks good."

Huh. He didn't have a makeup person making sure he was completely camera ready? Or even had a mirror in the room? That kind of surprised her. It helped that the man could probably roll out of bed and start filming that minute and still look good, but she respected that his focus seemed to be far more on the content he shared than himself.

He sat down behind the desk where he started all the Declan Talks Science videos that she'd seen and took a deep breath as he looked at the camera. He slid on the glasses that he wore in all his videos, then his eyes shifted to where she stood facing him, a bit back from the camera and just to his left. "I'm a little nervous doing this with you in the room."

She tried not to smile or feel like she'd won a point in whatever game they were playing by making the man nervous. "You could always kick me out and tell me to go shoot some hoops in the Beehive." She worried for a split second that he might take her up on that, but there was no way she was leaving.

He chuckled and shook his head. "We didn't bring you here for twenty-four hours just to be sent away from the action."

"Another option, then, is that I could make faces at you the whole time."

He laughed with that deep voice of his and the sound was thunder, rumbling deep and low across the night sky, being captured by the cushioned sound-proofing of the room.

Then he looked at her in a way she couldn't quite read and gave her a smile that she *could* read very well. Well enough that her knees buckled a little, so she sat in the chair they'd brought in for her. As soon as he looked away, she pulled the front of her shirt out a few times in an attempt to get some more air against her skin. Maybe she should've worn something cooler. Was this room smaller than it had been before?

Her phone buzzed, and she glanced down at it.

Mom: I just watched one of Declan Davenport's videos. That voice! I want to put it in my pocket and take it everywhere. WHERE HAS HE BEEN ALL MY LIFE?

Elle: Mom. Stop with the all caps. It makes it feel like you're shouting, and they're about to start filming.

Mom: Caps are for important things, dear. Things like MARRY THAT MAN. I can't believe you're in the same room as him. Seriously, get your flirt on.

Elle: MOM.

Mom: Look who's shouting now.

Mom: You should ask him if he's ever thought about narrating audiobooks. Romances, specifically.

She glanced up to see that Declan and Sam were ready to start filming, so she quickly typed out a text.

Elle: I've got to go now. I'm putting my phone away. Call you later.

She wondered if her mom had texted her "marry him" comment as a way of warning Elle away from Declan. Because that was exactly what her text did. She'd already lived the consequences of her mom going after someone because of his voice. Or his celebrity status.

Her phone buzzed again, and she was surprised to see Camilla's name instead of her mom's.

Camilla: Today is the day of your interview with Declan Davenport, right?

Camilla: [Gif of someone flailing their arms, squealing.]

CAMILLA: Get a selfie with him! And make sure
to send it to me!

Elle wasn't even going to respond. Well, maybe once
she was back in her room. The notification hadn't even
had a chance to disappear from her screen before another
came in.

SUMMER: So, how many times have you passed
out from hearing that magnificent voice while
staring into those green eyes of his?

She'd had her phone on silent, of course, but apparently, that wasn't enough. She put it in *Do Not Disturb*
mode and pulled out her iPad to take notes. As soon as the
tablet's screen lit up, a text appeared.

SUMMER: Because we've got a bet going on with
everyone in the Welcome Center.

She hurried and put the tablet in *Do Not Disturb*
mode as well. She looked up and saw Declan's eyes still on
her and her cheeks started to warm. She looked down at
her tablet just as Sam said, "Three, two," and then pointed
at Declan.

"Hey, all you science lovers! This is Declan Talks
Science, and I'm your host, Declan Davenport." It was the

opening he had to all of his videos, but apparently, he didn't like the way it came out, because after only a beat, he said it a second time.

Okay, now that he was filming, she could focus on that.

He said something introducing the episode, then started talking about worms and how they were older than dinosaurs, about there being about 1.4 million of them in a single acre of cropland, and that they could become paralyzed in as little as an hour if they were exposed to light.

There were a lot more cuts in filming than she had expected. During some parts, he talked for a couple of minutes straight. But for others, he kept trying until he was happy with his wording. There was a lot of conversation between Declan and Sam, too. Like Declan telling him which cut to use, and Sam saying things like "I'm going to zoom in on that part." Sam seemed to be jotting down quite a few notes about editing.

Then Declan started talking about how dirt and soil were different—soil was dirt plus organic material and air—and how much worms helped the soil. And somehow it was so entrancing even though the words coming out of the man's mouth were about *worms*.

That was exactly why Elle didn't generally watch his videos—other than the few she'd watched to prepare for the interview. She didn't *want* to be entranced by him right along with millions of others. It felt like when a movie star was all charming and attractive in a movie, just begging some magazine to name him "Hottest Man Alive."

Although, maybe it wasn't exactly like that. There was just something about Declan... an earnestness in the way he talked, as if he genuinely wanted everyone to know the interesting things he knew. Like the information was a gift he was holding out in his hands, presenting it to everyone, hoping they liked it.

All that combined with his deep voice and yes, it was entrancing. The dimples helped to sell it all, too. And the unassuming, open expression on his face. He was a male siren. (Was that a thing?) She needed to avert her eyes to avoid the danger. And somehow close off her ears. Because if there was anything she *didn't* want, it was to be sucked in.

He scooped a clump of dirt from the container on the desk behind him by hand, a single earthworm hanging out, and held it toward the camera. "Worms and other soil organisms eat the organic material in soil and leave behind nutrients that plants need. They also keep the soil well aerated, which helps it stay oxygenated and hydrated."

Yes, she told herself. *Focus on soil organisms*. That will keep her mind off Declan's... everything.

But instead of focusing on soil organisms, she focused on the way the slight curl to his dark hair gave it the perfect amount of lift and how his glasses perfectly framed those green eyes of his. It took a while to realize she hadn't paid any attention to what he'd been saying.

"This soil in my hand has more organisms than there are people in the world. In just the top six inches of an acre of soil alone, there are about twenty-thousand *pounds* of living matter. There are tens of thousands of different kinds of soil in the U.S., and I'm going to show you mine."

No one said "cut," but Declan and Sam seemed to have an understanding that the clip was finished. Sam looked down at his watch. "Our window of opportunity with perfect lighting in that southeast corner will close soon. Should we head out now and then come back to finish?"

Elle got her head back in the game and stood to follow Declan and Sam down the hall and through the door that led to his backyard. And wow—that was one backyard! It was so lush and green and beautiful and well cared for, with colorful flowers everywhere. Clearly, he was a man who knew a lot about soil and what it needed for things to grow.

Without even realizing she was doing it, she suddenly pictured him out there, working in the garden and having all kinds of science-y thoughts, with his shirt off.

Oh my goodness, why am I picturing him with his shirt off? It was picturing him having science-y thoughts, she was sure. She had always been super drawn to guys who did things like get lost in science-y thoughts. Or math thoughts. Or philosophical thoughts. Or any deep thoughts, really.

Once Sam got set up outside and they'd checked to make sure everything was positioned correctly for Declan's height, they started filming again. Declan stood at the corner of an impressive vegetable garden, pressing a shovel into the soil, then stepping on it to push it in deep. As he lifted the shovel to turn over the soil, Elle got a good glimpse of his shoulder and arm muscles tightening under his shirt. He might be a man who sat at a desk for much of his day, but that must not be all he did.

Why was she ogling him so much? And why was she having all these intrusive thoughts? She wasn't like this at all. She shook her head to clear her focus. She needed to stop watching him entirely. People got to be celebrities because they were nice to look at, and looks usually had very little to do with personality.

"When you're getting ready to plant a garden in the spring, this is the first step, right? Turning over the soil to make it nice and fluffy?" Declan broke up the chunks of overturned soil with the tip of the shovel. "Wrong. Turning it over like this is one of the worst things you can do to the microbiome of the soil.

"Remember how many organisms the soil in my hand had? More than there are people in the world. Those organisms are what make the soil healthy. If you turn it over like this, you expose all of those to the sun and the sun irradiates it, essentially turning it into dead soil. And dead soil is in danger of being washed away by your sprinklers or any windstorm that comes along."

Huh. Elle didn't know much about gardening, but that still surprised her. Then he started talking about weeds and how they were the earth's way of protecting the soil—helping to keep the sun off it and preserve the microorganisms below the ground. As Declan talked, she found herself getting more and more interested in what he was saying.

Declan spotted a worm in the dirt and got down on his knees. Sam turned the camera toward Declan and nodded, and then Declan brought his face right down close to the worm. "When you turn over the dirt, it also exposes these little guys to the light, and we know that's bad for them." He picked it up carefully. "Worms may be cold-blooded, but they have *five* hearts. That's a lot of love, so let's show them some in return." He tucked the worm under some dirt, letting it retreat into the soil.

Elle smiled, making sure she didn't chuckle out loud. She wondered if, at the next Monday morning team meeting after this episode aired, Jen would be pitching a line of merchandise with that quote on it. Maybe a t-shirt with a big cartoon worm with five red hearts and the words "Let's show them some love." She hadn't checked out Declan Talks Science's merchandise before and found herself suddenly very curious about it.

He moved over to some of his plants and talked about how they sent some of the energy from photosynthesis down through their roots, making the soil healthier, and how much planting groundcover could protect the soil.

She would have to tell her mom to watch this episode. They hadn't had a garden growing up, but her mom had started one a few years ago and seemed very enthusiastic about it—even if she struggled to grow anything. Based on her texts earlier, it wouldn't be hard to get her to watch.

Elle hadn't ever been interested in gardening before, but seeing Declan's passion for the subject ignited a passion that had been lying dormant in her. Although the HOA at her condo took care of the lawns, she did have a small area she could garden in. She'd always figured that someday when she had her life more together, she might try her hand at it. Listening to him made her want to try now.

Apparently, watching the man with the deep voice and the adorable dimples talk about science *did* make her interested in science, just like everyone said it would.

Well played, Declan. Well played.

Of course, there were songs her dad sang that she liked, too. That didn't mean that trying to get close to him was a good idea.

Chapter Six

DECLAN

*D*eclan did a decent job of filming when they were outside and Elle was standing just beyond his line of sight. Of course, just knowing that she was there threw him off a bit. Now that they were back inside, though, discussing how almost all the antibiotics used to treat bacterial infections came from soil microorganisms while he could see her from the corner of his eye, he was struggling to stay focused.

Why? He loved the stuff he was talking about. When he got in the zone, like he always did when he was filming or when he was researching, there was almost nothing that could pull him away. Probably because there was almost nothing that could even catch his attention enough to attempt to pull him away. His team always joked that if the Missouri River flooded again and threatened their area, not even the sound of water pouring into their offices would distract him.

Yet this woman's presence alone was doing it.

And she didn't even know she was doing it. She just sat in her chair, looking thoughtful, taking notes on her tablet. As if looking deep in thought wasn't attractive enough on its own, she would often bite her bottom lip, crinkle her brow, or tuck her hair behind an ear, exposing a beautiful cheekbone. He couldn't help but wonder what she was thinking about.

Declan finished saying the words he always used at the end of his videos—"In the immortal words of Albert Einstein, 'Imagination is more important than knowledge.' So until next time, keep imagining."

"Okay," Sam said, "now we need to record a part to go with the segment we filmed in the rain a couple of weeks ago."

"Oh, that's right." They had gone outside right when the rain was dying down and gotten some clips of all the worms that had come to the surface and crawled onto his pavement. It wasn't something he'd normally forget, but he wasn't on top of his game today.

This segment would start with his face on the screen, then go to a voiceover of the footage they'd already filmed. He cleared his throat and Sam gave him the thumbs up that the camera was rolling. He caught the smile from Elle just beyond Sam and tried to put it out of his mind.

"As strange as it may sound, worms have a natural predator other than the 'early bird.' Have you ever wondered why worms come to the surface when it rains, when they are creatures that like to stay away from the light? Moles think worms are a tasty snack to find when they're burrowing into the dirt, and we think that worms mistake the sound of rain—which can pound on the soil at twenty miles per hour—for the vibration of a mole coming their direction. So they race toward the surface in an attempt to stay safe."

He couldn't believe he got through that in a single take. Not that he usually couldn't—he just usually didn't have Elle in the room. And for whatever reason, it made him feel not only more likely to mess up but also made him want to be impressive.

"So," Declan said to her as Sam was taking the camera off the tripod, "what did you think of filming?"

Elle's eyes roamed the room, taking in the entire set before they met his again. "It surprised me how long it took to film a twenty-minute episode. That was"— she glanced at her watch—"about two hours, right? I didn't think it would be so intense. And it feels like you filmed a lot more content than what would fit in the video."

He breathed out a quiet chuckle and smiled a bit. "Not everything I say is worthy of the final cut."

"I bet your fans would say otherwise." The moment

Elle said it, her cheeks flushed, making him think that she hadn't meant to say it.

He held back a smile. "And there are a lot of pauses in the parts we do keep that need to be cut so that it keeps a quick pace. Even little pauses make a difference."

Sam, who was leaning over the desk doing something on the laptop, stood and said, "I'm going to open this on my desktop and make sure everything looks good."

As soon as Sam was out of the room, Elle pulled her chair over to sit right on the opposite side of the desk from him. Her expression was open, interested. He reminded himself that was a good thing and that he didn't need to have his guard up.

"How often do you film?" she asked.

"Twice a week, usually on Mondays and Wednesdays. If Halona has lined up an outreach visit with kids, we try to schedule that on Tuesday if it's local, Monday if it's not so we have travel time, then we just shift things around. Sometimes we have to film two episodes in one day. I can talk about science all day long, but it's rough to stay 'on' for that long. Especially because it's not a conversation about science—it's just me talking into a camera.

"But Thursdays and Fridays are research days for me. I prefer having two days together, and those days are sacred. We try to keep things from interfering if we can help it."

Elle nodded. "Research about what topics to cover? About what to put in an episode? Market research?"

"Just science research. I'm a scientist first—that's when I bury myself in what I love. I let myself go down rabbit holes and see where they take me."

If Elle thought he was a celebrity and lived a glamorous life like Jen and Halona seemed to believe his viewers thought, he hoped she wasn't too disappointed to find out that underneath it all, he was just a big science nerd, through and through. There was a time when he'd felt like he had to hide who he was, but that wasn't him anymore. She could accept it or not. It wouldn't change who he was.

You're still hiding, a voice inside him said.

He stood and grabbed the container of soil and worms from the desk behind him. "Would you like to come with me to free these little guys?"

Okay, so maybe he did continue to hide who he'd been as a kid. But that was the past him, not the present him. There was a big difference. He'd worked hard to become who he was today.

As the two of them walked through the door leading to his backyard, Elle asked, "So, do you plan what you're going to say in your videos or make it up as you go?"

"There's a lot of planning. I want there to be information in each video that will appeal to all age groups and that doesn't just happen. I don't memorize a script or anything—just have points I want to cover."

"Do you ever get any haters? You know, trolls in the comments?"

He crouched down and set the container on the soil, squinting up at Elle through the bright sun. "Doesn't everyone?"

"I guess."

"It's not something I usually see." He carefully poured the soil from the container onto a shady part of his garden. "Jen keeps an eye on the comments for me now and deletes any rude ones and lets me know if there are any that I need to see or respond to." He stood and they both watched as the exposed worms started burrowing their way into the soil.

"But when I first started, I didn't have the luxury of someone else reading the comments. And let me tell you, there were a *lot* of comments about my voice and dimples."

Elle laughed a really good laugh, then immediately put a hand to her mouth, shaking her head. "I'm sorry. It's just—"

"I know." Well, okay, he didn't know exactly what she was thinking, but he'd read enough of those comments to know that people liked his voice and his dimples. And some of them were very quick to say that they came for the eye candy, not the science.

"How did you handle it?"

He lifted one shoulder. "At first, I hated it. To be fair, I've hated comments about my voice ever since I was twelve and my voice started changing." He laughed. "And I hated comments about my dimples for a lot longer than that."

Elle gave a soft chuckle beside him as they both looked down at the garden.

"Eventually, I realized those two things made me memorable, and that was a good thing. But then I got to the point where those comments made me feel like people were coming to my channel to hear my voice or to stare at me, and I just wanted to reply to their comments, 'Hey! I worked hard to bring you *science!*' I wanted them there for that and not something I don't have much control over."

Elle was still looking down at the garden but he could tell that she was smiling.

"I take it you've dealt with similar things?" he pressed.

"Well, I can't say that I usually get people telling me that I have a super sexy deep voice, but yes. Enough to sympathize."

He raised an eyebrow. "*Super sexy*, huh?"

"Well, or so the comments say. That, and stuff about your hair."

"They are talking about my hair now?"

"You do have really great hair—of course they comment on it."

They were both bantering a bit, but she hadn't let it cross the line to flirting. At least he thought she hadn't. He wasn't sure if that made him sad or happy. Or both. It was definitely both. At the same time.

But it was going well. Except for talking about his looks, Elle was keeping the questions related to his channel and filming, not so much about him personally. That was good.

"Anyway, now the comments don't bother me. And if they come because of my voice or my dimples—or my hair, apparently—I'm grateful for whatever brought them, because that gives me the chance to get them excited about science."

The day was starting to get hot, but it wasn't quite there yet. As beautiful as Elle looked with the sun warming her cheeks and making her hair shine like polished bronze, she probably didn't want to stay in the sun. And the light likely made it hard for her to see her tablet screen.

All the worms had found their way out of the daylight, so he led her to a little table and chairs he had on the grass under a shade tree as she asked, "Did you always know you wanted to do this?"

"The science part or the YouTube part?"

She looked up for a brief moment, getting that same thoughtful expression he'd seen while he'd been filming that had pulled him in so fully, then she said, "Both, I guess."

He took a deep breath as he thought about his answer. Now her questions were getting a little more personal. Still, though, he could choose what he was going to share— he could share parts without getting specific. It was fine.

"The science? Yes. Ever since I was a kid, I was interested in science. I lived in a place where I had woods up to my doorstep, so I spent a lot of time outside. It was just me and my mom, and she encouraged my exploration of everything—from the tiniest things I could find in the soil to what was going on in the loftiest of trees."

Elle smiled as she wrote something down. "And YouTube?"

"No." He let out a breath of a chuckle. "That was never my goal. I was super hesitant about it for a long time and nearly talked myself out of it. But I think that science is important for everyone. The more you learn about it, the more it teaches your brain to think in different ways that help with problem-solving in every area.

"Learning about science helps people to have more organized brains, too, and helps with communication. And that's not even including the myriad of ways that scientific discoveries help everybody."

Elle wrote on her tablet, and then met his eyes. "And YouTube became a way for you to bring that passion to more people."

He nodded as he studied her. "Did you always know that you wanted to do what you're doing?"

She smiled at him. "This isn't a regular conversation," she said as she motioned between the two of them with her hand that held the tablet's pencil. "You don't have to make sure that the questions are evenly split between the two of us. That's not the way interviews work."

He leaned back in his chair and folded his arms. "You're here for twenty-four hours, though, and I'd love to know. If I'm going to be giving all the answers, I want some, too. Like if you always knew that you wanted to be a journalist."

Her eyebrows drew together for the smallest moment, then she just studied him. Eventually, she set the pencil down. "Okay, I'll answer. First, I'm not a journalist—I'm just an... *acting* journalist once a month. My official title is Admissions Counselor for Campus Recruitment Events. I knew I wanted a job where I got to plan big events, but no—I didn't know it'd be this job specifically. As a kid, I thought I'd be a wedding planner. It wasn't until I was in my last semester at LBSU that I realized how much I loved the school and wasn't ready to leave. A friend of mine on campus was a student ambassador in the Welcome Center and suggested I look there. The rest is history."

Interesting. From what he knew of her, he wouldn't have guessed any of that. Finding out just that little bit made him crave more. He wished he could turn this interview around and only ask her questions. "A wedding plan-ner, huh?"

She shrugged. "As a kid, it was the biggest kind of event that I could think of. Plus, it was an event with glitz and glamour. Some of the events I do now are just as big in scope, but sustained over several days." She laughed. "Minus all the glitz and glamour."

"And the interviewing portion of your job?"

"That part, I didn't seek out. Someone in the media department got the idea and, took it to my boss, and I got assigned to it."

"Do you like it?"

"Yeah. I mean in the Welcome Center, we are always looking for ways to help prospective students know they'll do well at LBSU. Showing them what our amazing gradu-ates have accomplished with their lives is a great way to do that."

"Did I just hear you call me amazing?"

"No—I'm only here because of the deep voice and the dimples."

He laughed the heartiest laugh he'd laughed in a while. "And the hair?"

She nodded, a solemn expression on her face. "And the hair."

He turned at the sound of the back door opening. Mato took a few steps across the patio and said, "I hate to interrupt, but it's time for lunch." Jen walked out just behind him, a grin spread across her face.

Declan turned back to Elle. "Unless we're out of town, we go to lunch together on Mondays and take turns picking the restaurant. Jen's a little excited because it's her week to choose and she picked a loud Mexican restaurant she loves. Are you game?"

She smiled. "Of course."

"Okay, but I've got to warn you that Halona always drives since she has a minivan with enough seats for all of us." He watched Elle's face for signs of hesitation. When he didn't see any, he added, "And she's got teenagers, so there's likely to be a few Burger Time and Taco Johns wrappers scattered about."

Elle seemed to be trying to hide a smile, so he continued. "Okay, then, this might be the deal-breaker. The person whose turn it is to pick the restaurant gets to ride shotgun, which puts us in the middle seats. But I don't mind driving us separately if you'd prefer the front seat."

One of her eyebrows rose in a perfect arch. "Are you implying that I'm a bigger diva than the celebrity himself?"

He chuckled as he rubbed a knuckle across an eyebrow. If he wasn't careful, this woman was going to plow right through all his carefully guarded walls.

Chapter Seven

ELLE

Elle walked out of Declan's house with the others, squinting into the bright sunshine as they headed toward the cars parked in his very large driveway. There was only one minivan—a blue Honda Odyssey—so she knew it was Halona's.

Jen and Halona opened the front doors and Elle followed Declan to where he slid open the door behind the driver. She climbed inside first. The two middle seats seemed to be on tracks so they could be slid sideways, though they were currently pushed together in the middle to leave a little space on each side.

Mato opened the opposite door, but just as Declan sat in the seat next to her, Sam tried to squeeze past him to the back seat. At the same time, Mato climbed in on her side and started to slide by. Elle leaned toward the middle to give Mato space right as Declan did the same. Her and Declan's sides pressed against one other and their heads came so close that they nearly collided.

And if that wasn't enough, Declan turned his head to say "Sorry" in that low, deep voice of his—except this time, it sounded a little ragged and did something to her stomach. For a moment their faces were inches apart, their lips nearly touching, and blood rushed to her head as electricity zipped up her spine.

She cleared her throat and sat up straight as soon as Mato passed, turning her attention to the front of the van to distract her body from all the extra sensations it was feeling. And to hopefully get her mind to do the same because she didn't see her body getting the message anytime soon if her mind didn't first. There were definitely a few Burger Time and Taco John's wrappers at her feet. A few stray fries, too.

Halona must've seen her notice them when she turned to back out of the driveway, because she said, "I told my kids that I'd be driving someone to lunch who worked at the college they might attend someday, so they should get this place as clean as they were okay with you seeing." She gestured at the wrappers. "I guess this is it."

That made Elle smile. She worked with teens a lot, so it kind of made her feel more at home. And seeing Declan here, sitting in this middle seat of a van that wasn't pristine, nearly made her laugh at how different it was from the image she'd had in her mind. She had pictured him having a driver who took him everywhere he needed to go, but she never imagined it happening like this.

"Do you eat lunch together every day or just on Mondays?" she asked, genuinely curious.

"Yes and no," Halona said.

Jen turned from the front seat enough that Elle could see the profile of her face. "We do Potluck Tuesdays and Delivery Wednesdays. And on Thursdays and Fridays, we bring our own or go out ."

"We can also raid Declan's fridge on Thursday or Friday," Sam said from the back seat, "since there are usually leftovers from earlier in the week. But the rule is that if you do, you have to bring some to Declan, too."

"I swear it isn't because I'm lazy or pretentious," Declan said quickly. He had the slightest bit of color to his cheeks. And was that an embarrassed expression on his face? It might just be.

"It's because when he's in research mode," Mato said, "he's not going to eat if someone doesn't bring it to him. He gets too focused."

"See? Not pretentious. Just"— Declan's eyebrows knit together—"forgetful. No, more like distracted."

It was pretty cute that he was defending himself. Like he cared what she thought of him, which was a far cry from the beginning of the day. She wondered which host was truly him—the one who cared or the one who didn't.

Not that she needed to know for the article. She was just... curious. That was all.

As they pulled into a parking spot at In Queso Hunger, Jen took off her seat belt and turned to Elle. "Have you ever been here before?"

Elle shook her head as she took off her seat belt. "I don't come to Sioux Falls often." Sure, it was many times the size of Lake Baldwin and therefore had a lot of stores that her small town didn't, but she only made the forty-five-minute drive every couple of months to go to concerts or conventions.

There were several groups of people either walking out of the restaurant or into it, and they all glanced over at Elle and her group. At first, she assumed everyone was just looking because that's what people did when they saw movement. But then someone would notice Declan and tell the others in their group, and then they all turned to stare.

Once Elle's group stepped into the lobby of the restaurant, Jen went up to the hostess to say that they had a reservation. She looked up the name before glancing at their group. It was clear the moment her eyes landed on Declan by the pink on her cheeks and the shy smile on her face. Others in the lobby were noticing Declan, too.

"Of course," the woman said. "Follow me."

She led them to a table for six at the back of the loud, colorful restaurant with walls covered in bright sombreros and cacti, and the entire way was the same—everyone turned to look at Declan and then whispered to the person sitting next to them. And Declan seemed oblivious to the attention.

She knew that Declan had a distinctive look—which also happened to be very attractive—and that his YouTube channel had millions of subscribers and that tens of millions of people watched each of his videos, but was he really so recognizable? Even when he hadn't said a word in that memorable voice of his? Or did he and his team just come to this restaurant often?

Elle leaned closer to Jen as they neared the table. "Is this normal?"

"What?" Jen looked around. "Oh, all the eyes on us? Yeah, you get used to it."

The hostess placed a menu in front of each of them. When she set one in front of Declan, she said, "Here you go, Mr. Davenport. Let me know if you need anything."

Calling him by his name seemed to clue Declan into the fact that she recognized him and his face lit up. "Oh, do you watch Declan Talks Science?"

The hostess told him how much she loved it and how she watched every single episode the day it came out. He asked her name and thanked her for watching. The hostess looked as bright as the sun as she headed back toward the hostess stand, turning to take one last glance back at him.

Elle couldn't help but think of her dad after seeing the

interaction. He probably made hostesses feel special, too. Especially if this many people were watching.

She needed to get those negative thoughts out of her head. Declan making the woman feel special was way better than him making her feel insignificant. Unless, of course, he also went around breaking people's hearts. She cleared her throat as she picked up her menu. "So, what's good here?"

Declan leaned over to point to a few things on her menu. Instead of the scent of cologne, like she would've guessed before today, she caught the scent of body wash and shampoo, both somehow better coming from him. Tingles spread up her arms and put her nerve endings on high alert.

Stop it, body! Brain, come on. You've got to help me out more here.

The goal was to keep from swooning over this man as the hostess had. Like half the room was currently doing. She thought she'd be a pro at it, yet there she was, not being any better at it than anyone else. She thought of her dad some more. And then she thought of her mom signing that NDA. There. That got all the tingles to go away.

Not long after they all ordered and the waitress set chips and salsa on the table, Declan said, "If you'll excuse me for a moment," and approached the waitress at the drink station right next to the kitchen entrance.

"Quick," Jen said. "What can we share about Declan while he's gone?"

Elle perked up. Should she get out her tablet for this? Grab her phone and turn on the voice recorder? No. That didn't feel appropriate. Instead, she just leaned in a bit.

"Oh!" Halona said. "We could tell her about that summer company party when we lined up a date for him with Sam's roommate's sister. What was her name?"

"Caprice," Sam said.

Halona nodded. "Yes, Caprice."

"Good one," Jen said. "Okay, we have this company party every summer where we all bring our families. Halona brings her husband and three kids, I bring my hubby, Mato brings his wife and his two daughters, and Sam brings a brother or a roommate or a friend. Our graphic designer even flies in for it. And Declan brings his dad and brothers but never a date."

Elle's eyes flew to Declan and the waitress. Was he flirting with her? She couldn't tell.. "Declan doesn't date?"

Jen shrugged. "He hasn't mentioned going on a single date since I've been here, and I just hit my two-year mark."

Mato looked a little uncomfortable, like he felt the need to defend Declan but didn't quite know what to say. "Declan, uh... chooses to focus on his business." He obviously knew the full reason but wasn't saying it.

Elle knew that Jen wanted to tell her story, but she suddenly felt the need to know more before Declan came back. "Doesn't he have events to attend that kind of require a date?"

"Sure," Sam said. "Like, he's been up for several Eddie Awards. Usually, he takes one of his brothers or even his dad. Once he took Mato's daughter since she was taking an events and facilities administration class in college and wanted to write a paper about it, but that wasn't as a date."

"Anyway," Jen continued, "so we all decided to line him up with someone. But we didn't think he'd agree to it, so we didn't tell him."

"So he just showed up and she was there?" Elle asked.

"Well, it didn't exactly go as we planned." Jen grimaced.

Halona raised an accusatory eyebrow toward Sam. "Probably because Caprice didn't exactly know how 'blind' the date was."

"Hey, don't look at me—I told my roommate. It was his fault he didn't share that info with his sister."

"And if he'd told her," Jen said, "we wouldn't have gotten quite the night of chaos."

Mato shook his head. "That was only part of the problem."

"Hey, in my defense," Sam said, "Caprice and Declan did go on another date after that, so it's not like it ruined everything."

"You're right!" Jen said. "He *has* gone on a date since I've worked here!"

Declan walked back to the table just then and Elle knew he had to have caught a bit of the conversation. Enough to know that they'd been talking about him, at least. She assumed they would try to cover it, but Jen just grinned and said, "We were just telling Elle the story of that one time we lined you up with a blind date for the summer company party. And how you don't date."

Declan's eyes flashed to Elle for a brief moment, and she caught a look of... embarrassment, was it? But then the look left his face, and as he took his seat, he said in a deadpan voice, "Oh. So kind of you to do that for me. Thanks, guys. And it's not like I *never* date—I just haven't had a serious relationship since college." Declan winced, then turned to Elle and in that gloriously deep voice of his, asked, "None of this is on the record, right?"

"Completely off the record," Elle reassured him. She was totally fine having some of the information she got during this twenty-four-hour thing be only for her enjoyment.

Mato held his hands up like he was trying to stop the conversation. "Hey, guys, remember how we want Declan to open up more on his channel? I don't think this is helping to encourage him."

Interesting. Elle had come to this interview not wanting to get personal at all, and she knew Declan wanted the same. But there was something about the way that Mato had said that the team had discussed Declan opening up that definitely made her want to get more personal with Declan.

Curiosity was the only reason, she told herself. It had nothing to do with her wanting to get to know Declan better. And nothing to do with how attractive it was that his team had just spilled information about him that he wouldn't have chosen to share, yet he didn't seem upset at them. They were all, Declan included, laughing about it. This seemed like a group of people who loved one another but still teased each other.

Kind of like a family, she realized.

Sam pointed at Jen. "It was Jen's idea."

Declan turned to Jen. "Then I'm *really* glad I just told the waitress it's your birthday."

"My birthday was last week and you had an entire elementary school full of kids sing to me."

"Yes, but we were out of town so it doesn't count the same. And since it's a week late, I also asked that they bring you the biggest sombrero they've got and have you stand up and shake the maracas as they sing to you." He smiled widely. "I'm extra glad I asked for that."

A young boy, likely about nine years old, walked up to Declan just then and tapped him on the shoulder. Declan turned to the boy, who said, "I know you. You came to my school."

"Right on," Declan said as he gave the boy a fist bump. "What was your favorite part about it?"

The boy smiled, and honestly, seemed just as mesmerized by Declan's deep voice as everyone else was. "When you talked about what makes the stems of plants grow toward the sun and what makes the roots grow toward the ground. It's because of the hormone auxin, right?"

"Good memory!" Declan said.

"That's not all. I remember what you said about phototropism and geotropism, too. And I did an experiment! I sprouted bean seeds, then planted half—the control group—pointing up like they should, and I planted the other half upside down."

"And what happened?"

"They both grew the right way! It was awesome. I felt like a scientist."

As Declan and the boy talked, Elle couldn't help but notice how good the man was at interacting with kids. Was it bad that right now she was picturing that deep voice of his singing a lullaby to their baby cradled in his arms? It was bad, right?

Yeah, she was sure it was bad.

He was a celebrity, and their public personas didn't always match how much—or how little—they cared about people.

"Will you sign something for me?" The boy looked down as if looking for an object for Declan to autograph. He held up his arm like he was going to ask him to sign that, and said, "No, it'll wash off. I know—my shirt!"

"I think you'd have to get permission for that."

The boy, staying right where he was, shouted, "Mom!" and waved his arm to get her attention. "Can Declan sign my shirt?"

All eyes in the restaurant flew to the boy next to Declan and his mom across the room. The mom blushed and said, "Yes."

"I've got a Sharpie," Halona said as she dug through her purse and then handed the marker across the table to Declan.

"Right here," the boy said, patting a hand against his shoulder. So Declan signed his shirt.

Honestly, even with none of their lunch being "on the record," Elle had enough material to write an article just from the team meeting, the filming, and the questions she'd asked Declan afterward. She didn't need a full twenty-four hours to gather what she needed.

But after seeing how he interacted with his team in this casual setting, hearing the details about him they'd shared, and seeing how he was with kids and people outside his team, she felt like she was just scratching the surface of who he was and hungered for more. Somehow, it felt like twenty-four hours wouldn't be nearly enough.

Chapter Eight

DECLAN

*O*kay, there had definitely been something between Declan and Elle at the restaurant, and Declan was pretty sure he wasn't the only one who'd noticed.

There was the electrical charge between them every time they made eye contact or brushed up against each other. The way they'd both sucked in their breath, gazes locked, when they'd gotten pushed against one another in Halona's van. The look in Elle's eyes when she watched him. The way she'd seemed to sit a little closer to him on the drive home than she had on the drive to the restaurant. All of it made him feel things he hadn't felt in a very long time.

It had been an equally long time since he'd last had such a strong desire to ask a woman out. But he wasn't looking for someone to date. Which was too bad, because if he was, she was exactly who he'd choose.

He opened the door to his office and stood back, motioning for Elle to enter first. As she walked past him, he caught the scent of lavender in her hair and tried to breathe it in deeply without being obvious about it. The scent seemed to open something inside of him that he hadn't known was closed.

The lights flicked on as she walked into his space. He spent so much time in this room, yet it felt different with her in it. He was suddenly hyperaware of how messy his bookshelves were and how many different soil and plant experiments covered the shelves in varying amounts of completeness and how many Post-it notes covered the wall behind his desk.

But the desk itself was clean. And so was the area in front of the bookshelves with two cushioned chairs and his side table and lamp. Elle folded her jacket over the back of the chair and took a seat, pulling her tablet and phone out of her bag.

She smiled up at him, and somehow it seemed more personal than it had earlier in the day. Maybe all the stories from his team had somehow created a bond between him and Elle. He thought everyone would've stopped with the stories after the one about his blind date, but no. They'd also told her how his voice sped up when he was passionate about something and about the running joke in the comments section that he should try doing rap.

And about the time—*the one time*—when his whole team left on a Thursday at the end of the work day without saying goodbye and he hadn't realized the time until they all showed up Friday morning. He'd been shocked to see them in different clothes, looking all bright-eyed when he was so tired, each of them wearing looks of shock at his disheveled, "mad scientist" look.

And they'd said that whenever his dad came into the office, they always managed to talk him into telling stories about Declan taking care of his brothers when they were little. To his embarrassment, they'd even shared the story of seventeen-year-old Declan changing his brother Ian's diaper for the first time and neglecting to put it on snugly enough. Declan had returned to their family room, where he had a group of friends over playing games, and handed Ian over to his mom—only to watch in horror as the baby's diaper slid off and landed right in the lap of the girl he'd had a crush on.

He should be furious that they shared so many stories when they knew he didn't want things to get personal. But he wasn't. And his team seemed to know that he wouldn't be. How had they known? He didn't even understand why he was okay with it himself. Did he somehow trust that this woman that he'd only known for half a day wouldn't share anything in her article that he wouldn't want to be shared? And did he *want* her to know so much about him?

But never did his team ask for stories about Elle. Not once.

Now it was just the two of them, and he was determined to discover more about Elle. He grabbed a couple of water bottles from his mini fridge and set them on the side table before taking a seat in the other chair. Elle might be there to interview him, but this time, he would get as much background from her as he was giving about himself.

She looked around the room. "So on your research days, you spend all day in here?"

He nodded. "All day" worked. She didn't need to know that he worked well into the nights on research days, barely leaving the room. "I like to have plenty of time for deep focus on whatever I'm working on."

She tapped the tablet's pencil on her lips, so many thoughts behind those eyes, and he could tell what she really wanted to ask was how often he worked through the night, like in the story his team shared. He liked that she didn't ask, though, like she respected that the information she got during lunch was off-limits.

"It sounds like you would've made a good research scientist. I understand you've gotten your doctoral degree?"

He grabbed one of the water bottles and twisted open

the cap. "I managed to start it at age twenty-three; I just finished this past May."

She raised a single eyebrow. "Finishing a doctorate degree by age twenty-eight is impressive. What was behind that drive?"

"I knew I wanted to do all of this, and I knew the degree would give me a lot more credibility and allow me to more fully accomplish my goals." She didn't need to know about the imposter syndrome he often felt, either—with or without the degree. "I know you graduated from LBSU, too. What degree did you get?"

"I have a double major in English and Business Management. English because I *was* good at it and business management because I *wanted* to be good at it."

A double major. He'd known she thought schooling was important because she worked at a college. The double major made him feel even more drawn to her. "And did you succeed? Do you feel like you're good at it now?"

She held up an arm, flexing her muscles. "Ready to take on the world."

He laughed.

"Okay, are you ready to start the 'interview' portion of our interview?"

He nodded, so she turned on her phone recorder and set it on the table between them. "Okay, let's start with something easy that will let readers know you're a real person. A way to connect to you. What were you most afraid of as a kid?"

That was her easy question? He thought they had an understanding not to get too personal. Partially to stall, he asked, "What age do you mean when you say 'kid'?" Because before age twelve, his biggest fear had been friends seeing his home. He'd always loved the small place where he and his mom lived, and she'd raised him to think that their unusual situation was the best thing ever. And he always knew it was. But it didn't take long to realize that he couldn't talk about it without judgment from others.

When he'd started kindergarten, he hadn't held back when telling other kids about it at all. They'd always loved hearing about how he got to spend so much time outside. First grade wasn't too bad, either. By the time he'd started second grade, though, he'd realized how judged he was by his situation, so he stopped talking about it. By third grade, he did everything he could to hide it. After elementary school, the need to hide it had gone away. Well, until college.

If she was asking about after age twelve, he was most afraid of being like his biological dad in any way. Declan knew how his dad had treated his mom and that half his genes came from the man. The thought was a good reminder that as much as he felt drawn to Elle, he didn't want to date anyone.

She shrugged. "Let's say middle school."

He put on the most serious expression that he could pull off. "I always worried that I'd have braces when an apocalypse happened and I'd never be able to go to the orthodontist to get them off."

She smiled, but he could tell by the look just under the surface that she knew he wasn't giving the true answer.

"What about you? What did you worry about most?" he asked.

"I thought we already covered this—that isn't how interviews work."

He tapped a finger on his chin thoughtfully. "And did we already cover that if you want answers, you have to give them, too? I can't remember."

She shook her head, chuckling. "Okay, fine. An answer for an answer." She only thought for a moment before she said, "Since my name sounds like the letter L, I feared walking down the halls in my elementary school and having kids hold their fingers in the shape of an L on their foreheads."

"Did that really happen?"

"A lot. I mean, it was elementary school, so kids only had the mentality of elementary students and the joke was just right there, waiting for them. It was hard to resist."

She picked up her water bottle and took a sip. He studied her face and could tell that her answer was the truth, but it wasn't the thought that had first entered her head when he'd asked the question. But since he hadn't shared his true answer, she hadn't shared hers. He wanted to know what the real answer was. They might have bonded a bit over lunch, but they hadn't built that kind of trust yet.

She set the water bottle back down and held the stylus over her tablet. "You have seen a great deal of success in your life. More than most people can ever hope to achieve. I'll highlight some of those successes in the article. But what I want to hear about is which success gave you the greatest sense of pride in your accomplishments."

If she wanted to go for an easy question, it was this one. "Hands down, it was getting my first real subscriber on YouTube."

"Your first?" she asked, sounding a bit surprised. "Not your one-thousandth or one-millionth or ten-millionth?"

He chuckled. "Admittedly, those were pretty great. But no, it was my first that was the best. It meant I was on the path. And I knew my mom would be proud of me. Sometimes, getting started is the hardest part. There are many mental obstacles and many things you have to do just to feel like you're at step one. That was how it was with my channel. It took months—no *years*—before I had everything planned and ready to go. Starting was a big deal, and getting that first legit subscriber made it all feel real."

"Huh. So much for people calling your channel an 'overnight success.'"

He shook his head just thinking about all it had taken to get started. Which made him think about how far he'd come since then. The process felt overwhelming, even just looking back on it. "Now it's your turn. What was something that made you proud?"

"We're going to do this for every question?"

He smiled. "Every single one."

Her eyes were on his for a long moment, and he met that gaze, memorizing the way her brown eyes had golden facets that he hadn't noticed before. Her eyes were so expressive, yet only offered a glimpse of all that he could tell was going on behind them. He could keep this up for as long as she could, and he would enjoy every moment of it.

"It was my mom's wedding to this guy named Benny," she began. "They were only married for a year, and I knew from the start that they wouldn't last. It was painfully obvious for everyone who wasn't my mom, actually.

"But that doesn't matter. What matters is that I asked my mom if I could plan her wedding. She said yes, and I pulled it off. I was only thirteen at the time, so it was pretty impressive that she agreed in the first place. But they originally planned to get married at the courthouse, so maybe she figured that if I made a disaster of it, it couldn't be much worse than not having a reception at all.

And I only had a two-hundred-dollar budget, so it wasn't like they'd be out a lot of money.

"I was so resourceful and found a great outdoor venue for free. I made invitations on a school computer and found a place to print them for next to nothing. I talked a friend's mom into letting me use her big kitchen and they even helped to make the food. I borrowed folding tables and tablecloths from neighbors and even one from my English teacher.

"It was pretty darn amazing and I stayed within budget. After all the compliments came in from the people who attended, I felt like I could do anything. And my mom felt the same, which was also a pretty great feeling. She even let me plan the wedding to the guy she's married to now."

"Wow!" He looked up at the ceiling, shaking his head in amazement, and then met her eyes again. "Thirteen? Really?"

She nodded, and he could see the pride written all over her face. He was proud just hearing her tell the story. "Now I get why you wanted to major in business management."

She waved her hand as if trying to wave the story away. "Enough about me. Oh my goodness, this is not what we are here for."

It was exactly what he was here for.

Technically, he was here because Mato had lined up

an interview and he'd agreed to it. But he was all in now because what he wanted most from this interview was what Elle was saying about herself, not what she was writing about him.

She looked at her tablet for a moment, then met his gaze again. "You've seen a lot of success—you've won a coveted Eddie Award for the quality of your content, a National Science Amplification Award for making science accessible to the masses, you've published several peer-reviewed papers, you have tens of millions of viewers who watch each of your YouTube videos to learn more about science—and I could go on and on."

He wished she wouldn't, though. Those things took hard work, sure, but they also took a lot of luck. Lightning striking in the right place.

"I'm sure our readers would love to know what or who was the inspiration behind that success."

Okay, that kind of question he could handle. "Easy. My mom."

"Yeah?"

He nodded, leaning back in his chair. "She was pretty great. She helped me to believe that I could do anything." He hadn't always thought his mom was perfect—he was a regular kid, after all, and thought that she was being mean when she'd make him go to bed before he was ready or when she said no to eating candy before dinner. The usual stuff. But he'd also understood at a fairly young age that he had lucked out in the Mom department.

"We had the woods practically right out my back door, and she and I spent a lot of time outside, exploring everything. She always told me to keep studying things and paying attention. Almost every day, she'd motion to all of our surroundings and tell me that I had no limits out there and I had no limits in life. That I could learn and do anything."

He paused a moment, just letting himself relive the feeling of being in those woods with his mom, alive with the possibilities of where his life could take him. "And I believed it. My whole life, I grew up knowing that I would one day do big things, and I felt like my mom knew it too. It's a gift I'm grateful for every day."

"She sounds amazing."

"She was." He hadn't wanted to get personal in this interview, but he never had a problem talking about his mom. He wouldn't be where he was if it weren't for her, and it felt really good to share that with Elle. "She always told me that I had the ability to use my voice for good and that with a voice like mine, I'd be able to direct that good toward a bigger audience.

"She would've been happy if I'd become a research scientist. I probably would've, too. But I had to make a choice, and I had a dream to bring science to more people. When I told her I wanted to start a YouTube channel instead of a regular science job in a lab, she didn't once try to talk me out of it."

"She didn't give you the whole 'Sure, you can do that on the side, but you'll need a real job to pay for everything' talk?"

He laughed. "Nope. I missed out on that one completely." It was probably a good thing that she hadn't given him that talk. He'd been so nervous about starting his channel and so worried that it would flop. If he hadn't had her undying faith in him, he might have taken a "safe" job instead and never gotten started at all.

"Instead, I got the 'rejection isn't failure' talk. The one where she told me that if I try and fail, then I'm no worse off than I was before. She said that I'd spent nearly twenty-four years *not* having a successful YouTube channel, so if I tried and it failed, I knew just how to deal with that. But if I never tried, then I'd have to spend my entire life wondering if I would've been successful but never knowing for sure. And that would be so much more difficult to deal with."

"I can't help but notice that you refer to her in the past tense. Has she—"

He nodded. "She died in a car accident four years ago. Right before I started my channel."

"Oh." Elle looked like his words stabbed her in the heart. "I'm so sorry."

He loved talking about his mom, but not this part of it.

"She knows how the dream I shared with her has grown." He had to believe that. But he didn't want to keep talking about her. "So how about you? Are you very close with your mom?"

Several emotions crossed Elle's face in quick succession. Probably because she was trying to transition from hearing about his mom and her passing to talking about her own mom. It wasn't the nicest thing to throw at her, but he did need to change the subject. And he did want to hear more about this woman sitting across from him.

There was a quiet knock on Declan's door before Mato opened it and poked his head into the room. "I apologize for interrupting. Declan, I've got a woman who needs to talk to you."

Yeah, she was sitting right here in this room with him, and he really wanted to listen to her. "Who?"

"I've been on with Delaney from Kids Camp Nation about the partnership for your kids' science camp. Her boss has some questions and she'll only speak with you. Normally, I would tell her that we need to schedule your chat for later, but I know we're close to getting them on board and waiting might jeopardize that."

They'd had more than a few times over the years when something like this required immediate attention to keep things from falling apart. He turned to Elle, hoping that their conversation didn't fall into that same category, yet fully knowing it wouldn't be wise for him to connect with her any more than he already had. "Do you mind if we pause our interview for a moment?"

"Not at all."

Declan stood to leave the room, but she said, "No, you can take it in here." She turned off the recorder on her phone and picked up her tablet. He watched her face, trying to see a hint of her being as regretful as he was not to be continuing their conversation.

Declan nodded to Mato. Then, to Elle, he said, "When I was about to start filming, you said I could send you out to the Beehive to play basketball. I didn't think I'd take you up on that offer today."

She laughed. "Oh, don't worry—I didn't offer to leave so I could play basketball. I did it so I can see if any of your team members want to spill more juicy details about you."

He gave her a mock worried look that felt a little too real. But honestly, he just wanted work and all other responsibilities to stop for the day—something he *never* wished for—so he could talk with Elle, undisturbed.

Which probably meant that the disruptions were a really good thing.

Chapter Nine

ELLE

*E*lle *had* hoped to get juicy information about Declan from his team. But it wasn't exactly what she got.

She found out from Sam how long editing took (three times as long as filming did!) and how he kept the website updated. Jen told her what was involved with keeping the front end of the business going—and Elle also learned that if she ever decided to start her own event planning business, she needed to hire a Jen.

And she learned from chatting with Halona that Declan's true passion was his local children's science weekend camp that he wanted to take nationwide. That was the big project they were working on now and the one that he was currently on the phone about.

Why did that make her stomach flutter? So the man had a soft spot for kids. It wasn't like that was. . .okay, it totally was adorable. Did he have a soft spot for puppies, too? Because she was picturing that man sitting on the floor while playing with a preschooler (theirs, of course) and a puppy (also theirs) and laughing in that deep voice of his. Suddenly she needed a fan and a long drink of ice water.

Halona also told her that they'd created a YouTube video about the science weekend thing and had so many excited parents comment that it was helping to get partners and sponsors on board.

The feedback about the science weekend possibility and how fun it would be was so positive that Declan's team even discussed hosting a modified version for adults at some point. Elle was going to have to ask him about that.

What she'd gotten from the day so far was good, but she hoped for something a little more personal for the article.

Okay, maybe that wasn't it. She tried to get something personal from everyone she interviewed, and the part about Declan's mom inspiring him fit the bill. So maybe the personal details she wanted weren't so much for the article as for her. Which completely caught her off guard, since she'd walked into this interview wanting nothing personal at all.

My, what a difference seven hours could make.

Mostly, she just wanted to get back to the interview. As much as she didn't want to admit it, she was craving that voice of his. She had a hard time not excusing herself to go to the restroom or grab something from her guest room or her car just so she could listen to some of his interview recordings and let that voice soak into her bones.

She didn't have much time to carry out that plan, though, before Declan and Mato came out of his office and Jen clapped her hands together. "Okay, it's time to film some social media!"

Jen led them into the room where Declan had filmed earlier, but now the set desk was moved to the side, leaving lots of open space in the middle of the room. A cell phone was set up on a tripod at the front, facing the shelves at the back.

As Jen adjusted the tripod and the phone, she said, "We try to spend an hour or less filming for Instagram Reels, YouTube Shorts, and TikTok videos. I grab clips and photos from filming during the week, add text, and pair them with trending music. We do a lot of science-related stuff in those, but in the short clips that we film, we just try to show Declan's personality."

She finished pulling up the phone's camera and met their eyes, hands on her hips. "Sometimes we do a lip sync, sometimes a trend adapted to his brand, sometimes a trending dance, or just something silly that we came up with. Declan, are you ready?"

"Wait," Elle said, turning to Declan, "you do trending dances?" Why hadn't she thought to check out his social media before? Because that was something she really wanted to see.

Declan shrugged and gave her a little smile that showed only the dimple on the left and good golly was it attractive. "I know surprisingly little about social media and Jen knows everything. When we're filming, I just do what she says."

Jen grinned. "And don't you think I don't use that to my advantage. Okay, tell me if you've heard this sound before."

She tapped on her screen and a sound that was part song, part spoken words played. Declan shook his head, but Elle nodded in recognition. "Yeah, I've heard it a ton. People use it while shaking their shoulders, or their hips, or sometimes their booty, and list three unusual things about themselves with text on the screen."

"Yep! And Declan, we are going to use it in a video with you and grasshoppers. We'll switch off between you doing the shaking dance and a clip of a grasshopper rubbing its legs together and have the facts be about the grasshopper."

Elle caught the glare Declan shot Jen and her returning grin, which made Elle want to know more about what a social media filming session was like when Elle wasn't there and what Jen was doing differently this time.

"Perfect," Declan said with gritted teeth. But the man must've still been willing to do what Jen asked, because he added, "But don't think I'll be shaking anything other than my shoulders."

As Elle watched Declan doing the shaking-his-shoulders part, a laugh accidentally broke free. She couldn't help it, though! Declan was just so different from the tense man she'd expected to encounter at this interview.

When Declan's eyes met hers, an eyebrow raised, Elle said, "When you said 'Perfect,' I think you hit the nail on the head. That clip might be the greatest thing that will ever hit the Internet."

Declan didn't say anything—he just scrubbed his hands over his face and turned back to Jen.

They filmed two more clips—one lip sync and another that was just a bunch of reactions or actions that Jen said would go with a video she'd taken earlier in the week that needed a few more segments.

The videos were very different from his longer science ones on YouTube. She loved seeing this more playful side of him.

Jen was silent as she re-watched the video on her phone, her smile getting bigger and bigger as the twelve-second video played. At the end, she clapped her hands once. "Fantastic! Okay, the next video we're going to film is a trending dance, and I think you should both be in it."

Declan rubbed a hand on the back of his neck. "I don't know about that. This twenty-four-hour thing is a test to see how sharing more background on me goes on a very small scale, right? I don't want to announce that's what Elle is here for and make it a bigger test than we'd planned."

Oh. Elle crossed her arms. That's all he saw her as—a small-scale test of a marketing strategy? Was that the only reason he and his team had said yes to this interview? Elle hadn't planned on being in a video with him, but now that he was throwing out Jen's suggestion, she bristled at his unwillingness to be seen publicly with her. She tried not to roll her eyes.

Plus, she had been hoping that Declan would want to share the article on his social media so they could reach his audience, too, instead of just the audience that Aquamoose Rising already reached. It had the potential to draw a lot of students to their college and it was a huge disappointment to know that he wanted to hide it.

Jen put a hand on Declan's shoulder. "You've had plenty of other people in your videos—your dad, your brothers, each of us, and other YouTube, TikTok, and Reels celebrities that you've collaborated with. People won't suddenly go 'Oh! I bet that means he's being interviewed for an article with his alma mater. I should go find it.' We don't even have to say who Elle is or who she's here representing."

He nodded. "You're right."

Jen let go of Declan's shoulder and turned to Elle. "So, what do you think? Are you in? I swear it'll be fun."

So Jen wanted her to be in the video because she thought it would build Declan's audience, but Declan was unwilling to let the spotlight shine even a little bit on LBSU? Ugh. *Celebrities*. They only looked out for themselves.

She nearly put her foot down and said that she wouldn't do it if they didn't at least tag LBSU in the video caption, but then it hit her how much of a hypocrite she was being. She was there interviewing Declan, hoping that his celebrity status would help out LBSU's recruitment efforts. She had asked him to agree to this interview out of the goodness of his heart and offered him nothing in return. The least she could do was agree to be in a video with him.

Plus, he was waiting for her answer with such a hopeful expression. It had a hint of vulnerability behind it too, and it was overwhelmingly endearing. She was beginning to realize that there was a lot more power in those intriguing eyes than in his dimples, his voice, or his hair. His comments section should definitely be full of comments about his eyes.

"I'm in."

Besides, if her article only reached the audience she would've been able to reach anyway, it might still help to have her in a video with Declan. She could link to it in the article, and it would offer an extra connection in people's minds between Declan and Lake Baldwin State University.

What? She was looking out for the school's interests since she was there on their behalf. It wasn't the same as looking out for her own interests.

Elle, Declan, and Jen all gathered close to Jen's phone to watch the dance she and Declan would be doing. It was probably no more than fifteen seconds long, so it couldn't be too hard to learn.

Yet she suddenly felt panic rising. What if she looked like a dork in the video? These were Declan's fans who would be seeing it, so they'd be gracious in their judgments of him, but they didn't know her. And he had a *lot* of fans. Spread out over all walks of life. What if the comments were filled with people making fun of her or calling her ridiculous names or saying she was awful?

Why had she said yes before thinking this through? Oh yeah. Because she had been too focused on petty matters. Or maybe because he'd turned the power of his pleading eyes on her and they were impossible to resist. The look he was giving her right now made her knees feel not exactly full of strength and capable of holding up an entire body.

How was she supposed to pull off a trending dance with knees that couldn't even support her when she stood still?

"You seem… uncomfortable with this," Declan said.

Was she broadcasting her feelings on her face? Or was he just being extra observant? "Just a bit," she said, holding her thumb and pointer finger an inch apart, hoping her tone came across as brevity and not the anxiety that surprised even her.

He cocked his head. "I'm confused. You run big events at LBSU, right? You get up in front of everyone?"

She nodded, not trusting her voice to come out as strong and unwavering as she wanted.

"Okay, so you're comfortable in front of a crowd. How big of a crowd? Generally speaking."

She shrugged. "Anywhere from fifteen to six hundred."

His nodding was slow and thoughtful. "So why are you not comfortable here, in front of a camera, where it feels like only Jen is watching?"

That was a very good question. The truth was, she loved being in front of a crowd as an Admissions Counselor. The bigger the crowd, the more exhilarating. She'd often wondered what it was about her personality that made her crave that so much, especially since she'd always been such a shy kid. Maybe it was because she liked the feeling of everyone listening to her, knowing she had important things to say.

But this wouldn't be getting in front of a hungry audience and having important information to share. And the audiences she normally spoke to were very specific ones—high school students checking out colleges with their parents, and college students who were part of the student ambassador program or Sterling Scholars. Declan's videos went to people of all ages all over the world.

She cleared her throat. "When I'm in front of a group, I can see their reactions immediately and adjust. When it's in front of a camera and people will be watching it later, I don't know what their reactions might be. They could all be at home, hating me. And people are a lot nicer in person than they are online."

Declan studied her for a long moment, and she could swear that he was seeing right into her soul. Like he now knew all the things she'd just thought and not said aloud. And she was suddenly glad that she hadn't been thinking about how it made her heart rate kick up and the heat level of her entire body increase to have the force of Declan's concerned eyes turned upon her. It felt like he cared. About her.

She had to stop thinking like that! *Come on, nine-year-old Elle! Think of your dad's rejection and his NDA! You're slacking on the job!*

"For what it's worth, I think people are going to love you. I think they'd find it impossible not to."

Why did that sound so genuine? And why did it make her heart do a warm, fluttery thing? It was the deep voice, she was sure.

But deep voice trickery or not, her body seemed to listen and the anxiety fled. "Okay."

"Yes!" Jen said, clapping once. "Let's get this party started. You two stand right there. Good. I'm going to play this at half speed until we get the dance down pat. Then we'll speed it up to normal and we'll try it with both of you wearing lab coats."

Elle breathed in deeply. *Don't think about who's going to watch this later. Just focus on the music, the dance, and the people here in this room.*

Then she met Declan's eyes and her knees reminded her that Declan was their Kryptonite. *Okay, maybe don't focus on the man in the room so much.*

The dance was simple. She'd seen it in enough videos to practically have it memorized. But just because it was simple didn't mean it was easy. She'd played plenty of sports growing up, so she was fairly coordinated. But dance classes cost money—money they'd never had.

Elle's dad's band was a little more "rock" than "boy band," so he didn't have to get up on stage and dance—or at least he didn't in his music videos. With upbeat songs like his, he could dance on stage and it wouldn't be weird.

But he didn't. Maybe her lack of dance coordination came from him.

She knew her dad was far from perfect, even if the media didn't see it, so it made her smile to know that the genes she'd gotten from him weren't perfect, either.

After a lot of takes, a lot of bumping into each other, a lot of laughter at all the ways they'd managed to mess up a fifteen-second dance, and a lot of accidental touches and eye contact (that she managed to only let affect her a little), they got the dance down.

And once the movements were natural, it only took twice of practicing it at normal speed before they nailed it. Jen bestowed the lab coats on them like bouquets of flowers to celebrate a stellar performance.

Stellar, it wasn't. But she was having fun.

They did the dance once in the lab coats. It went well, but when they were done, Jen just studied them, a finger on her lip. "It needs something more. How about at the end, Declan, you put your arms out like this, as if you're holding a big load of laundry. And Elle, you jump into Declan's arms."

Elle eyed Jen suspiciously. She'd been asking them to get closer and closer for the past forty minutes, like she was trying to nudge things into happening between the two of them. Which was going directly against what Elle wanted to have happen. (Or at least what her brain wanted to have happen. Her body wasn't always getting the message. Okay, sometimes her brain wasn't, either.) "That's not part of the trend."

"You say that like there are rules for using a trending dance or sound," Jen said. "Anyone can tweak the trend. Especially when you've got as many followers as Declan does. It's going to add that extra zing at the end that gets people to hit that heart or favorite or follow or share. Trust me."

Declan looked at Elle. Maybe it was the adrenaline from the dancing, but she gave him a shrug. "Yolo."

So Declan turned to Jen. "We'll try it once and see how it goes. Then we'll decide."

So they did the dance at normal speed with the lab coats on. And when they got to the end of the dance, she jumped up, putting her arm behind Declan's neck and across his shoulders as he caught her in his arms.

"Oh my goodness!" She might have said the words in her head or she might have breathed them. Being in his arms, one just under her knees and the other across the middle of her back, holding her close to his chest, felt like being cradled in a cloud. If the cloud had strong muscles and a great smile. She could feel each of his deep breaths against her, his heart beating against her arm, their faces only inches apart. She had caught whiffs of his scent as they practiced, but now she breathed it in deeply as her heart pounded away, her own breaths coming fast.

And with that joyful smile on his face that mirrored

her own—one of happiness and an immense feeling of victory at getting the dance right—being so close, she knew those breaths of hers weren't going to slow anytime soon.

Declan cleared his throat, like he suddenly realized the two of them shouldn't have their arms around each other with their faces close enough that they could kiss if she only tilted her head a bit. He set her on the ground.

"Oh, wow," Jen said.

"You think we should do it for the actual video, then?" Declan said, his voice coming out even deeper and huskier than his voice sounded naturally. Elle wasn't okay admitting what that sound did to her insides.

"I think we should use that last take. It was perfection."

Elle's eyebrows rose. "You were filming that one?"

"Of course I was. And I'm so glad—that was lightning in a bottle right there. Unrepeatable no matter how many takes we do."

"Show us," Elle insisted.

"No," Jen said as she removed her phone from the tripod. "I've got to finish editing and adding the words and captions. You can see it when it's posted on Friday."

Maybe it was good that Jen wouldn't let them see the video right then, because Elle knew two things.

One, that she was going to watch that video later and fully let herself relive that moment because Jen was right —it *was* magical. The kind of magic that birthed fairy tales and inspired songs. And not everyone got to experience that, so it felt irresponsible not to let it live in her head for a while.

And two, that she absolutely couldn't allow herself to get into a position where she was that close to Declan again, because apparently, his closeness was Kryptonite to *all* of her, not just her knees.

Nine-year-old Elle, I'm going to need you to step up your game over the next little while, or we'll be in trouble.

Chapter Ten

DECLAN

Declan followed Elle and Jen out of the filming room and headed toward the Beehive where Halona, Sam, and Mato all sat at the round table, working on their laptops. Mato looked up as they entered and said to the group, "I need to let the restaurant know a final count for dinner tonight. Sam?"

"Oh, sorry, I'm going to have to bow out. My sister and her husband have tickets to a show tonight and her babysitter fell through. I need to watch my niece."

Mato nodded. "Jen?"

Jen looked at Declan, her mouth turned down in a frown. "I'm going to have to miss, too. Brady said that they're having an 'all hands on deck' moment at the firm and he's going to be there late into the night. He asked if I would bring him dinner."

"Well," Mato said, "we don't want him to starve. Halona?"

"Kateri has an early soccer game tonight and I've got to go. She still hasn't forgiven me for missing last week when she scored a goal from midfield."

"Tonight?" Declan asked.

"Yeah. It was supposed to be tomorrow, but something about the field and grubs and pest control coming tomorrow."

"That's too bad," Mato said, shaking his head. "Because my oldest just texted that her water heater went out and she needs my help installing a new one."

Declan eyed Mato. His sentence was true, except for the "just" part. Her water heater had gone out last week and Mato knew that Declan knew that, so it was his way of being "honest" with Declan while providing a reason to Elle.

Declan looked around at his team. "I thought you were all staying for dinner tonight."

"I thought we were, too," Halona said. "So weird that something came up for all of us."

Declan eyed her. "Yes. *Weird,*" he said in a flat voice. It was as if they were all conspiring to get Declan and Elle alone together. Even Mato, the guy who knew how impersonal Declan wanted this interview to be.

Mato cleared his throat like he was trying to clear the

guilt from his conscience. "Don't worry—the restaurant should still have the food delivered for the two of you on time."

At least his team stuck around until the end of the work day so that Elle could ask any questions that had come up and laugh and joke around with her a bit, obviously trying to get her to overlook the whole leaving early thing. And they were being so darned charming that it appeared to work.

As soon as it was quitting time, though, everyone except Mato left pretty quickly. Then Mato said, "You two go talk about interview stuff and I'll hang around until dinner gets here and set it all out."

"Mato, you don't have to do that."

"No, it's okay. I have more to do before I leave anyway. Go talk about your plans to take your science weekend national or answer Elle's questions."

So they did. Declan and Elle talked enough that there was no way they'd let her write an article long enough to cover it all. And he was pretty proud of himself for staying on track with the questions and not getting too personal. Which was a strange thing to be proud of himself for—he'd been worried he'd struggle to open up at all, not that he'd open up too much.

The food came, and Mato went to the kitchen to "get everything set out" before saying goodbye and leaving.

And then it was just Declan and Elle, standing at his dining table that was set beautifully, including lit candles.

Candles.

He was going to have to talk with Mato. And was that seriously Barry Manilow coming through his speaker system?

He kept hearing a buzzing sound that he knew wasn't coming from his phone. Elle seemed to be ignoring whatever texts she had come in, though, and she picked up a note that Mato had left on the table and read it aloud. "'Dessert is in the fridge. Enjoy!' Oh, that's sweet of him."

Yeah... sweet.

Elle stood at Declan's side, staring down at the table setting and the fancy meal. "This looks like a date."

He squeezed the bridge of his nose between his thumb and fingers. "I know. This is completely unprofessional, and on behalf of my overzealous team, I apologize. I'll turn on the lights and change the music to... anything else."

It wasn't that he didn't want to be alone with Elle—he very much did. That was the problem. He'd decided back in college, after how things had gone with his last girlfriend, that he wouldn't get into any more relationships, yet that was exactly what he wanted to do with Elle after having known her only nine hours. The length of a single work day. How was he going to keep thoughts of her and a possible future together in check if he spent even more time with her? Especially in a setting like this.

He was opening his mouth to tell his smart-home device to make some changes when Elle said, "No, really, it's fine."

But he still asked it to change to his road-trip playlist and increase the lighting by twenty percent. There was no need for this evening to feel any more awkward . . . or plant more ideas into his head.

"I want you to know that my team's enthusiasm in arranging all this is because they like you. They wouldn't have done it otherwise."

She smiled, pulled out her phone, and gave it a little shake. "I get it. My people are being a little enthusiastic, too. Maybe it's been too long since either of us has dated and they thought they needed to step in."

He chuckled on the outside, but on the inside, all he could focus on was that she hadn't been on a date in a while. What did she consider "too long?" Two weeks? A year? He wasn't looking to date this woman, so why was that all he could think about?

Mato had already plated their salads, so they both sat down, picked up their salad forks, and placed their napkins on their laps. How had Mato even known where all this stuff was in his house? If Declan ever had a sudden need for fancy place settings, he'd have to search for everything—he never set his table this fancy.

As he stabbed his fork into the Caesar salad, he tried to think of conversation topics that would keep things professional and not romantic. And then he immediately had to push from his mind the memory of Elle jumping into his arms earlier during filming. Just that flash of a thought of her lips being so kissably close made him want to get that close to her again.

"You still owe me a story about you and your mom," he said. That was a good one, because not only was he curious, there was no topic like parents to keep things from getting romantic. He stuck the bite of salad into his mouth. Okay, so it didn't quite fit into the "keep things professional" category, but it was better than being zero for two.

She swallowed her food. "Oh! I forgot about that." Her brow crinkled, like her mind had been going another direction and was suddenly pulled back. "Um, I don't even know where to start. I guess with the fact that we didn't get along very well growing up?"

"You didn't?"

She shook her head. "I spent a lot of my childhood being mad at her and definitely not understanding her. But then I moved out and went to college. In my second semester, I took a Psych 101 class because I realized I wanted to get where she was coming from."

"Did you have Professor Feinmore?"

Elle's eyebrows shot up. "Yes! Did you take her class, too?"

He nodded. "My first semester."

"And like every Psych 101 student, I started seeing and armchair diagnosing the problems in everyone else's lives—"

"—and never your own," Declan finished.

"Exactly." Elle studied him for a moment with a small smile on her lips and he could practically feel their connection strengthen. Then she chuckled and glanced down at her plate. "I never made much progress on the 'figuring myself out' thing that semester, but it helped me with my mom. I realized in that class that a lot of my childhood frustrations were related to my mom's belief that she didn't have enough worthwhile DNA in her, so she never believed in herself."

"That's really sad." He couldn't help but think of his own mom. She'd gone through a lot. If she'd had to do it without faith in herself, it wouldn't have gone well for her or Declan.

"Yep. And it made me feel like I'd been treating her unfairly pretty much my entire life. So I started trying to help my mom change her mindset and eventually talked her into seeing a therapist. Somewhere along the way, she overhauled her life and we managed to overhaul our relationship. She and I became friends.

"And she's doing so much better now! She even found a guy, Duane, who treats her well and they're very happy and very much in love. Which is great, because the guys she dated or married for most of my life were bums. She and Duane got married four years ago. She's got everything all figured out and it makes me so happy."

"I can tell." The smile she wore was genuine. So was the blush that brightened her cheeks when she saw him noticing. "So what I'm hearing is, you went to college and it changed your mother's life."

She laughed. "We should start putting that on our recruitment materials."

Looking around at the table, he said, "Do you know what? This isn't me." He'd be happy to take Elle to a fancy restaurant sometime—that wasn't out of the realm of possibility. *If* he was looking for a relationship, which he was not.

But having this fancy meal pushed on him while with someone he was not dating and wanted to keep a semi-professional relationship with just wasn't right. "I'm much more at home outside. And the sun hasn't even set, so the candlelight feels wrong. What do you say we take this..." he looked at the main dish and made a guess, "...Tuscan chicken out to the patio table? That's where I eat most of my meals anyway."

The face she made at his suggestion told him she was relieved. Once they'd picked up their plates and gotten settled outside, the compliments she gave him on his yard made him feel like a rock star. Seeing the golden light of the evening sun on her face made him feel things he had long ago given up on feeling.

He cleared his throat. "When Mato suggested this day-in-the-life interview, he had things planned down to the minute. If I remember correctly, after dinner with *all of us*, there were going to be games while we all socialized. Card games, probably." Now that it was just him and a woman he'd sworn to keep things professional with but felt increasingly attracted to, the rest of the evening seemed like an impossibly long time to fill.

"I can play card games with the best of them," Elle said as she stabbed a piece of chicken with her fork, "but what I want to do is beat you at tetherball." She motioned to his tetherball pole with her fork before sticking the bite into her mouth.

He smiled. "I installed that because once I introduced the game to my little brothers, they became obsessed."

"Define 'little' brothers. Because my 'little' brother is just two years younger and has a good six inches and fifty pounds on me. Please tell me you're used to only playing with people shorter than me so my height won't be such a disadvantage. How old are they?"

Chatting about family was good. It was a normal topic of conversation and a way to connect in a friendly manner. That was all they could be. Friends. "They're nine and eleven. My mom married my dad when I was sixteen.

Well, he's my stepdad, but from the very start, I've always called him 'Dad.' He was exactly what my mom needed. He's a pretty great guy."

Elle gave him a curious look when he mentioned his dad, but he couldn't tell why, so he just forged ahead, hoping to figure it out.

"They had their first kid together, my brother Ian, when I was seventeen. So a year before I left for college. My brother Hayden was born during my sophomore year. And to answer your question, you've got Hayden beat in height. Ian, though?" He shrugged.

"So you're saying the eleven-year-old is taller than me."

"And he's pretty good at tetherball."

He didn't miss the gleam in her eye. She was clearly up for the challenge. And suddenly he wondered if that look was only referring to tetherball.

She broke off a piece of one of the crusty rolls. "So you have a stepdad. Was your biological dad married to your mom before that?" Her eyes met his, bread chunk raised halfway, and he could tell that she knew to be cautious in asking the question, but there was also a strong curiosity. Those alluring eyes of hers grabbed his focus and he felt powerless to break free.

He cleared his throat and looked down at his plate. "They divorced when I was four." He took a bite of chicken, hoping it would stop that line of questioning. It didn't.

"Do you see him often?"

After he swallowed the bite, he shook his head. "Not once since the divorce."

"Do you still have memories of him?"

All he had was a vague memory of fighting and things crashing to the floor. "Nope." He wasn't going to let his mind relive the past, though, especially when he had a present that included Elle. And tetherball.

As soon as they'd finished eating, they played more rounds of tetherball than he'd guessed they would—until the sun set and it was too dark to play any longer. And before he knew it, they were flushed with the rush of exercise and competition and back inside, sitting on his couch, playing cards while talking about random things. Non-interview things. Like how they managed to spend the same four years at the same college, their paths constantly crossing, without ever having met.

They each sat on the couch with one leg bent so they were facing one another, and it seemed that the later the night got, the closer together they inched. The space between them where the cards went shrunk smaller and smaller and the electricity between the two of them grew bigger and bigger.

They had played quite a few different games together, but as the night wore on, Elle suggested a game that he was pretty sure she'd made up on the spot that felt like offspring of the games Speed and Memory, where they both played at the same time. Their hands moved quickly among the same overturned cards.

And then they both leaned forward simultaneously to grab the same card, her hand landing right on top of his, and the game based on speed suddenly slowed to a crawl as they met each other's gaze. Her hand was warm and soft on his and sent pulsing energy up his arm and straight to his heart, where it seemed to zap him at a constant pace, his chest heating up more and more with each zap. Her lips were just inches from his, and when his eyes did manage to leave hers, they couldn't seem to stray from her lips. They were so perfectly smooth, her pink lipstick faded from earlier.

But he sat frozen, just feeling the zaps and the softness of her hand and the pull of her captivating eyes. It felt like they would always be paralyzed in that position, unable to move away from its magnetic pull—until the moment Elle did.

She cleared her throat, but her voice still came out rough. Strained. "It's getting late. I've got notes to type up —I should probably get to my room."

He nodded, trying to tamp down all the emotions that had been building up inside, and started scooping the cards into a stack. "I should get to bed, too." He hoped she didn't notice that his voice also came out a little strained.

Declan reminded himself not to let Elle affect him that way.

He struggled to get the cards back into their box as he watched her walk toward the hallway that led to his guest room, wondering if he would be able to sleep tonight, knowing that she was only three doors away.

Chapter Eleven

ELLE

Elle woke up in the darkness with a full bladder and reached over the right side of the bed for her phone before remembering that she was in Declan's guest room and her phone was on the left. She found it and opened one eye long enough to see that it was 3:19 a.m. and that she had a slew of texts from her mom, Camilla, and Summer. She put it face-down on the nightstand and stumbled out of bed to the door.

When she reached the hallway, she headed toward the main area before looking around, confused. Where was the bathroom again? Her mostly-asleep brain remembered that it was in the hallway, not out there. She went around the corner to the hallway again, feeling for the wall in the darkness so she could mostly keep her eyes closed and not risk waking up fully, and promptly ran into something hard. She squinted at the same time as her hand flew to the object she'd run into and realized it was skin. Smooth skin over hard muscles.

Her eyes flew open, and she screamed and stepped back, heart hammering in her chest. In the dim light, she could see that it was Declan, wearing only a pair of gym shorts, his hair ruffled from sleep, his expression as shocked as hers must surely be.

"What are you doing?" he asked.

"Looking for the bathroom. What are you doing?" Her eyes weren't on his face as she asked—they were on his abs. And she was definitely fully awake now. It was probably a good thing for her state of mind yesterday that she hadn't known that a six-pack was hiding under his shirt.

Did he get that from doing yard work? Or maybe he had a gym in his basement? His house was pretty big, and he didn't seem like the gym-going type. Or the super vain type. But it also didn't seem like all that came from gardening. Oh. It was probably because he was a scientist, so he knew the science behind making bodies work optimally.

He was a really good scientist.

He rubbed a hand over the back of his neck, looking... sheepish, was it? "I, um, woke up hungry. Are you?"

Was she? She was too tired to tell. But she nodded anyway.

"Okay, I'll go, uh, put on a shirt. Sorry about that."

"And I'll..." she hooked a thumb toward the door she was now sure was the bathroom, "...head to the bathroom."

By the time they both made it to the kitchen, Elle was feeling a little more alert. Or at least less likely to get lost.

"What are you hungry for?"

Those words in his deep, inviting voice at this time of night were almost too much. She picked up the note that Mato had left for them last night about dessert being in the fridge. They'd had so much fun that it hadn't crossed her mind that they hadn't eaten it. "How about this? I mean, we don't want to just leave it in the fridge and make Mato feel bad that we ignored it."

"True. Eating it would be the kind thing to do." Declan opened the fridge, pulled out a white pastry box, and read the label on the side aloud. "Chocolate vanilla berry panna cotta tart."

She had no idea what that was, but it sounded delicious enough that her sleeping belly woke right up and started rumbling.

Declan opened up the sides of the box. The tart looked kind of like a pie but smaller. After getting out two forks and two plates, he cut the tart into four slices and put one on each of their plates.

The crust looked similar to a pie crust but darker. That must be the chocolate part of the name. The filling was white, silky smooth, and creamy. The top was covered with a berry sauce and sprinkled with strawberries, raspberries, and blueberries.

The moment her rear touched the seat of the barstool next to Declan, she pushed her fork into the dessert and got that piece of deliciousness into her mouth. The flaky chocolate crust, the sweetened cream of the filling, and the fruity topping mixed to create an experience worthy of heaven itself. "I can't believe how good this is," she mumbled.

"I can't believe I never knew this existed," Declan said after a bite of his.

After a few minutes of them sitting side by side, fully enjoying every bite of the dessert, Elle licked some of the topping off her fork and then twisted it around slowly, examining it. "I have to admit that when Mato asked me to do a twenty-four-hour interview with you, I pictured it going differently."

"Oh, yeah? Different in what way?"

She shrugged and pushed her fork into the sweet goodness again. "Flashier, I guess."

"Jen assured me that home offices were flashy. I feel lied to."

Elle laughed. "I guess I just thought you would be showing off connections more. You know, famous people you are friends with. Name dropping. Having every moment of your day spoken for, with people to get you to each thing on your schedule. Wardrobe changes. Fast cars. Getting into fancy restaurants."

He forked another bite of the tart. "Hey, I got you into In Queso Hunger."

"I'm pretty sure that was Jen's doing."

"Okay, you're right. My team is much better at opening doors to opportunities than I am. If you think Jen is impressive, you should see Halona in action with anyone who can get us in to share science with kids."

"You seem pretty passionate about working with children." He nodded, so she continued, hoping to get more details. Typing up her notes last night—or, well, just a few hours ago— had helped her to see some gaps in her knowledge of him. "Is that because of the way you grew up?"

"Probably."

"What was your home like?"

The way he pressed his lips together and drew his eyebrows together for a quick moment told her that he didn't like that question. She wondered if he might share if she just gave him a minute, so she stayed quiet.

She looked down at her empty plate, then glanced at the other side of the counter where the other two pieces still sat in the box. The dessert was just so tasty and not heavy at all, and their pieces were rather small, and she really wanted to keep eating it. She probably could've eaten the entire tart herself. "It looks like we have seconds waiting for us."

He tilted his head to the side, his eyes soft and amused. "I think those should maybe go back in my fridge."

They were both going to eat a second piece—she knew it and he knew it. His tone was teasing. Just making her want it even more. Which was probably an impossible feat, because she already wanted it at the maximum level.

So she eyed him, then got up and headed around the island counter to the other side. He jumped, hurrying in the opposite direction around the island, racing to get to the dessert first. But she ran and grabbed the spatula before he could. "Where are your manners, Mr. Davenport?"

"Still asleep, I guess."

He reached clear across the wide countertop and retrieved both of their forks. She didn't miss the way his T-shirt revealed an inch or two of the skin she'd seen just a bit ago. She wished Mato's note wasn't clear over on the table so she could fan herself with it.

He held the fork out to her, eyebrow raised in question, so she put down the spatula and took it from him. Who needed plates? She had no problem standing next to this man, eating something sweet and delicious right out of the box.

But it was clear that his mind was no longer on her question, so an answer wasn't going to be coming. Not that it could fill in any gaps in her article—it suddenly hit her that the NDA covered things about where he grew up.

Just because she couldn't put it in the article, though, didn't make her any less curious. Maybe if she told him about her childhood home, he'd open up about his. "I grew up in a trailer home."

He glanced from the tart to her and back to the tart. "Oh, yeah?"

She nodded as she ran the edge of her fork back and forth over the filling, smoothing the surface. "It wasn't a bad place to live, but Gertrude was *old*."

"Your trailer home's name was *Gertrude*?"

"Me and my brother, Levi, named it when he was seven and I was nine. We figured the place was like a sweet old grandma—it kept us safe and protected and was a good place to call home. But it was also worn out, the carpet and wallpaper looked like they had hit their prime fifty years earlier, and it had seen far too many hard days in its life."

"Let me guess. Gold and green color palette?"

"I can see you're picturing it perfectly. It had a stale smell, too. But it also smelled like baking cookies a good part of the time. We didn't have any firsthand experiences with grandmas—our mom didn't get along well with her parents and we didn't know either of our dads' parents at all—so we had to go on our knowledge of grandmas in TV shows and movies. And Gertrude was the most grandma-ish name we could come up with."

She took a bite of her dessert, hoping that would give him the opening he needed to talk about his home. But instead, he asked, "How about your biological dad? Was he ever married to your mom?"

"Nope. One night stand."

"So he wasn't in the picture at all?"

She set down her fork and leaned against the counter. "Nope. My mom was a groupie—one of those women who would put on a skimpy dress and hang out backstage at a concert or at an on-site filming location, trying to get invited to mingle with the band or with an actor. Sometimes it worked. And sometimes it produced a child. In my mom's case, twice. Me and Levi."

"How did she feel about getting pregnant when the guy wasn't likely to hang around?"

"That was what she'd gone there for."

"To get pregnant?"

"Yeah. It took me a while to stop judging her for it. And she is a different person now. She just... grew up with parents who failed at life in pretty much every way. They belittled her a lot, too, so she grew up believing that she didn't have much to offer the world.

"Of course, she'd internalized it all in a way that made her think she was never enough to attract the kind of good man—an amazing person who would be an amazing dad—

that she was attracted to. And it had been a self-fulfilling prophecy. She dated losers my entire childhood."

"Abusive?"

Elle shook her head. "Nothing like that. Just people like her parents—no ambition, could rarely hold down jobs, spent most of their time drunk in front of the TV—stuff like that.

"But she wanted kids, and she wanted us to have a better chance at everything than she had. So she sought out men who she thought were as talented as she thought she was untalented, in the hopes that they would balance things out for us. That they'd contribute the stellar genes she felt she lacked."

She studied Declan's face for signs of judgment but didn't see any. So she continued. "Maybe she sought out guys who were only looking for a one-night stand because she didn't feel like she could keep the attention of someone like that for more than a couple of hours. But it was never intending to snare the guy or to get money or anything. The whole goal was to provide 'better' genes for us."

"So she was looking out for you before you were even conceived."

Elle was grateful that he saw that side of it. She didn't tell the story to many people, but when she did, people only saw the flip side that made them dislike her mom.

"So do you know who your dad is?"

"Yep. Corbin Flint." She paused a moment to let recognition wash over him before continuing. "My mom wanted Levi and me to know that we had those good genes, so we both knew who our dads were pretty much from the start. When I was nine, my dad came out with the song *A Dad and his Daughter*. Do you know it?"

Declan nodded.

"I heard it on the radio, and I felt it connect to my soul." She touched her knuckles to her heart, somehow still feeling that same emotion she'd felt as a little girl. "I came home and looked up the music video. I found out later that he wrote the song because he and his girlfriend were expecting and she miscarried."

She picked up her fork again, mostly for something to do with her hands, but she didn't want another bite of the dessert. "He was a dad in the video. And he was so caring toward the daughter, and it seemed like he was the most perfect dad ever. He wore a white button-down shirt and dress pants, no tie, the top button open. His hair was nice and trimmed and everything about him was so different from the guys my mom dated or married. I re-watched it a million times, looking into his eyes and seeing how much love he had for his daughter."

She couldn't believe that she was telling him all this. It wasn't information she shared. Yet she couldn't seem to stop, either. Maybe because he was looking at her with those understanding eyes that seemed to *want* to know the story. It was almost as if they had the power to coax the story out of her.

Those eyes were going to be the death of her.

"I wanted that same love aimed in my direction. I just *knew* that he'd have that much love for me once he knew about me. Especially since I was *actually* his daughter—I found out at some point that the girl in the video wasn't."

The emotions for that washed over her, too. She noticed that her fork was starting to tremble, so she set it down.

Then Declan reached out and put his hand on hers, giving it a little squeeze of comfort. She swallowed hard as she looked down at his thumb running across the top of her hand. It felt so caring. Like he got it. Like he wasn't judging.

But still, she never shared this story. Something in her current state of tiredness combined with being loaded up with sugar was making her share. She looked down at the dessert. "Is there truth serum in here?"

He chuckled softly but stayed quiet, urging her to continue. The same thing she'd tried earlier to get him to talk. Obviously, he was much better at it than she was because she continued. She didn't even remember deciding to do it.

"My mom was with a guy named Travis then, and he was so bad at pretending to be a dad that it made me want a real one. So I wrote my dad a letter and found out just how much of that video was him showing off his acting skills."

"What happened?"

"I told him that I was his daughter and I wanted to meet him and wanted him to be my dad. I poured my heart and soul and hopes and dreams into that letter, all written in my best nine-year-old handwriting. I even included a picture of myself. My mom always said I had my dad's eyes, and I was hoping that he would see those eyes and just know me. To feel that connection, I guess.

"Apparently, he did notice the eyes and believed my story. Looking back now, I realize I probably was far from the first surprise child he'd heard from. Anyway, he didn't write back, but his lawyer did contact my mom and offered her nine thousand dollars to sign an NDA stating that she wouldn't tell anyone I was his daughter. Or, I guess, anyone *else*."

"Oh, that must've been hard."

"I was devastated. I ran home from school that day, hoping to find a letter from my dad, and instead, I found his lawyer standing by my kitchen table as my mom sat and signed the contract. To me, it felt like she was signing away any chance I'd ever have of a relationship with my dad. She'd traded a chance for me to have an actual dad for money."

He gave her a soft look and asked in a quiet voice, "Why do you think your mom signed?"

"She just saw the situation very differently. She had sought my dad out so she could give me a leg up. It's why she sought out Levi's dad, too. My dad offering her money did the same thing. It allowed her to pay off Gertrude so she could get rid of her crappy boyfriend and her crappy second job and be there more for Levi and me. She said he was never going to hang around and be a dad no matter how much I wanted it.

"It stabbed me in the gut at the time, but I eventually understood that reality. She hadn't traded my relationship with my dad for cash—that contract represented my dad fully rejecting me."

Elle realized she wouldn't have told Declan all that if he hadn't put his hand on hers and been so sweet. So she pulled her hand back. "It took me a while to understand that. I mean, I should've known before sending the letter— my dad was used to being in front of a camera and expressing emotions that didn't exist. I should've known not to trust what he wanted everyone to see."

Declan didn't say that her dad would love her if he knew her, that he'd be proud of who she'd become, or that it was probably best that he wasn't in her life, or anything else she'd heard from others since childhood. Instead, he pulled her into a hug, wrapping his arms firmly around her.

His embrace was strong without being tight. She leaned her head against his chest, feeling the exhaustion of the late hour and the emotional strain. His breathing and the beating of his heart and the steadiness of both made her own heart, which was beating too fast and too hard, start to calm. Like it knew it was safe and peaceful here.

She stifled a yawn as the exhaustion grew. He made her feel so comfortable that she could probably fall asleep on her feet, right there against his chest. "He's how I got my name, you know," she said, her voice coming out muffled against his shirt.

Declan pulled back a bit. "He chose it?"

She shook her head. "It was from the album he was promoting when my mom went to that concert to meet him—*Luck, Love, Last, Live*. The album cover had a big L in the middle, and since the title had four four-letter words all starting with L, she thought that Elle, a four-letter name, was perfect."

"Well, for the record, I do think it's perfect."

She gave him a very sleepy smile that she felt with her entire face. She was such a weird mix of tired and yet exhilarated being with Declan. Maybe her body was asleep and her mind awake. Or was her mind asleep and her body awake? Neither sounded right. Both sounded right. But her nerve endings? They were definitely awake. "I shared too much."

"No, you didn't."

"Yes, I did. I'm pretty sure that was the textbook definition of oversharing, and I can't be the only one who does. It's your turn now."

"You already know about my family. My parents divorced, my mom was single for a long time, and then married my dad, Gary, a dozen years ago, and he's great. She died four years ago and I have brothers who are also great and I get to see them several times a week."

"I need more than that. That's like level-two sharing. Mine was more like level ten."

"That may be true. But I think the sugar crash from that dessert is hitting you and you're going to fall asleep right here if we don't get you to bed."

Okay, that may be true, but it didn't make her want to hear about Declan any less. But oh, was she tired. She could barely keep her eyelids from closing. So quickly she didn't even have time to stop it, Declan scooped her up into his arms.

"Declan! I don't need to be carried to bed!"

"I know."

Yet he still walked toward the hallway that led to her room. And just like when she'd jumped into his arms while they were filming, it felt glorious. She could fight him to walk there herself, but did she want to? Earlier, she'd been scared of the feelings she'd had while in his arms, pressed up against him. Now, though, she just wanted to close the distance between their faces.

He set her onto her feet just outside her room, but

their bodies were still so close together. She had reasons not to fall for him. Not to kiss him. What were they again? They felt so fuzzy and far away.

She leaned in closer, her head tilted up, her eyes locked on his. The moonlight filtered through a window somewhere and cast just enough of a silver glow on his face to see his dark lashes. The spot where a dimple would appear the moment he smiled. They were so close she swore she could still feel his heartbeat. Close enough that all she had to do was rise on her toes and her lips would meet his.

The look on his face told her that he wanted her to kiss him as much as she wanted it. But then he breathed, "You're on the clock. I'm pretty sure it's bad manners for me to kiss the person who came to interview me. Or to take advantage of someone under the influence of sleep deprivation and truth serum."

"Oh, now you care about manners. Where were they when I wanted more chocolate berry deliciousness tart?"

He smiled, still so close to her that they only needed to whisper. "You plan to leave at nine in the morning?"

She nodded. Declan wrapping his arms around her in his kitchen, her head resting against his chest, him listening to everything she said, carrying her to her room— all of it had felt like a spell had been cast over them. The reminder that she was leaving in the morning seemed to make the magic dissipate. Would she even see him again after tomorrow?

She'd thought about trying to convince him to stay with her longer. But before she could, he said, "I make breakfast in the mornings. Eight-fifteen, if you're interested."

And then he turned and walked away, leaving her wondering how she would ever get back to sleep with thoughts of his lips on her mind.

Chapter Twelve

DECLAN

"Good morning," Elle said as she entered and sat at the bar across from Declan, who was slicing oranges and keeping an eye on the biscuits in the oven and the sausage gravy simmering on his stove. He stopped with his knife mid-cut, feeling like his whole world stopped a bit when she walked in.

Gone were the thin T-shirt, baggy pajama pants, and messy bun from the middle of the night. This morning, she was wearing an LBSU Welcome Center polo shirt and jeans, and her hair fell in beautiful waves down to her mid-back. It didn't matter what she wore or how messy or polished her hair was—she was beautiful in all of it.

"Good morning." He smiled at Elle, surprised at how happy seeing her in his kitchen made him. Her eyes had been intriguing from the start, but now that he knew more about her, he craved to know even more of what was behind those eyes. All the feelings he'd had last night as they had talked came rushing back and he wanted her to stay today, too.

She was smiling, but he could tell that there was something else behind her smile. He wondered if she also felt the same things from last night whenever she glanced at the spot where they'd stood at the counter, eating the tart.

Mato, Sam, and Halona had already arrived and were looking hungry except for Sam, who was already chomping down on one of the pastries that Mato had brought with him. Somehow Declan had forgotten to text his assistant that plans had changed and he didn't need to bring donuts.

The front door opened and before they could even see Jen, they all heard her call out, "Is that Declan's famous biscuits and gravy I smell?" Jen rounded the corner, saw Elle, and paused, mid-step, as she was putting pieces together. Then, unfortunately, she decided to voice the leaps her brain had made. "I thought you weren't making breakfast if Elle was here, but you are and she's here. Oh my gosh, did you two—" and pointed back and forth between Elle and Declan.

"What are you implying? Jen, no," Declan said, heat rushing to his neck and face. "Wow. This was an interview —what do you think happens during interviews?" He glanced at Elle and caught a look of surprise and question on her face and a blush on her cheeks.

"I am so sorry," Jen said, holding her hands up like she was trying to stop the words that had already tumbled out of her mouth. Then she turned the gesture to Declan. "My bad. Pretend I didn't say anything." But Jen was still smiling like she knew things had gone well last night.

Then he saw Mato smile into his coffee cup.

Declan wiped the orange juice off his hands with the towel hooked at his waist and stirred the gravy. "Guys, don't make it awkward. This is just a normal breakfast like any other day of the week. Elle just happens to be joining us this time. Everything else is the same."

"Yeah," Halona said, "so just drink your wheatgrass juice, Jen."

But he could see that Halona hid a smile with her coffee cup, too. Everyone on his team was being so enthusiastically unhelpful. Well, all except Sam, who wasn't reacting to anything other than the second maple bar he was biting into. Maybe it was a good thing that Mato had still brought pastries.

He threw Elle an apologetic look, but she just smiled. And then yawned. He felt bad that she'd gotten so little sleep last night.

But only a little. He wouldn't have changed any of it. In fact, Elle being here made him feel more bright-eyed and bushy-tailed than normal.

"Oh!" Halona said, looking at her phone. "I just got an email from Kids Camp Nation. Apparently, your call with them yesterday went well because they're meeting in just over a month to make a decision."

Declan smiled with excitement and relief. He'd been hoping they'd bring it up at their next board meeting.

"We have a lot of work to do before then," Halona said.

He nodded. They really did. But that could wait until the work day started. "And it's ready!" he said with a wave of his spatula.

This was his favorite time of day. He knew it wasn't common for a boss to open up the "home" part of his home to his employees, or to make them breakfast, but his employees felt like family. And never as much as when they all gathered in his kitchen for breakfast. It wasn't a formal affair here—his team all crowded in like a pack of hungry beasts and loaded up their plates. He decided to plate it for Elle, though, so she wouldn't have to enter the fray. And possibly because he wanted to make it look extra nice.

He opened a biscuit and rested one half on the edge of the other to make it look just right, and then poured the gravy across the top. He fanned out a few orange slices, then set the plate right in front of where she sat across the bar and handed her a fork.

"Mmm. It smells so good! I'm impressed."

"Well, don't get too impressed. Breakfast is the only meal I can cook."

As he was plating his food, Halona sidled right up to him and said in a low voice, "You seem awfully chipper this morning, and I don't think it's just from the Kids Camp Nation news."

"What can I say? I'm a morning person."

She nodded slowly. "Yeah... I'm sure that's all it is."

Everyone started chatting as they found spaces at the bar or the table with their food, mostly discussing the day ahead like usual. Despite the conversation being centered around the work day, Elle was still right in the middle of it. None of it seemed forced, either. As much as it had felt like an intrusion to have her peek into their comfortably-oiled machine yesterday morning, she seemed to fit in now. It surprised him how natural it felt to have her there.

Elle looked down at her watch. "Oh! I'd better head out. We've got a team meeting in the Welcome Center on Tuesday mornings."

It also surprised him how sad he was to have their twenty-four hours come to an end. And, honestly, it also surprised him that it was Tuesday. And that life was just going on like normal. As if something that felt so huge, so life-changing, hadn't happened.

"If you have any questions as you're writing the arti-cle," Mato said, "please feel free to reach out to me."

Sam nodded. "And if you have any questions about

editing or the website, you can reach out to me." Mato gave Sam a look, who said, "What? She could have computer questions."

"And I will reach out if I do," Elle said, which made Sam smile.

Jen, who was standing next to the bar as she ate, said, "If you have any questions about Declan or his life, or want the inside scoop on anything, or even if you have a question that you're pretty sure he won't answer, reach out to me." Her eyebrows rose twice and she winked.

Declan rubbed his forehead. His team was killing him.

"And if you need someone to set you straight after talking to these guys," Halona said, pointing to everyone else on his team, "reach out to me."

Declan shot his team a look before meeting Elle's gaze. "How about you just reach out to me. For all of it."

He didn't miss the smile that crossed her face.

Mato looked past the great room to where Elle had placed her bag against the wall near the foyer. "I can walk you to your car."

"I've got this," Declan said, pulling free the towel at his waist and placing it on the counter. "I wasn't there to walk her in—I want to walk her out."

Elle picked up the jacket she'd worn when she'd first arrived yesterday from the top of her bag and hooked it over an arm. He took her bag and they headed out the front door. As they walked across his driveway, he glanced at her. "Is everything okay? You seem a bit... off."

He caught a slight blush brightening her face before she bit her lip. She didn't say anything, though. She just pulled out her keys, unlocked her car, and opened the door behind the driver's seat. He placed her bag inside and she put her jacket on top before closing the door and leaning against her car.

He stayed quiet, eyes on hers, barely breathing, hoping that she would give him a clue as to what was up.

She looked out at the road in front of his house for a moment before releasing a breath and meeting his gaze again. "When we were filming that video yesterday and I jumped into your arms, I kind of wanted to kiss you."

His eyebrow rose.

"But I mostly didn't want to."

Kind of was something, at least.

"And when we were sitting on the couch last night, right before going to bed, I kind of wanted to kiss you more."

He stepped a little closer to her.

"But I still kind of didn't."

He couldn't take his eyes off her, willing her to continue.

"Then, in the middle of the night, when you carried me to my room, I definitely wanted to kiss you."

He held back a smile even though he was jumping in

the air and pumping a fist internally. "Yeah?" He closed the gap between them a little more. "What about now?"

"Now? I'm embarrassed about last night."

Embarrassed that she wanted to kiss him? "Why's that?" he breathed, his voice coming out low, feeling himself getting pulled even closer to her.

"All that stuff about my dad? I don't share that with anyone. *Ever.* But give me a glimpse of your abs, feed me sugar, and talk to me in the middle of the night with that deep voice of yours, and I spill all my secrets."

The smile he was trying to hold back broke free. Strangely, relief also washed over him that the same thing hadn't made him share about his own biological dad.

"You were the one being interviewed, but I feel like we're ending our twenty-four hours with you knowing more about *me* than I know about *you*."

He moved even closer. A couple of inches were all that separated their bodies now. All they had shared during the night made him feel closer to her than he'd felt to another human in a long time. "I'm going to need a lot more than twenty-four hours to learn everything I want to learn about you." His voice came out low and deep, but he couldn't help it. He could see how it affected her by the way she sucked in a breath and parted her lips slightly. "When can I see you again?"

She hesitated a moment, their gazes locked. He wondered if she was feeling that their relationship was hovering on the brink of change as much as he was. Then she said, "Come to the Aquamoose Days kickoff concert in the park. It's a joint event put on by my town and LBSU. My coworkers and I are going as a group."

He'd spent his LBSU years on campus but he'd spent the summers at home with his family in Sioux Falls, so he'd never actually been to any of the town's summer events. "I'll be there." He pulled out his phone. "Can I get your number?"

He entered it into his phone as she told him, then sent her a quick text that said *I'd say I'll be there with bells on, but I think it'd be more appropriate to be there with Aquamoose antlers on* so she would have his number too. It made him smile to think of her reading it later.

"The interview is over," Elle said.

"Yeah." He looked back up at her and slipped his phone into his pocket, trying not to feel the sadness of that fact.

"So, I'm off the clock."

"Yeah?" This time the word came out as a question as he tried to decipher her meaning.

Somehow, they'd moved even closer together, and those eyes of hers that had been so vulnerable and open over the past twelve hours searched his eyes for a long moment before she whispered, "That means you should kiss me already."

Tingling electricity zipped up his spine. He smiled

and his own voice came out a low whisper, too. "Because you 'kind of' want it or 'definitely' want it?"

He was teasing her and she knew it. Her chuckle was quiet and her gaze only left his long enough to glance at his lips. He could tell by the way she leaned forward, lips parted, the effect that his delaying the kiss had on her. He was feeling it himself. He hadn't been with another person who was so intriguing and had so fully seemed to *get* him. Their connection had grown so strong that it felt like it was pushing them together.

Then she grabbed his shirt in both fists and pulled him against her, pressing her soft lips against his.

A soft moan escaped him. He put one hand on the top of her car's doorframe to brace himself and wrapped the other around her waist, holding her close. Her hand glided from his chest around to the back of his neck, like she was trying to hold him close too. As if he needed any coaxing. With each kiss, he could feel her melting into him a little more.

"Declan," she breathed, and he didn't think he'd ever loved hearing his name on another person's lips so much before.

He trailed a few kisses along her jawline, and when he got to her ear, he breathed, "I guess that means you 'definitely' wanted the kiss?"

He felt her chuckle more than heard it. She placed a smiling kiss on his lips. "That I did."

She pulled back and closed her eyes for a long moment before opening them. "I should probably get to work." He could hear how much she didn't want to leave in every word. Maybe because he felt it so much himself.

"I probably should, too. Please tell me my team isn't watching us through Jen's office window?"

Elle's gaze shifted to behind him. "I can't tell you that."

He closed his eyes and shook his head. "Next time, we won't invite them."

Elle shook her head, smiling. "Nope. Next time it'll just be my co-workers."

He let out a soft laugh. "I can't wait." He placed one last quick kiss on her lips, then he reached out and opened her car door for her.

Before she got in, though, she said, "Oh, hey, just in case you were thinking of getting that panna cotta tart delivered daily, I think I should leave you a warning to watch out for the truth serum."

"That's very good advice. Thank you."

She sat down in her seat, then quickly added, "Unless I'm going to be there. Then eat lots. Don't watch out for it at all."

"Got it." He smiled and soaked in the smile she gave him in return. Then he stood in his driveway as she backed out and drove off. He watched her until she turned out of sight, the morning sun shining brightly.

Chapter Thirteen

*E*lle pulled into the faculty parking lot at Lake Baldwin State University, turned off her car, and sat there without getting out. Yes, the Welcome Center's staff meeting had already started and she should be in there already, but she had just kissed Declan Davenport, and she was struggling to focus her mind elsewhere.

Maybe if it had been an ordinary kiss instead of an incredible one, she could still function fine. But there was nothing ordinary about Declan—she should have guessed that his kiss would be extraordinary too. She'd kissed plenty of guys over her dating years, but no kiss had ever felt like that.

Maybe because she'd never connected with a guy as strongly as Declan. She already felt closer to him after a day than she usually did after dating a guy for months. So many things about him just drew her to him. Like there was an invisible thread around her heart and he was the only one who had ever found it and pulled her closer. Would this be the last time she had a first kiss? She already knew that no other would ever be able to compare. And all she wanted was to experience Declan's kisses for the rest of her life.

She shook her head. It was dangerous to think like that. Even though it was a wonderful, spine-tingling, heart-thrilling, oh-so-sweet thought to have. She wanted to drown in those thoughts.

Why was she so drawn to him? Okay, he was kind and brilliant and thoughtful and a good cook and smart and charismatic and business-minded and good-looking and passionate about kids and their education. But he was also a celebrity, and she didn't trust celebrities.

He was constantly recognized in public. But at his house, he hadn't seemed like a celebrity at all. Maybe that was what had allowed her to let her guard down. Maybe that was what had kept nine-year-old Elle from sounding the alarm.

Looking back now, that kiss felt inevitable. Like it wouldn't have mattered whether she had her guard fully up or what else happened that night; they were still going to end up with their lips pressed together in a kiss at the end.

But if it hadn't been inevitable, if she'd known they

were going to kiss right after the interview concluded, would she have done anything differently going in?

No, she would not. Because it had been... she thought back... yep, definitely a lifetime since she'd been as affected by a kiss as she'd been by Declan's.

She looked in the direction of the Student Center, even though another building blocked her view from the parking lot. She was dying to see Declan again, but why in the world had she thought it would be a good idea to invite him to the Aquamoose Days kickoff when she knew all her coworkers would be there? She'd been inundated with texts from everyone from work—not just Summer—while she'd been at Declan's. The concert could end up being nightmarish.

And why had she invited him to something a full three days away? Somehow, after spending twenty-four hours with the man, she'd gotten used to him being nearby. How had that made the prospect of going three days without seeing him feel so long?

Letting out a huge breath, she got out of her car, closed the door, and started walking.

Come to think of it, maybe she *did* want everyone there because they would keep her from doing anything stupid. Or any stupider than letting a relationship begin to develop between her and a celebrity. Nine-year-old Elle hadn't been strong enough to stop it, but the combined power of her coworkers would be.

———

AFTER THE MEETING, Elle brought Summer to her office for their Ambassador's Retreat planning meeting. Elle loved her office. The décor, especially the items on her bookshelves, was an eclectic collection of quotes she had hand-lettered and framed alongside trinkets she'd found at flea markets, most of them in lavenders and silvers. Maybe no one else in the world would feel the same, but she loved all of it. It was relaxing to enter her space after the stressful team meeting.

Not that the subject matter of the meeting was stressful. It was the fact that not only had she been very late, but everyone had immediately guessed—maybe by whatever expression she wore—that she had fallen for Declan. It probably hadn't been the best idea to show up to a meeting full of people with whom she spent eight hours a day so soon after that kiss. They knew her too well. Of course, they'd figure it out.

As if that hadn't been bad enough, the moment Elle had walked in, Deja had said in a voice that sounded like a coming storm met a southern drawl, "Oh, lawd, you two kissed!"

Elle hadn't exactly confirmed it in words, but apparently, her face had confirmed it all on its own. And then everyone started hooting and cheering. Elle needed to work on her poker face. Did they have online classes for things like that? Maybe she should talk to Tora over in the registrar's office and make a course recommendation.

She and Summer sat across from each other and Elle moved everything on the desk between them out of the way. She looked around for her notebook, then remembered it was in her bag and pulled it out. "Oh, I should grab the file." As soon as she turned toward her file drawer, she remembered that it contained nothing that wasn't already on her computer, so she pulled out the laptop instead.

Summer leaned back in her chair, arms folded, watching Elle. "You're seeming a bit scattered."

"Sorry."

Summer sat up straight, resting her folded arms on the desk. "Obviously, it's about Declan. And *obviously,* we should talk about that first, or we won't get much work done."

"And *obviously,* you just want to hear more details."

"Well, yeah. I mean, that goes without saying. Now, tell me—what *didn't* you say that's still on your mind?"

Elle took a deep breath and looked down at her notebook without really seeing it. The forty-five-minute drive from Sioux Falls to Lake Baldwin hadn't been nearly enough time to process everything. All she knew was that it left her feeling embarrassed. Not because she'd told Declan that she wanted to kiss him—she still stood by that. But she'd done it after sharing things about her life with this man she'd barely gotten to know. And she didn't open up that much to anyone. Yes, it had given them a strong connection, but she was also feeling...exposed.

"I shared more personal stuff with him than I wanted to. I couldn't even tell you why. There was just something about him." The word *safe* popped into her mind. Was that it? She'd felt safe sharing with him? She didn't know. But that in itself wasn't enough of a reason.

"That sounds like a good thing. Right?"

"Summer, I opened up about *both* my parents! I was just spilling secrets left and right. I don't know how I'm going to feel facing him again." Especially in the light of a new day. And Declan was such a flashy and obvious person to fall for. Everyone fell for Declan. Even people who hadn't met him in real life.

"And, sure, he seemed to like me, too, but our twenty-four-hour thing didn't feel real, you know? Now that I'm back, it feels like a fluke. Something magical that could only have happened in that situation. The longer I'm back here in real life, the more I'm realizing it's something I shouldn't expect to continue."

Summer asked, "Do you want it to?" just as Everett walked in.

"No, I don't *want* to like Declan."

Everett looked back and forth between the two of them, as if knowing that he was interrupting something important. Whatever he'd come in to say, it seemed less critical than it had a few seconds before.

"Why not?" Summer asked. Then realization crossed her face. "Oh. Because he's a celebrity?"

Everett's eyebrows drew together. "You've got something against celebrities? Why? Did you have a bad run-in with one or something?"

"Something like that."

Summer knew who Elle's dad was, but she didn't know the whole story about Elle sending the letter and the NDA. All she knew was Elle's dad had never been in her life. And Elle hadn't told the rest of her coworkers about her dad at all. She'd only told Summer because it was hard to keep a secret like that from someone who was not only a great friend but someone she'd worked with closely for so long.

Ironically enough, the person who knew more than Summer was a man she'd only known since nine a.m. yesterday morning.

"I sense a story behind that," Everett said.

"But not one I want to tell." Before Declan, when was the last time she'd told someone as much of the story as she'd told Declan? Camilla knew most of it. And before that, it was probably Hannah Hales back in fifth grade. They'd been friends for years, and Hannah had always wondered if Elle was adopted and her mom just never told her because everyone in her family was so different from each other. But Elle had always known who her parents were. She was the only person in existence who had her same mom and her same dad, and it *did* make her feel different.

Hannah had been her best friend and they'd shared everything, so eventually, Elle had told her about her dad and the letter she'd written in third grade. And about all the emotions she'd experienced then and every day since. She'd felt so much lighter, just knowing that someone else knew her story and she didn't have to carry it alone.

Then, not too long after they'd started middle school, Elle had overheard Hannah telling her new friends all the secrets about Elle's life that Elle had shared with her. And about her fears and dreams—the things she felt in her core. And Hannah and her friends were laughing at it all, like there was something fundamentally wrong with Elle.

The betrayal had destroyed Elle. At the time, it had felt just like the incident with her dad. She'd opened up to him about who she was, and he'd turned his back on her. It felt like Hannah had done the same thing.

But that had been a long time ago—she hadn't even thought about it for ages. It made her wonder for a moment if that experience was what made her skittish about telling people. She hadn't even thought about it being a possible reason until now.

"Anyway," Elle said, turning the subject firmly away from her dad, "I'm just glad that I found out he doesn't date anymore. Because how awful would it be if he had a long list of women he'd dated, and I was just one more on that list who fell for him?" Especially when she'd specifically planned not to. "It's embarrassing enough that he knows all the personal stuff I shared with him."

Everett studied her for a moment. "What was Declan's reaction?"

"When I just opened up and spilled everything?"

He nodded.

She thought back to the moment when she'd told him and the look of care and concern on his face. The way he listened without judgment. The way he seemed to understand. "He was so sweet. It was the middle of the night, and he knew how tired I was."

"Is that when he kissed you?" Everett pressed.

She shook her head.

"Then he isn't a tool."

"And it was me who kissed him, but not until right before I left this morning."

"You go, girl!" Summer said.

"And how did he react this morning when you first saw him?" Everett continued.

"Again, super sweet."

"And he kissed back?" Summer asked.

Elle tried not to blush as she thought of him leaning in close, his hand on the car just beside her head, his other arm wrapped around her waist. The way it felt to have him so near, the sound of his breath against her ear, the feel of him trailing kisses along her jaw. Her face heated at the memory. "He definitely did."

"So he's not a guy who dates," Everett said, "but he clearly likes you. Did he ask to see you again?"

"Yes. He's coming to the concert on Friday."

"Do you want a guy's opinion?"

She nodded.

"You didn't scare him away with your secrets. He feels more connected to you because of them."

"You think so?"

Everett nodded. "I can pretty much guarantee it."

Okay, so maybe she hadn't scared him away. But she still hated that he knew.

Chapter Fourteen

*E*lle dropped her pile of folded blankets onto the grass in Downtown Park, then picked up the top one and spread it out on the ground. There were a few others also setting out camp chairs or blankets for the concert, but not many since she was so early. The band was still setting up their equipment.

She picked up the second blanket and spread it out too, letting its edge touch the first. Her group was attending this event as Welcome Center and Admissions Department coworkers, and any one of them could've come early to claim their spot. Elle could have said yes to Declan's offer to pick her up and drive her to the concert. Yet, instead, she'd offered to come early to save a place big enough for all of them to watch together. Why?

Maybe because she was still so wary of a relationship with Declan, and a real date was a step in that direction.

Well, okay, so was chatting with him in the middle of the night instead of just going back to bed. And kissing him in his driveway. Those, admittedly, were definite steps in that direction, too. But that had all taken place in a bubble that had disappeared once they'd stepped out of it. She still wasn't sure where things stood now that they were in the real world.

And she wasn't sure where she *wanted* things to stand with him now that she wasn't directly under his spell. Or now that things might be awkward between them after she'd trauma-dumped on him in the middle of the night.

Once she got the final blanket spread, forming a big island of blankets for all of them to sit on, she plopped down. If she'd been thinking, she would've brought her laptop or her tablet so she could work on writing the article about Declan. Her week had been so busy that she'd barely had any time at all to spend on it.

Instead, she pulled out her phone. And then she immediately sat up straight because the moment her screen lit up, she saw two notifications—one from TikTok and one from Instagram—both saying that Declan's accounts had just posted a new video. She nearly dropped the phone in her scramble to tap one and get the phone angled at her face so it would unlock.

It was the video of the trending dance they had filmed

together. She put a hand over her mouth and laughed at the surprise ending of her jumping into his arms and seeing how it looked from the camera's point of view, all edited. Objectively speaking, it was pretty great. If she'd been scrolling TikTok and come across the video, she definitely would have stopped to watch.

Her eyes flicked to the side and saw that the likes were already at 21,000. Then her gaze went to the bottom—it was posted more than an hour ago. Why had TikTok waited so long to notify her? Didn't they get that she'd wanted to see it the very second it was up?

She watched the video a second time, seeing the two of them moving together, their actions synchronized. All her earlier feelings of connectedness and exhilaration while practicing filled her, along with all the joy as they'd laughed and made mistakes. And how it had felt when he was holding her in his arms and she was close enough to feel his racing heartbeat, his quick breaths, his strong muscles.

She wanted to keep watching it over and over, reliving all the emotions of the experience again and again, but curiosity about the comments people might be leaving was strong enough to get her to click on them.

The first comment said, *I don't know who this mystery woman is but you two clearly vibe.* That comment itself already had 1,615 likes and had the "liked by creator" tag. Had Declan been the one to like it? Or had he not even seen the comment and it was Jen who did?

The next comment, with more than a thousand likes, said, *Lucky girl! Not me being super jealous.*

The third comment, though, was the one with the most likes. Her eyes went wide when she saw over two thousand seven hundred likes on it so far before she read the comment itself. *The most impressive thing about this video isn't the fact that they almost hit every beat. It's the size of the smile on Declan's face.*

The comment already had dozens of replies, all mentioning how happy he looked, how authentic his smile was, and how it was, indeed, a larger smile than usual for him.

Was that true? She tapped on his profile and watched his previous video. Then the one before that and the one before that. Then the five before that. She tapped on the video they had made together again—and confirmed that his smile *was* much bigger with her. Her stomach did somersaults as she watched it through again, her eyes staying on his smile the entire time.

Oh, that was a beautiful smile.

"Hi," she heard in that gloriously deep voice of his. She was so focused on the video that it took most of a second before she realized the voice came from the man standing above her rather than the video of him on her screen. She shielded her eyes from the setting sun.

"Declan!" she said as she tried to both swipe out of the app and turn off her phone at the same time, causing the phone to practically leap out of her hands and land screen-side-up on the blanket in front of her. She'd neither managed to exit the app nor turn off the phone, so the video continued looping right there for him to see.

She grabbed it and turned it off, starting to stand just as he started to sit, so she sat again, too, managing to fumble the execution of that as well. "What are you doing here already?" More people were trickling into the park now, but this place wouldn't be fully hopping for at least another twenty minutes or so.

"I didn't want you to have to hold down the fort by yourself, so I came right after we finished up for the day."

Oh, that voice. She'd become acclimated to it on Monday after being around it so much, but somehow she'd lost that over the course of three and a half days of not seeing him. So it hit her with its full, powerful force.

And he had chosen to sit down so close to her, too, his right knee barely touching her left knee, his right hand nearby on the blanket. It put him close enough that her body reacted to his nearness, making her feel lightheaded and slightly dizzy. She had lost whatever acclimation she'd had to that, too. So she was getting the full force of *all* of Declan, and it nearly overwhelmed her.

"Well, you're in luck because right now the job is fairly easy."

Declan held a hand up. "Feel that breeze?"

"This very slight breeze?"

He nodded. "That kicks up, and you'll be glad for another body to help keep these blankets from being taken up in the whirlwind."

Her attempt to hold back a smile wasn't very successful. "Then I'm very lucky that you came early."

His eyes flicked to her phone and back to her. "I see you noticed that our video was posted."

"I did." She glanced down at her phone, and then looked out toward the parking lot. Declan had to have spotted her from quite a distance away—had he seen her being fully sucked into watching it? What had that looked like to an observer? She'd been so focused on the phone that she couldn't even guess. She cleared her throat. "We did pretty well."

"That we did. I checked it in the car moments ago—it seems that everyone else thinks so, too." He paused for a moment before adding, "Maybe we can do it again sometime."

Why did her mind immediately go to her jumping into his arms and how it felt to have those strong arms around her?

"Excuse me," a tentative and very sweet but very high-pitched voice said.

Elle put a hand up to shield her eyes from the sun low on the horizon to see who was talking as Declan did the same. It was two girls, probably fifteen years old, one clutching a notebook.

"Hello," Declan said in that gloriously deep voice of his, which made both girls squeal.

"It *is* you!" the shorter one said before turning to her friend. "I told you it was." Then she held her notebook out to Declan. "Can we get your autograph? We *love* your show. We even convinced our science teacher to let us watch in class each time a new episode came out."

"I'm glad you enjoy it," Declan said, then asked them what class on their fall schedule they were most excited about. He was adorable with them which, at this point, didn't surprise her. They were still kids, after all.

It wasn't long after the girls left before a woman in her thirties came over and asked for an autograph, too. It *did* kind of surprise Elle that he was just as gracious with adults. Which was a good thing, because before long, he had half a dozen people of all ages lined up to get his autograph.

Elle looked around at the park. It was maybe half full of people now, and she tried to picture her dad greeting fans like this. She couldn't, though. *At all.* From what she knew about him, he would never leave himself so open to just anyone coming up to him.

Which made her wonder how quickly Declan's patience would last. Who knew? Maybe they wouldn't even make it to the end of the concert. Maybe, if things between them ever turned into a relationship, they wouldn't ever attend events like this.

"Avery!" Elle said, scrambling to her feet just as her friend and her friend's fiancé, Nicolas, neared the blankets. "When did you get back in town?"

Avery looked at Nicolas. "An hour ago? We haven't even unpacked yet."

Elle turned to Declan. "I'd like you to meet my coworker, Avery, and this is Nicolas. They got engaged not too long ago. Since then, they've been splitting their time between here and Belgium where Nicolas lives."

As soon as Declan said "It's nice to meet you," Avery's eyes lit up in recognition. Elle was impressed that Avery didn't start fangirling—she hadn't even been in the team meeting when Elle had made everyone promise they would treat Declan like a normal guy and not like a celebrity.

Declan and Nicolas barely had time to start talking about their careers before Elle spotted the rest of her coworkers walking across the grass toward them. Good. She hadn't even been with Declan long and she was already feeling her resolve to hold back waning.

Elle introduced each of her coworkers and their significant others to Declan and could see that he was struggling to keep track of names. Everyone had shown up tonight. Well, except for Joy's boyfriend. But Elle was starting to think that was normal for them.

She was surprised at Everett's girlfriend though. He didn't bring dates to get-togethers often so she didn't know what his type was, but she wouldn't have guessed someone like Paige. She just had such a serious air about her—as if her tight bun, pencil skirt, heels, and dry-clean-only shirt were all part of a uniform she'd never be caught without. She was holding Everett's hand but looking down at the sea of blankets (and lack of chairs) with an expression that told Elle she thought they were all Neanderthals.

Since the concert hadn't started yet, they all sat down in a very misshapen circle. She and Declan were sitting next to each other again, both leaning back on their arms, their hands almost touching. When would that dampening of reactions from exposure to Declan kick in and make being around him not feel so intense? Because right now, her heart was beating so strongly that she could feel each beat and her nerve endings were tingling. It took all the willpower she had to keep herself from scooting into that bit of space between Declan's arm and his torso.

She'd kissed him. She'd chosen that. She hadn't just kissed him back—*she* had kissed *him*. Why was she questioning everything so much now, just because they were back in the real world?

Maybe because over the past three and a half days, logic had been figuring into the equation more. Back at his house, she had been running on pure emotion.

Declan stretched his hand enough to give her pinky a

little finger hug and that teeny little movement sent the best kind of shivers all up her back. Who needed logic? She was okay with drowning in feelings and reactions.

Mariana, the woman job-sharing with Avery who'd spent the last three months working in the Admissions side of their offices, turned to Avery. "How is wedding planning going?"

"Well, Nicolas's mother doesn't seem to hate me anymore, which is great. But that doesn't mean she isn't a bear to plan a wedding with."

"It's bad," Nicolas added in his slight accent. Dutch, was it? "My brother got married without her there so she knows this is her only wedding, and it has turned into a massive event."

"And whatever you're picturing for 'massive,'" Avery said, "double that mental image. And the stress associated with it." Then Avery grinned. "My parents are going to be there, and they'll hate every second. I think the comedy of that is what will get me through it."

Nicolas chuckled. "I don't think it'll be anything compared to the comedy of my parents coming to our reception here, though."

Even though Elle didn't have the time to plan an entire wedding reception, the planning parts of her brain lit up, thrilled at just the thought of doing it.

"True," Avery said. "They are going to hate it so much worse than my parents will hate the fancy one! We plan to make it as low-budget and country as can be. Well, we will when we get to that point. We don't even have a wedding planner for the reception here yet."

Deja pointed at Elle. "Elle could be your wedding consultant."

"I definitely have experience planning the most low-budget country wedding ever."

Declan jumped in. "She planned her mom's wedding when she was only thirteen, on a budget of two hundred dollars. If that isn't impressive, I don't know what is." And he was giving Elle the most admiring smile too. Both dimples even made an appearance.

Why did it make her feel taller just hearing him say that?

Avery caught Elle's eye and mouthed *I really like him!* Elle really did too. If only she knew whether that was a good idea or a bad one.

"Weddings are so much work," Summer said.

Brock squeezed Summer's hand. "*So* much work."

"But you're only two weeks away!" Joy said.

Summer smiled. "Then it'll all be off our shoulders and we can just move on to the happily married part." She and Brock shared a kiss.

They were such an adorable couple. Even though neither Brock nor Summer had seemed to guess that they would eventually fall madly in love, Elle saw it coming from a mile away. They were just so well paired.

She was surprised to realize the thought made her hopeful. Usually, when she spent time with Brock and Summer, she always felt like something similar would never happen to her. Interesting. She'd have to think about that some more.

"I loved our wedding," Pavani said and turned to look at Zane, who gave her an equally sweet look back before kissing her temple.

"I loved yours, too," Deja said. "It was the first traditional Indian wedding we'd ever been to, and one of the most fun. All the bright colors, the henna patterns on your hands and feet and on the bridesmaids, the groom's procession. Everyone grinning like a possum eatin' a sweet tater and fine as a frog hair split four ways. *Ahh.* I loved our simple ceremony, but after yours, I nearly told Trent we needed to have ours all over again."

What kind of wedding would Elle have? She sneaked a look at Declan. She wasn't going to marry a celebrity, so it was a moot point—but just for fun, she thought about what a wedding for her and Declan might look like. Fancy like Avery's was going to be? Big like Summer's? Neither seemed like Declan's style. And neither felt like her, either. She had looked at more than her share of wedding magazines over the years, but she still wasn't sure she knew what a reception that was very "her" would be like.

As if Everett's girlfriend, Paige, had heard Elle's thoughts, she said, "I know exactly what kind of wedding I want, and all I can say is that my mother and my future mother-in-law better both stand back and keep their opinions to themselves."

"And your husband-to-be?" Declan asked.

"He can voice his opinions, but he better stand back too."

Everett laughed that big, hearty laugh of his, but Elle wasn't sure Paige meant it as a joke. And Elle didn't have a clue what to say in response. Based on the way everyone else stared at fun-loving Everett and lay-down-the-law Paige with confused expressions, she wasn't the only one.

Everett cleared his throat. "What about you, Grant?"

Grant shrugged. "I don't know. I haven't dated anyone lately who made me think about it. But back when I dated this girl, Lauren—*the one who got away*—we discussed a reception on the beach."

The mayor stepped up to the microphone and welcomed everyone to the kickoff event for Aquamoose Days, which would run through next week. They all shifted to face the stage.

As the band started playing, Declan leaned in close and said, "I always went home for the summers, so I've never been to any of Aquamoose Days. I know that Aquamoose is the university's mascot, but why do they base the town celebration on the same thing?"

She turned her head to answer him and gave a sharp intake of breath. His face was so close to hers that she could've kissed him instead of answering. And if she'd had any less self-control around this man, she might have. "It's also the mascot for the elementary school, the middle school, and the high school. I have been an Aquamoose since I was five. It's so much a part of this town that it couldn't be anything else."

She'd shared too much with him while drunk on tiredness and sugar and his nearness, but it still felt so right to be there with him as they sat side by side listening to the music. As they ate the Aquamoose Tracks ice cream that the college and the town had paired up to provide for free at this event. As the band asked them all to get up and dance, and as he swung her in a circle and pulled her close.

How could everything feel so right? How could she feel so comfortable with him? At the end of the song, everyone sat down, panting from the exertion of dancing.

Elle looked at Declan. "Do you go to many community events in Sioux Falls?"

"I don't. I think I get the draw, though—"

Declan hadn't finished his sentence before the lead singer of the band said, "I have it on good authority that Declan Davenport is in the house. Is that true?"

At least half of the crowd had noticed because they turned to stare and point him out. The other half of the crowd now knew too.

"As those of you who watch his YouTube videos probably know," the lead singer said, "Declan gets talking a bit fast when he's excited about something, and his fans have been dying for him to do a rap. What do you say, Declan? Come make up a spur-of-the-moment rap with us as your accompaniment?"

Declan leaned in close. "There's not an easy way to get out of this, is there?"

Elle shook her head and grinned. "Not that I can think of." Plus she wanted to see it herself, so she started chanting for him to go on stage right along with everyone else.

Declan stood and people all around cheered. So he wound his way through the mess of blankets and camp chairs until he made it to the stage and climbed the stairs. He was immediately handed a microphone by one of the backup singers.

He held the mike to his mouth and his silky deep voice was suddenly amplified through the park, sending shivers down Elle's spine. "You know there's a difference between talking fast about science and rhyming and being on beat, right?"

The lead singer nodded. "We get it."

"And rapping is a skill I do not have."

Declan was being a good sport, saying everything with an amused smile on his face. It was so adorable she was practically swooning.

The man chuckled. "Don't worry. We won't judge you harshly. Right, everyone?"

There were enthusiastic cheers from the crowd, and a small group on the right-hand side started chanting, "Rap. Rap. Rap." Okay, a few of her coworkers were chanting it, too, and shouting things like "You've got this!"

Elle shook her head. She'd hoped their presence would mean a barrier of protection for her heart and that they'd help her keep from falling further for Declan, but her coworkers were nothing but welcoming to Declan, proving they were even less strong than nine-year-old Elle was.

Well, they hadn't kissed him, so maybe they were stronger than she was. She should've known better than to think they would save her from falling for him—they'd been the ones pushing her to interview him in the first place.

Avery scooted into the space beside her that Declan had vacated and grinned meaningfully at Elle.

"If you talk fast when you are excited about something," the lead singer said, "all you have to do is rap about something that excites you."

Declan thought for a moment, then said, "Okay, I've got it." Then he looked out over the sea of people and met Elle's eyes and she no longer remembered how to breathe.

Chapter Fifteen

DECLAN

If Declan had been at this event with his dad and brothers or his team, he'd never have gotten up on stage. He would have just stood, waved, and said something along the lines of "Nah, I won't torture you with that" and sat back down. It was the fact that Elle was cheering for him that made him go up. Even if she did seem as unsure about their relationship as he was.

But now that he stood on stage in front of most of the town, he was rethinking the wisdom in that. Because he was the opposite of Elle—Elle liked being in front of a crowd more than a camera. But he much preferred being on camera because not only could the footage be edited and have multiple takes, but it would be seen by people who chose to watch it.

These people hadn't chosen to listen to him. They'd

come tonight because they wanted to listen to the band. Seeing the sea of faces made him nervous. He looked out again at Elle, meeting her eyes. She just had a way of making him feel more grounded in the moment.

"Right before I came up here," he said into the mike, "I was about to answer a question about why I think events like this have so much power to draw people in. I don't want to be rude to my date by not answering, so that's what I'll rap about."

It seemed like every head in the entire park turned in Elle's direction the moment he said the word "date."

"Perfect," the lead singer said as the drummer began to play a quiet rhythm. "You go ahead and start when you're ready, and we'll try to keep up."

Declan rubbed the back of his neck. He was going to make an utter fool of himself. "Okay, but I should warn you all that the last time I wrote poetry was for English 201 back in college."

The crowd laughed.

"I got an F on that assignment," he added. The laughter grew louder, so he went on. "And that one didn't even rhyme."

The crowd's laughter swelled and continued for several seconds. At least they were prepped for what they were about to get. For as much as he smiled at the comments on his videos that suggested he should rap, they'd never actually made him want to try. But he was enjoying this event more than he thought he would—he could rap, or fake-rap, really, about that.

He cleared his throat and began his attempt.

> *I don't come to things like this*
> *Always found a reason to miss*

Okay, that came out sounding a little bit like rap. But really, the band was carrying it more than he was.

> *I got the brochure*
> *Never understood the allure*
> *But now I get it, sure*
> *Lives intersecting*
> *People connecting*
> *An opportunity*
> *To feel community*

People were clapping along to the beat now. Some even stood and started dancing along.

> *You can't dance in a crowd without the throng*
> *You can't sing along without a song*
> *There's nothing like people doing the same thing,*
> *same time*
> *So sing*
> *And rhyme*

Who cares
If at poetry you . . . failed

The crowd laughed. Well, if nothing else, at least he was entertaining them.

Together, our emotions amplified, don't hide, enjoy the ride,
side by side, get swept up in the tide
Great people, great fun
Especially one
In particular, I like...

An audible happy sigh came from half the crowd, right as the realization hit that he'd said that. Out loud.

I'm glad they handed me the mike

No, no he wasn't.

This is my first town event
Of hopefully many more

For as quickly as the rhymes had been coming so far, he was suddenly unable to think of a single thing to say next. Probably because his brain was still back on the part where he'd said he liked Elle.

Someone in the crowd called out the suggestion, "But

your rhymes we adore!" Immediately afterward, someone else shouted, "You made my grandpa snore!" and sure enough, the old man sitting next to them was indeed asleep in his camp chair. It made him chuckle.

Then he came up with his own ending.

I'm going to sit down now
Before they throw me out the door.

The band got that it was the end of the song, so they finished with a flourish and Declan took a little bow. "Thank you, everyone, for not throwing things at me. Rotten tomatoes, insults, camp chairs.... Remember to tip your waitress."

Then he turned and thanked the band for the impromptu magic they'd pulled off, shook hands with the lead singer, and handed the microphone back before making a beeline for the stairs leading to the grass.

He liked keeping his personal life private and didn't want his fans to know more about him than he was willing to tell. He'd have never guessed that he'd come to this event and tell a big group of people that he liked Elle.

He actually couldn't believe he was doing any of this. Getting personal. Pursuing a woman after he'd already decided that he wasn't going to. What in the world was he doing?

As he neared the blankets with Elle and her coworkers, they let out a chorus of *Awws* and hooting and cheering. Elle stood and gave him a bright enough smile that he suddenly wondered if there was anything he wouldn't do for another smile like that from her. Then she wrapped her arms around his neck and gave him a kiss on the lips that was both as perfect as a kiss could be and not nearly long enough. And because of the powerful pull she had over him, he didn't even mind that everyone saw. Or that half the town responded with their own cheers.

They both sat down and the band started playing their next song. Elle turned to him, her cheeks looking flushed. "Will you be my plus one at Brock's and Summer's wedding?"

He'd just made up an impromptu rap song in front of a crowd for her. He realized that he would probably say yes to anything this woman asked.

———

DECLAN DRIBBLED a basketball across his gym floor and shot a basket . . . and missed. It wasn't even a half-court—just the empty space on one side of his basement gym that had a basketball standard. But it worked just fine for small games.

He looked down at his smart watch—8:05. He'd planned to leave in a couple of hours to spend the day with his dad and brothers like he did every Saturday, but the concert last night had left him needing a hard-played game this morning. Something to expend some energy on and hopefully make him feel less scattered. So he'd texted his team to see if anyone was up for a game. He let them know that he'd be in his gym at eight, ready to play. They knew they could just come in.

No one had shown up yet.

Thankfully, though, Jen walked in at 8:08 with her husband, Brady, both wearing gym clothes and looking very awake and ready to destroy him at basketball. A minute or two later, Sam showed up in a T-shirt, basketball shorts, and his sports glasses—not looking quite as ready to take on the competition, but eager to play nonetheless. Good. They could play two-on-two.

It didn't take long before they were all sweating, the competition intensifying, everyone playing hard. Then he mostly accidentally pushed Jen's arm while she was shooting a basket, and the other two agreed that it was a foul.

As Jen had her eye on the basket, preparing to make the free throw, he said, "I went on a date with Elle last night."

Jen didn't even flinch. She kept her eye on the basket, shot, and made the basket with a quiet swish. Then she turned to Declan. "Did you really think that would make me miss? I'm your *social media manager*. Of course, I know you went on a date with Elle—I saw the videos posted online."

"Oh." Why hadn't it occurred to him that people would take videos and post them? Maybe because he hadn't gone on a real date since hiring a social media manager.

"I also know that you admitted that you like her. Not just to a couple hundred people in the crowd, but people all across the world."

His stomach was doing some weird things right now. "Yeah... I still can't believe I did that."

Jen shook her head, attempting to appear somber, but the teasing glint in her eye gave her away. "Me, neither. I mean, we had an office bet going, but the odds were not looking good."

"You did?"

"No. We just speculated. But we should have!"

Sam passed the ball to Declan and said, "I'm not even your social media manager and I still knew about it."

Declan fumbled his dribble. "You did?"

Sam nodded. "It showed up on my For You page. Twice."

Declan passed the ball to Sam. As his website manager dribbled toward a layup, all Declan could think about were all the reasons he never shared anything personal—once it got out on the Internet, the information could no longer be controlled.

After Sam made the shot, he said, "Maybe I can get Mato to set me up with someone, too."

Declan froze, ball in hands. "What?" Then he turned to Jen. "Mato set us up?"

Jen's hands were on her hips, breathing heavily from the game. She shot Sam a look before letting out a breath and turning to Declan. "I mean, yeah. Why else would he have requested a twenty-four-hour thing? Elle could've gotten what she needed just by spending a work day with us. But after talking with Elle to work out the details, I think he could tell that she'd be perfect for you."

Declan was stunned. He hadn't guessed that was the case at all. So many thoughts ran through his mind. But mostly that it was a very good thing that he'd had enough experience with Mato over the years to know that the man always had Declan's best interests at heart, otherwise Declan might've been worried about how well the man had pulled it all off.

As Jen was passing the ball to Brady, she asked, "So, I'm guessing you've kissed her?"

"Oh, come on. You know—you were watching from your office window."

Jen stopped guarding him and put her hands up defensively. "I swear I wasn't. I *tried* to, but Mato made me stop."

"He didn't *make* her stop," Sam said. "He offered to let her go first in the meeting next time it's his turn."

"Same thing," Jen said. "But oh, wow. You kissed her. And you went on a date with her. That's huge for you!" She gave him a playful punch in the arm. "So things are getting pretty serious, huh?"

Brady missed a basket and the rebound came right to Declan. He caught the ball and held it against his hip with his wrist. "I don't know. I guess? It all kind of just happened."

He wanted to be all in with Elle. So much had happened between the two of them in that twenty-four-hour interview, but it was still only one day. There had been no time to simply ponder things. He just felt swept away by the romance of it all. Like he was going with the flow instead of making a solid decision. Reacting, not acting.

Jen studied him for a moment. "And now that you've gotten up in front of her town and rapped about liking her, you feel like it's time you made the actual choice instead of just rolling with things?

"Exactly." Before going further, he had to decide not to let all his fears stop him. "I need to actively choose to be all in instead of passively getting there."

"Is that what you're going to choose?" Brady asked.

"I want to."

Jen grabbed the basketball from under his arm and started dribbling it. "But whatever it is that's kept you from dating for as long as I've known you is making you ques-tion it?"

He shrugged, but then nodded. He'd spent his whole life worrying that he might be like his dad, simply because he was his father's child. But somehow, Elle made him feel like he didn't need to fear. Without her even saying the words, he knew that she believed in him and knew every-thing would be okay. And, as surprising as it was to him, he believed it too.

"She's pretty cool," Sam said. "And she likes you, right? You like her. It seems like a simple choice to me."

Maybe it was that simple.

"Okay," he said as he stole the ball back from Jen, mid-dribble. "Decision made. I am choosing to be all in."

Chapter Sixteen

ELLE

*E*lle fingered her sky-blue gown. It was identical to the nine other bridesmaids who stood around her, also watching with anticipation as Valeria, Summer's best friend, pinned the veil onto Summer's hair.

"You look beautiful!" Elle said.

Summer beamed as she looked at her reflection in the tall mirror. Then she turned to face them. "Can you believe this day finally arrived? Oh, I'm just so happy!"

She pulled all of them in for a quick hug. Even Summer's mom joined in from where she'd cornered the wedding planner, telling the woman about the places she'd traveled and how they had the most amazing *everything* that she wished Summer's wedding had. Apparently, Summer hadn't seen her mom in years. Despite the woman's humble bragging and pointing out every deficiency she saw in her surroundings, Summer still seemed happy that she'd come.

There was so much happiness in the air that Elle could almost feel it. And like everything in her life lately, it made her think of Declan. Over the past couple of weeks, Elle had definitely gotten to know Declan better.

She'd gotten to know how it felt to kiss him on her doorstep (so sweet and blissful), on a blanket while watching an outdoor movie in his backyard (so loving and accepting), and on the shore of Lake Baldwin under a sky filled with stars. (If she'd thought it hard to keep her knees from buckling while preparing to film a TikTok dance with him, it was nothing compared to having Declan run his fingertips down her neck, across her shoulders, and then down her arms, all while listing the reasons he thought she was amazing).

But more than finding out exactly how much everything about him was her kryptonite—and not just his deep voice, luscious hair, adorable dimples, and the raw power of his eyes—she'd soaked in so many new bits of information about him. If she'd felt like she hadn't gotten enough details about him during their interview, he'd rectified that over the past two weeks as they'd texted, talked on the phone for hours, attended the Aquamoose Days Parade, enjoyed the early-morning launch of the hot-air balloons, gone bowling in Lake Baldwin, visited Falls Park, and biked on the trails in Sioux Falls.

She'd learned that the glasses he wore in his videos and while he was working were computer glasses, not prescription glasses. And before he'd built the team that worked for him, he'd once spent three days straight researching. He'd barely eaten anything and had fallen asleep at his desk a few times, but otherwise, he hadn't known how much time had passed. It was while working on a project his senior year, and a fellow project partner had finally knocked on his door loudly enough to pull him out of the research hole.

She'd learned that his mom had worked as a maid for a wealthy family while he was in elementary school and had to be at work by 6 a.m., so he would shower and get ready for school in the rich family's pool house.

And she'd learned that his biggest fear in going away to college had involved not being there to protect his little brothers. At some point during his first semester away, a coyote had attacked his toddler brother, Ian. That kind of thing was extremely rare, but his dad hadn't hesitated even for a second before jumping in to draw the animal's wild attack to himself, saving Ian. After that, Declan knew his family would be okay no matter what happened.

She'd found out that his favorite color was green. Which wasn't a surprise—as much as he worked with growing things, it would've been weird if it was anything else.

She'd learned how drawn to him she felt whenever he

was around. And the heart swelling and weak knees and racing pulse weren't just limited to him being physically around—even a text made her stomach flutter and rendered her brain unable to form complete sentences.

With every piece of the Declan puzzle that she discovered, she hungered for more. Lately, that meant she was thinking about him pretty much all the time. Especially as she worked to take all her research, formal and otherwise, and turn it into an article for the LBSU magazine that felt worthy of who Declan was.

She glanced at the clock on the wall of the bride's room as she sat on a padded bench and was once again surprised that Declan hadn't arrived yet. The ceremony would start in just a few minutes, and he'd planned on being there a good forty-five minutes ago.

A voice she'd long ago stopped listening to but apparently was still making appearances and had popped up several times over the past couple of weeks. It usually said something along the lines of, *You're just like your mom—you'll make a million bad choices before figuring things out. Declan is probably one of them.* And, even worse, the other destructive voice would chime in to say, *You're not worthy of love.*

She forced them both away. She knew how harmful it was to listen to those voices. Then she reminded herself that she felt nothing but love when it came to Declan.

The wedding planner walked over to Summer and

said, "It's almost time to start. Are you ready?" Just then, Elle heard her phone buzz with the text sound she had set only for Declan, and her heart gave its own buzz of excitement. She went to the pile of phones on the counter and grabbed hers.

In the noise of the room, she'd somehow missed a text he'd sent over forty minutes ago, apologizing profusely for being late and saying he was on his way. The latest text said he was walking into the building now. She set the phone down and hurried out into the hall.

The door at the end of the long hallway opened, and she saw him silhouetted in front of the bright afternoon sun. As soon as the door closed behind him, cutting off the blinding light, she caught the man striding toward her in a breath-catching suit.

As she went to meet him, she said, "We're going to need to turn up the A/C if you're going to come in here all smoking hot in a suit like that."

That smile that she loved spread across his face, and then she saw his eyes take her in from the top of her fancy up-do to the bottom of her silver heels. "I thought that bridesmaid dresses were traditionally unflattering. You look—" He shook his head. "You look incredible. I did not fortify my defenses enough for this."

She felt the same. Although she wasn't sure that she could have fortified her defenses enough for Declan to say sweet things to her in that deep voice of his while wearing such a well-fitted suit.

He leaned in close, wisely avoiding her glossed lips, and she could feel his breath caress her ear. "It would be entirely unacceptable if we snuck off to a closet somewhere, right?"

She knew he was teasing and couldn't help the smile that spread across her face. "Well, there are ten bridesmaids, so I'm sure I wouldn't be missed." After pausing a moment, she pretended to tap a finger on her lips (to avoiding touching the gloss) and said, "Except for the fact that there are only four of us who will be standing by Summer during the ceremony—Valeria, Brock's twin sisters, and me."

Declan's eyes shifted behind her as she heard the door to the bride's room open, bringing a sudden swell of talking voices. "Well, they've already spotted us, so there's no escaping now."

Elle gave him a playful shove toward the chapel and said, "Go. Get in there and grab a seat."

By the time the bridesmaids and Summer made it to Elle, all the groomsmen were joining them, forming two lines. She and Everett, one of the groomsmen who would be standing by Brock, were near the front of the line. Then the music started, the doors opened, and they walked down the aisle toward the arch where Brock stood, looking like he couldn't imagine anything greater than this day.

The four groomsmen and bridesmaids took their spots at the front while the others took their seats in the first two rows. Then the music changed and Summer started walking down the aisle. She looked so vibrant and beautiful, her dad beaming at her side.

When Summer reached the front and she and Brock gave each other a look filled with indescribable love and care and happiness, Elle dabbed at a tear with her knuckle. They looked so confident in their love for each other. She hadn't realized how much she'd been craving that same kind of confidence in love for her entire life.

As the officiator started talking, Elle gazed out over the large crowd now sitting for the ceremony. Between Summer's expansive friend base and Brock's expansive family, all of whom were being added to a normal-sized wedding group, there were a lot of people in attendance.

She looked at her coworkers and their plus ones, mostly dressed in wedding party attire. Avery sat snuggled up next to her fiancé, Nicolas. Pavani was with her husband, Zane. Deja with Trent. Tess with Dane. Each couple held hands and looked so happy that Summer and Brock had found what they had found.

Then there were her single coworkers—Joy, Mariana, Grant, Everett. And her. Maybe it was all the love swirling in the air, but she hoped they were all on their way to finding it too. Maybe Joy would with her boyfriend— although he hadn't come to this event, either.

And maybe Everett with Paige. Paige sat with perfect posture, wearing a fitted knee-length navy sheath dress with a jacket that could've been office attire if it wasn't made of satin and lace. Elle glanced at Everett, who also stood at the front, his suit pants covering the bright, sky-blue socks she'd spotted while he was seated, like his personality was so big and happy that it couldn't help but find a way to shine through. She had a hard time picturing the two of them in place of Brock and Summer under the arch.

Then her eyes fell on Declan and that sweet smile of his—dimples included—and those expressive eyes. She had RSVP'd with a plus one weeks ago, planning to either attend with a random date or show up with her mom if that didn't work out. It was so infinitely better being at the wedding with Declan. He was just so much more incredible of a man than anyone she'd ever dated. Than anyone she'd ever known.

Yes, but do you really deserve a relationship with a man like that?

The thoughts hit her hard as she smiled back at Declan. With a metaphorical bulldozer, she plowed them right out of her brain. She wasn't sure whether she deserved it or not, but she would soak in every moment with Declan for as long as she could.

Chapter Seventeen

DECLAN

eclan moved with Elle along the dance floor, her arms on his shoulders and his on her hips, as they talked about the wedding and the people there. He'd loved being there with her during the ceremony, the dinner, and the toasts, and now he enjoyed the dancing and mingling. She was an incredible woman and so fun to be with. He couldn't believe he'd almost missed out on all of it by letting himself fall into a research rabbit hole.

When the song ended, they headed off the dance floor to find a drink. As they passed Summer and Brock, they overheard someone—for at least the fourth or fifth time tonight—ask Brock and Summer if they were going to have kids anytime soon.

Brock said, "I've got five nieces and nephews with

another on the way, all from four siblings who are younger than me, so we have some catching up to do!"

Declan nodded toward two three-year-old girls and a toddler boy living their best lives on the dance floor. "Are those Brock's nieces and nephews?"

Elle nodded. "Plus that baby over there and. . ." She turned and glanced around the room. "That baby over there. Those are his parents. Have you met them yet? They're super sweet."

He would've liked to say that he'd seen the same people tonight that Elle had because he'd spent every moment at her side, which was where he wanted to be. But the truth was that he'd been pulled away by people who had recognized him from his YouTube channel plenty of times. Summer's mother had been the biggest offender all night.

He'd decided long ago that he would always be kind to people who came up to him. But he was there as Elle's date, to celebrate Summer and Brock, and it felt rude to not have his attention on Elle and the newly married couple. He had to figure out how to balance those two conflicting goals better.

Both Declan and Elle turned when they heard Summer's voice through the microphone. "Where are my single ladies? Come gather around up here—I'm about to toss the bouquet! Single men, stay close because Brock is going to toss the garter right after."

As they walked toward the front, Elle grinned at him and said, "How good of a catch do you think I am?"

He kissed her temple and then winked. "I think you're the best catch there is."

She laughed, winked back, and went to join the other single women gathering in front of Summer.

Everett stepped up next to him, his eyes on the single women too. Probably because his girlfriend, Paige, was among them. "You as nervous about Elle being out there as I am about Paige?"

Declan chuckled but didn't answer. Mostly because his answer would be yes. Because he could see that behind Elle's smile and look of casual indifference, a part of her—even if it was small—was hoping she would catch that bouquet. And that did kind of scare him.

Not because over the past couple of weeks he hadn't already pictured a life with Elle more times than he could count, but because he wasn't sure if he would be good at that. He had only gotten okay with dating less than three weeks ago—he wasn't to the point of being okay with marriage yet.

Both he and Everett watched with wide eyes as Summer turned her back and tossed the bouquet over her shoulder. It was headed in the general direction of Elle, but Paige dropped her poised demeanor, pushed Elle and Joy aside, and leaped into the air, catching the bouquet. Declan heard Everett's audible swallow next to him.

Neither Elle nor Joy had been shoved hard enough to fall or anything, but Declan still went immediately to Elle's side. As he passed Paige, she held up the bouquet triumphantly and called out to Everett, "You better fight for that garter now!"

A breath of a chuckle escaped Elle's mouth. "She sounds pretty serious about that. You might want to watch out for flying arms and possible pushing when that garter is tossed."

He very much did not want to participate in the catching of the garter. But the woman he was dating had just participated in the bouquet toss, so how could he bow out without sending the wrong message?

So he stood with the other single men, right next to Everett, and pushed his hands into his pockets as Summer sat on a chair and Brock removed her garter to much hooting and cheering from the crowd. Then Brock turned his back to them and shot it like a rubber band up into the air.

All of them looked up as the garter seemed to move in slow motion, arching through the air above them before quickly picking up speed as it fell. It was coming right at Declan, but his feet felt rooted to the spot. Maybe because this was a huge wedding, so there were a lot of single guys vying for the garter without much room to move side-to-side.

Instead, hands still in his pockets, he leaned back and to the side so it could sail alongside him and to the man standing right behind him. It didn't. Declan felt the garter hit his arm like it weighed fifty times its weight, tucking itself right into the crook of his elbow. The roar in the room was instant and loud. He grabbed the garter with his other hand and held it high in the air as everyone cheered.

His gaze found Elle, who was laughing to the point of dabbing the tears escaping her eyes. He was glad that was her reaction and not the one he imagined Paige having if Everett had been in Declan's shoes.

When Declan reached Elle, she placed her hands on his chest. "Those were quite the impressive maneuvers you showed there. You were channeling that one scene in *The Matrix*, weren't you?"

"Just testing out my limbo skills," he said as he placed a kiss on her lips and pushed the garter into his pocket. "But really, it's human nature to move out of the way when objects come flying at you."

They both turned when Deja placed a hand on each of their arms. "Holy guacamole if that wasn't the most entertaining thing I've seen in a while. Let's just say— somewhere far down the line, of course— that you two end up getting married. If that happens, come to me. I have the perfect video to play at your wedding of you, Declan, hands shoved in your pockets like you were trying to scratch your knees, evading that garter like it was a grease fire and you were water. And you, Elle, are perfectly lined up in the background, laughing so hard you're clutching your stomach."

Declan laughed, but it didn't stop the heat from rising to his face.

Zane and Pavani joined the group of Elle's friends starting to surround them, and Zane reached out to give Declan a fist bump. Before long, Summer and Brock were there too, Brock slapping Declan on the back like he was welcoming him officially to the group. His mind was whirling.

"Oh!" Pavani said, a hand flying to her pregnant belly.

Everyone seemed to hold their breath, waiting, as they looked at Pavani, her eyes wide but focused.

Then she looked at her watch before meeting Zane's eyes, her own wide and unblinking. "That's four in the past hour. Honey, I don't think these are false contractions —I think this is premature labor."

Zane's eyes widened in shock for the smallest moment before the adrenaline kicked in. "Okay, I've read about this —we need to get you lying down on your left side as soon as possible."

"The bride's room has a couch," Summer said, concern making her words come out in a rush. "Let's go."

Zane bent to pick up Pavani, but she hissed, teeth gritted, "You. Are. Not. Carrying. Me."

So he nodded and they all, as a group, followed the bride toward the nearest door leading to the hallway.

"Water!" Zane called out. "Dehydration can cause contractions!"

"I'm on it," Declan said, jogging toward the bar.

A minute later, he was in the bride's room with Elle's coworkers and their plus ones and the wedding couple, all gathered around the couch where Pavani was lying on her side. Zane knelt beside it as Pavani sipped the bottle of water.

Elle reached out and slipped her hand into Declan's, and he gave it a squeeze.

In a quiet voice, Pavani said, "The contraction stopped."

Everyone in the room seemed to let out a relieved breath at the same time.

Tess glanced at the clock on the wall. "We should watch it for fifteen minutes after the previous contraction started to see if they've all stopped."

"You all don't have to stay in here with me," Pavani said. "Zane and I will be okay. Go! Enjoy the wedding!"

Summer reached out and squeezed Pavani's hand. "We're going to stay right here until we know you're okay."

They all nodded and stood around, waiting. A sense of concern filled the room and Declan was starting to understand that they were all more than coworkers. Maybe even more than friends. This felt like family.

Declan studied Zane as the man knelt next to his wife, worry on his face, then his gaze went to Elle's hand in his. If it was her on that couch with early labor pains, would he be able to handle watching her in pain and deep in worry about their unborn child?

It had only been probably ten or twelve minutes, by Declan's best guess, when Pavani gasped and put her hand on her stomach again.

"Another contraction?" Zane asked.

Pavani nodded, eyes wide in fear.

"Okay. The moment this contraction stops, we are taking you to the hospital."

"Zane, I'm only at thirty weeks!"

He ran a hand in circles on her back, over and over. "I know. It'll be okay, honey. They'll know what to do."

Moments later, they were all outside, helping Pavani into her car.

Declan put his arm around Elle as they watched the car pull out onto the main road and speed away toward the hospital. She leaned her head against his chest, eyes still on the retreating vehicle. "She'll be okay, right?"

He was far from a medical doctor, but he'd also had plenty of biology-related classes while earning his degrees. And he knew that what Elle wanted wasn't a medical diagnosis—it was hope. He nodded. "They'll probably give her an IV of Magnesium Sulfate pretty quickly, keep her in the hospital overnight to give her a continuous dose. They'll get the labor stopped."

She turned her head to look up at him, eyes so full of trust, and smiled.

Chapter Eighteen

ELLE

$\mathcal{E}$lle stood beside Declan at his car, as Gary, Declan's dad, pressed a fancy wooden box into her hands that she knew contained two decks of cards. Elle ran her fingers across the smooth wood and the words carved into the lid—*Science does not know its debt to imagination. –RWE.* Words that now made her think of both Declan and his dad. She smiled and looked back at Gary. "Oh, I can't take this."

"I saw how much fun you had as we all played games together. Call it an early birthday present. It's coming up on Tuesday, right? Besides, making things like this is a hobby I enjoy precisely because I like to see people having fun with them. I'll enjoy making another. Please—I want you to have it. As Ralph Waldo Emerson says, 'The greatest gift is a portion of thyself.' Enjoy—maybe even play a few more games with Declan." His voice was like a breeze across a forest floor. Quiet, yet strong and grounded.

She looked back down at the box again. "Thank you. I love it."

She gave Gary and Declan's eleven-year-old brother Ian and nine-year-old brother Hayden hugs and said goodbye before Declan opened his car door for her to slide in. Declan always spent Saturdays with his family, and this was her first time joining him.

They had played soccer in the backyard (where she gave them all a run for their money) before his brothers had taught her how to play a racing video game (which she'd been terrible at). Then they'd played some crazy card games (which she'd loved) and just spent time together. One day with them, and they were already on a hugging basis. She almost didn't want to leave to go to Pavani's baby shower. But of course, she didn't want to miss that either.

She fastened her seatbelt and looked down at the box resting on her lap. "I take it your dad is a Ralph Waldo Emerson fan?"

Declan nodded, chuckling, as he pulled onto the street. "He's got quotes hanging up all over the house. In his woodworking shed too."

"Oh yeah? What's his favorite?"

Declan's answer was immediate. "'It is not the length

of life, but the depth.' It became his favorite not long after my mom died."

Elle could see why. Just thinking about the day and the lovely box she held in her hands made her smile. "I want your dad for my dad."

"Right?" he said as he turned the corner. "I thought the same thing when my mom started dating him. It took a full year of him proposing to her before she worked up the nerve to tell him yes. I respected her waiting, but I was still rather impatient." After a moment, he asked, a little hesitantly, "Did you ever reach out to your dad again? It's been a long time since you were nine. You might get a different response."

"I did," she said and turned to look out her window. "I mean, not recently, but I never will again."

When he stayed quiet, she looked back at him. He was clearly waiting to see if she wanted to talk more about it. And strangely, she found herself wanting to tell him. Not because it was the middle of the night and her brain was tired or because she ate a dessert that was the equivalent of truth serum, but she realized it was because she trusted Declan with the story.

"The summer between high school and college, Camilla and I decided to take a road trip to St. Paul to celebrate being newly graduated. To hang out at the pool, catch a festival, shop, gorge ourselves on banana cream pie —did you know they're famous for it?— and revel in finally being adults. Anyway, I knew that my dad was on tour for his new album and he had a concert in St. Paul that summer, so I made sure the dates we went coincided with his concert.

"Then I sent my dad a letter telling him I would be in town at the same time as him. And I told him that I was eighteen now, so he had no legal or financial obligation to me—I just really wanted to meet him and say hi. So I could have met him face-to-face, been in the same room as him, had his attention on me—if only for a single minute, you know?"

Declan's eyes were on the road, but he nodded, his brows drawn together a bit.

"I wasn't even asking for a relationship. But I never got a response back from him. Not even a 'no.' Just a continuation of the ghosting he'd been doing my entire life." She hadn't thought that telling the story would make her emotional—it had been a long time since she'd worked through it all. Yet even now, she had to swallow down the emotions that bubbled up. In a voice that came out quieter than she'd expected, she said, "I never told anyone I wrote to him, that I tried again to connect. Not even Camilla."

"Why?" His voice was low. Quiet. Gentle.

Her dad didn't want her. She wasn't worthy of his love —he'd made that clear. And she couldn't help but think that eventually, Declan would come to the same conclusion.

But rather than saying any of that out loud, she shrugged and looked out the window again. She might trust Declan with the story—she even trusted him enough that she didn't feel the need to ask him not to share it with anyone else. But apparently, her earlier feelings of worthlessness hadn't retreated as fully as she thought.

The car's tires moved loudly across the rumble strip at the edge of the road, drawing Elle's attention to Declan as he maneuvered the car to the gravel on the side of the highway. Her eyebrows drew together in confusion. Without a word, he put the car into park, got out, and walked around to her side of the vehicle.

He opened her door and held out a hand expectantly. She unbuckled her seat belt and got out, still not understanding what he was doing.

Until he pulled her to him and wrapped his strong arms around her in the most comforting hug she had possibly ever experienced. For a long moment, he just held her close, not saying anything, letting her feel safe and protected and loved.

Then he kissed her temple and said, "I am sorry. You deserve so much better than that."

And she soaked his words in like she was the desert and he was the long-awaited rain.

———

ELLE AND DECLAN parked and had just gotten out of his car outside Pavani's and Zane's small house when Declan stopped in his tracks. "It occurs to me that this—a shower for one of your coworkers, attended by your co-workers and their dates—is the type of thing you would help plan. I apologize. I didn't even think about that when I invited you to spend the day with my family. Did that mess everything up?"

"Nope, because you didn't take into consideration how deep my planning goes. I came over early this morning to decorate and bring my part of the refreshments and I dele-gated out the other parts and the games."

"You are inspiring," he said as he wrapped her hand in his. They walked along the side of the house toward the backyard, her decorations lining their path.

The shower had to take place at Pavani's house because she was on bed rest, but she had a teeny home that could never fit all ten of the Welcome Center and Admissions Department co-workers and their plus ones. Luckily, Pavani and Zane had a decent backyard patio, a grassy area, and weather that was currently cooperating.

Summer and Brock had returned from their honey-moon just three days before, but Summer had enough contacts that even in that short amount of time, she had managed to borrow a hospital-type bed on wheels with a back that could raise for Pavani—which made it easier for her to be outside for the party.

As Elle and Declan rounded the corner to the back-yard, they saw Pavani sitting up in the bed on the patio, overlooking the yard like a queen, Zane by her side, both looking like they were ready for the party to arrive. The shade umbrella was positioned over her, and the cute baby stuffed animals that Elle had hung from the umbrella's spokes with blue ribbon made it look almost like a baby's mobile.

All the other decorations in the trees, on the chairs, lining the refreshments table, and in the balloon backdrop were various shades of light blue—which also happened to be Pavani's favorite color.

Elle went straight to her resting coworker and friend and leaned down to hug her. "You look beautiful. And congratulations on making it past the thirty-two-week mark! I know the doctors said that was important."

"Thanks!" Pavani said with a grin. "Now we'll see how close to thirty-seven weeks we can get."

Elle adjusted a few of the decorations and then headed inside the house to grab the food from the kitchen and bring it out to the refreshments table. Declan jumped right in and washed his hands before helping to arrange finger foods on platters. It was nice working alongside him. There was a natural rhythm between them as they worked. She'd never experienced that before.

And just having him standing next to her, their move-ments almost a dance, made her want to grab him and pull him close and run her fingers through that luscious hair of his while kissing him until they were both dizzy.

Based on the smile that tugged at one side of Declan's mouth as he arranged sausage pinwheels on a platter, he could tell exactly what she was thinking. He peeked at her from the corner of his eye and that grin turned into a full smile—dimples and all—as he turned, put one arm on her back, lowered her into a dip, and kissed her in such a captivating way that it left her smiling and breathless.

"Well," she said as he lifted her upright and started putting the last of the pinwheels on the tray, "you know how to leave a girl unsure if she can stand steadily."

He picked up the platter of pinwheels and the one she'd been filling with bruschetta. "Don't worry. I've got your back."

As they carried the last of the refreshments out to the tables, the guests started arriving. The sound of chatter filled the yard as everyone mingled and hugged Pavani.

"Is Paige not coming?" Elle asked as Everett joined them in the backyard without his girlfriend at his side.

"We, uh, are no longer together."

Grant clapped him on the back. "That's a bummer. Sorry, man. Did you break up with her because she caught the bouquet or did she break up with you because you didn't catch the garter?"

Everett chuckled, but kind of in a self-conscious way. Like he knew Grant's question was a joke but at the same time, it also hit close to home. "In a weird way, a little of both. And kind of neither. I think we just figured out that things weren't going to work out between us."

"Oh, that's too bad," Tess said for all of them, even though Elle wasn't sure a single one of them believed it. Not that Paige was a bad person at all—she just seemed to be for Everett.

Even though Pavani knew she wouldn't be able to play them, she had requested active games for the shower. So they did baby stroller races (which became much more competitive than Elle had expected and led to a show-down between Deja and Avery, of all people). Then they had a baby pacifier hunt where everyone, including Zane (the one who'd hidden them all through the backyard) and Pavani (the one suggesting where he hide them) couldn't find the last three. And then blindfolded diapering (which Brock won, hands down—a good thing, because it was no secret that Summer wanted a lot of kids).

Afterward, as the guests chatted and filled their plates with vegetables and dip, chicken puffs, and blue macarons, Elle grabbed the empty tray of stuffed mini peppers and took it into the kitchen to get more.

Tess followed her inside and said, "I'm impressed with Declan."

Elle smiled. That was pretty much the state she was living in lately.

"I just love how well he gets along with everyone,"

Tess continued. "It kind of feels like he's always been a part of these gatherings."

Elle pulled more stuffed mini peppers out of their container and put them on the tray. "Yeah." And then she voiced a fear that had been niggling at her that she'd managed to keep hidden. "So that means something's about to go wrong."

Tess's head pulled back in surprise. "You've never really struck me as someone who is so doomsday about things. Generally, you're pretty optimistic. Are you doing okay?"

She chuckled as she placed the last pepper on the tray. "I'm only doomsday-ish when it comes to relationships with celebrities."

Summer walked in just then and said, "*Only* with celebrities?"

"Ouch!" Elle said, laughing, but mostly on the outside. Okay, so she was twenty-eight, nearly twenty-nine, and her longest relationship to date had lasted three months. She pushed the tray into Summer's arms. "People who point out painful truths have to do the carrying."

But Summer's comment made her think about something else that had been bothering her for the last little while. Was she only that way with romantic relationships? Or all relationships? The last person she had shared so much with was Hannah Hales, her friend in elementary school who had betrayed her and laughed as she exposed

Elle's innermost secrets to her new friends. Summer knew a lot, and Camilla knew even more. But neither knew as much as she'd shared with her childhood friend.

Elle had a lot of friends now. But she no longer let anyone get to know her on as deep of a level. Long-term relationships, though, required opening up to deepen. Was that where things were headed with her and Declan? Yes, yes they were. She had already shared so much with him, and he always made her feel accepted wholeheartedly when she did. Could she trust that he'd always be like that?

When they walked back out to join the others, she met Declan's eyes across the yard and gave him a smile like everything was okay. Because right now, it was.

As she walked over to Declan, Everett asked Zane and Pavani, "So do you think you'll want to face the possibility of this again," he gestured at the bed Pavani was in, "or do you think it'll make you want to stop at one?"

"Everett!" Deja said. "I can't believe you asked that!"

"Nah, it's all right," Zane said. "It's a fair question." He smiled at Pavani. "We've always wanted two. We just hope the next one won't be quite so eager to get here."

"Two is a good number," Summer said. "Of course, ten is even better."

Everyone laughed, but the funniest part was that Elle knew having ten kids would probably thrill Summer. She still couldn't picture it herself, though.

And then everyone started chiming in with how many kids they thought they would have one day as they snacked on mini cheesecakes and mini blueberry eclairs. Elle had always wanted kids but had never come up with a solid number. Two felt natural, since that was how many had been in her own family. But maybe she would like three? She could picture her and Declan walking to a park with three little ones, all of them holding hands, maybe one of them on Declan's shoulders. And maybe Declan singing a silly kids' song in that deep voice of his as a dog walked alongside them all.

She glanced over at Declan and recalled how much he loved being around kids and how good he was with them. She swallowed. Maybe the number he wanted was more along the lines of how many Summer wanted. Maybe she should start talking herself into being okay with more than three.

Then she caught an odd expression on Deja's face from the corner of her eye. Deja wore a bit of a smile on her face, but it didn't look like it was there without a lot of work. Underneath, she just looked sad. She met Deja's gaze and asked, "Is everything okay?"

Deja gave an even sadder smile before briefly glancing at her husband, Trent. "Every once in a while, things just hit a little harder—we've been struggling for a while now to get pregnant."

"Oh, Deja," Elle said. "I had no idea."

Tess reached across their circle and squeezed Deja's hand. "If you ever need to talk to someone who understands, come to me—we've been trying for the past four years to give Ava a sibling. It's hard. We have one child though, so I know it's not the same. But I'll be a listening ear anytime."

Deja nodded and Elle's heart hurt for her. And for Tess. She wanted to hug them both.

But Deja waved her hand like she was trying to banish the emotions, and said, "But enough about me and sad things! This is a party! Um. . ." She glanced around the group. "Declan! We haven't heard your answer yet. How many little ones do you want?"

Declan chuckled in that deep voice of his, but there was something behind it. Discomfort, maybe? "I'm pretty sure this isn't one of the official shower games, so playing isn't mandatory."

"We should make it an official shower game, then," Pavani said.

"Okay, I'll answer, but only because this is your shower, which makes you the boss." Declan rubbed the back of his neck. "I enjoy other people's kids, but I don't plan to have any of my own."

Elle was so stunned by his answer that she just stared at him, unable to comprehend the words. Did he really not want any kids when it was clear he had the potential to be a "Dad of the Year" kind of father? Or was he just saying that so Deja wouldn't have to hear about all the children in everyone's futures?

Elle stood rooted in place, trying to find the lie behind his words, but he wasn't making eye contact with her. From what she could see, it was no lie. It looked like truth.

Chapter Nineteen

DECLAN

$\mathcal{D}$eclan awoke and jerked to a sitting position in his bed, covered in sweat, heart racing, and breathing heavy. The nightmare was one he'd had often as a little kid, but seldom since. He was four, hiding under the side table pushed up next to the couch, squeezing his eyes shut tight and covering his ears to block out the sounds of yelling and objects crashing to the ground.

The nightmare was based on the one memory he still had of his biological dad—although he'd had the nightmare enough times that he was no longer sure how much of it came from his memories and how much came from his dreams.

In the dream, just like in real life, he'd peeked out from behind the couch, terrified of what he would see yet needing to see anyway. But today was the first time that, instead of seeing his biological dad standing there, he'd seen himself.

Although he hadn't looked crazed with anger like his bio dad always had. He'd just stood there, looking at four-year-old Declan with a sad expression on his face.

He threw off the covers, swung his feet onto the floor, and sat on the edge of the mattress, pushing the sweaty hair off his forehead. He closed his eyes and breathed in through his nose for the count of four, held it for the count of four, and released it for the count of four. Then he did it again, trying to calm his heart.

Declan hadn't had the nightmare for years, but this was the third night in a row of waking up to it. He knew without a doubt that he was having it again now because of the look on Elle's face when he'd said he didn't want kids. There was the shock and surprise he'd expected to see, but her expression had held something more.

He'd replayed that expression in his mind while lying in bed last night and decided that it had been hurt on her face. Like she'd taken it personally. Maybe she thought he didn't want to have kids *with her*, specifically.

But that was so very far from how he felt. This was all on him.

The edges of the blinds covering his windows told him it was still dark outside but that the sky was just beginning to lighten. He grabbed his cell phone from his bedside table and looked at the time—5:07. Close enough to when his alarm would go off that he shouldn't attempt to fall back asleep. Good. Because he was never successful at falling asleep again after a dream like that.

What he needed was a run.

His eyes fell to one of his notifications—an email from Kids Camp Nation. The subject line read *Our partnership has been approved!* and the preview text started with *I'll give you a call in a few hours to discuss details and celebrate, but I wanted to let...* before it cut off.

He stared at it, stunned. The project he'd been working toward for years was greenlit. They'd been struggling to make it a reality for so long that it had felt forever out of reach. Now it was actually going to happen.

The email had come in sometime while he was asleep. So either the board hadn't come to a conclusion until very late or Delaney, their point of contact, had woken during the night and decided she was too excited to wait until daytime to give the news.

He didn't even go into the email. His emotions were too freshly frayed from the nightmare—and from the three nights of terrible sleep—to handle news so big. Instead, he padded down the hall to his kitchen to make himself a smoothie. Maybe the noise from the blender would drown out any remnants of the nightmare from his brain. And hopefully, give him the kick he needed to start his day while so exhausted.

By the time he was dressed in running clothes and

stretching in his driveway, the emotions from the nightmare had been slightly overpowered by fears and doubts that Kids Camp Nation would decide he was either inadequate or a fraud.

He walked out to the road and turned the slightly uphill direction at a brisk walk. Why did something like having his greatest dream come to fruition make imposter syndrome hit him so hard?

Probably because the only reason Kids Camp Nation had agreed to the partnership was the sense of legitimacy his doctorate provided. It wouldn't have happened at all, though, if they'd known how he'd grown up. That knowledge would've removed all sense of legitimacy, doctorate or not.

He started running now, hoping his feet pounding on the pavement would help stomp out all the negative feelings. He'd worked hard to overcome those feelings of inadequacy before. But the fact remained that he had a past that was looked down on. He knew the key to overcoming those feelings was a matter of mindset and how he framed the situation in his thoughts. Logically, he could tell himself that it was all in his head. And there was a part of him that believed it and tried to convince the other part of him that his fears were unfounded.

But he could never fully persuade that other part of him. There had been too many instances of being looked down upon to really, truly believe his fears were unfounded. In middle school and high school, he'd convinced himself pretty well.

But during college, he'd moved back to what felt like square one. He and one of his roommates, Justin, were working on the same degree and had the same plant ecology class. They'd been doing a project together, testing which plants could survive in a mainly carbon-dioxide environment, when Declan had confessed his thoughts of having a more public career than working in a lab or land management fields.

He'd also told Justin long before about his humble beginnings—something he hadn't shared with anyone since the first grade—and Justin had said, "If you came from nothing, what makes you think you can ever become something?"

That comment, that phrasing, had shown Declan that Justin had never truly been his friend, and he eventually realized that Justin had his own issues of inadequacy. Nonetheless, Justin's words had stuck in his head ever since.

Who was Declan really, to think he deserved millions of followers? To have his dream career? To set a goal as ambitious as his kids' camp and have meeting that goal within reach? He had come from nothing. It was hubris to think that he could become "something." He started running up the steepest part of the road, pushing himself as fast as he could at the memory of the question.

Maybe it had hit him so hard at the time because it was only a couple of weeks after he and his girlfriend had broken up. That had been its own kind of trauma because it made him question his genes. Justin's comment had served as a reminder that his history was because of his dad. And that he couldn't let people know about it or they would judge him harshly and try to make him feel like he could never make it.

Maybe he believed he was worthy of success. After all, his mom had told him he was his entire life. But Justin's comment reminded him that *other* people didn't have that same belief.

Sure, people didn't usually say things like that to him. But even when people knew his background and said nothing about his lack of potential, they could still be thinking about it.

So on came the imposter syndrome whenever anything big happened. Even with the best big things—like Elle being in his life. And just like the double whammy that had hit him in college with his girlfriend and Justin's comment, he was not only worried about his relationship with Elle and whether he might be like his bio dad but about Kids Camp Nation still believing in him if they discovered his background.

He slowed his pace, panting and gasping for air, and eventually came to a stop. He put his hands on his knees and tried to catch his breath. Tried to banish his worries. Tried to tell himself that everything would work out.

———

BY THE TIME work was over, including his phone call with Kids Camp Nation, he felt only slightly better. Today was Elle's birthday, though, so he blasted music on his drive from Sioux Falls to Lake Baldwin in an effort to forget about his worries for a while.

Elle's mom, Tina, had called him a couple of weeks ago to say that she was planning a surprise birthday party for Elle and wanted his help. He'd been more than excited about helping to make the day special for Elle. Elle's best friend, Camilla, was secretly flying in from Chicago and would be getting Elle to the party. Declan's job was to help at the party itself.

He arrived at the shore of Lake Baldwin—the lake, not the town— before the rest of the guests to help Tina and Elle's stepdad, Duane, put up all the decorations. He'd spoken on the phone with Tina several times, but they hadn't met in person before now.

Tina wore skinny jeans and a bright pink flowy blouse. Her face lit up when she saw him, and he instantly knew where Elle had gotten her smile from. Not the hair, though—Tina's was permed and big and much blonder than Elle's. She shuffled over to him in uncomfortable-looking platform wedges and gave him a tight hug.

Then she pulled back but kept her hands on Declan's shoulders. "Oh, I'm so happy to finally meet you! I think I fell in love with you a bit when Elle had me watch one of your videos, but I've fallen even more as I've heard Elle talk about you. Nothing makes a momma happier about who her daughter is dating than hearing how sweet he treats her and seeing the big smile on her face any time she talks about him."

Declan grinned. "Elle has said wonderful things about you too. I'm glad to meet you." He reached out and shook Duane's hand. "You, too, sir. It's clear that Elle thinks very highly of you."

Why was he so nervous to meet them? Was it just because Elle wasn't there and didn't know they were meeting for the first time? Or was it all of his other fears spilling over into something that shouldn't make him nervous at all?

Duane gave him a once-over, as if he was trying to decide for himself if Declan was a decent enough guy to date Elle, then said, "Good to meet you. Thanks for coming to help out."

The three of them worked quickly to set up a couple of shade canopies, a table for refreshments, a big banner that read *Cheers to 29 Years*, and lots of lavender and silver decorations, which were Elle's favorite colors. He hadn't even known that. There were still so many things about her that he didn't know and wanted so badly to know. Was he going to get the chance to find out everything?

As soon as everyone arrived, he pulled out the Sharpie and package of stick-on name tags he'd brought, and said, "Okay, I want each of you to take one of these—"

"Uh," Everett said as he looked around at the group of people gathered under the shade canopy, "I'm pretty sure we all know each other."

Declan nodded. "But I don't want you to put your real name. Instead, choose a name that sounds like a letter. Like the way 'Elle' sounds like the letter 'L.' For example." He picked up the Sharpie, wrote on his name tag, and then stuck it to his shirt. "For tonight, I'm 'Jay.'"

He didn't want to tell them the whole story about Elle being made fun of as a kid because her name sounded the same as a letter or explain that he thought she would get a kick out of seeing the people who loved her all wearing names that sounded like a letter for the evening.

A few of them looked at him rather strangely, but Summer smiled and winked at him before saying, "I call 'Gigi.'"

"I call 'Bea,'" Avery said.

Elle's stepdad said, "Can I go by my initials, 'DJ'?"

As soon as Declan nodded, Nicolas said, "Oh, we can do a name that has two letters? Then I'm 'Casey.' Get it? KC?"

Declan grinned. They were on board and seemed to be getting it.

"What if I can't think of one?" Grant asked.

"Just make one up," Brock said. He peeled the backing from his sticker and put it on his shirt. "From now on, you can call me 'Aych.'"

Grant rose an eyebrow. "A-y-c-h? Really?"

Tina started flailing her hands. "Everyone, she's coming! Camilla said they just parked." Then she pulled out her phone and brought Elle's brother Levi up on a video call so he could join in from Baltimore.

They all looked up to watch the place where the edge of the parking lot met the rocks sloping down to the sandy shoreline, everyone seeming to hold their breath.

Then they saw Elle's head of light brown wavy hair and Camilla's much darker, longer hair bobbing in the distance. The moment Elle's eyes fell in their direction, they all started waving their arms and shouting, "Happy birthday!"

Elle glanced at Camilla with wide eyes, then hurried down the rest of the slope to where they all waited, looking genuinely surprised. "Oh, I can't believe you're all here! And that you kept this a secret. Especially you, Everett!"

Everett looked around at the group. "Wait. Is that why no one told me about this until today?"

Everyone laughed, and Elle wrapped her arms around Declan and kissed him on the lips. Then he put his mouth right up to her ear and whispered, "Happy Birthday." He felt her shiver at his warm breath against her skin.

Then she pushed back with both hands on his chest. "You told me you were going out of town for an event today!"

He grinned. "I *am* out of Sioux Falls, and this *is* an event."

She shook her head and looked around at everyone present. He could see the moment that her eyes fell on the name tags. Her eyebrows drew together and she cocked her head. "Deja, why does your name tag say 'Deedee?' And Joy, why does yours say 'Em'?"

Then she drew in a sharp breath. "Oh! All of you have names that sound like a letter!" Her hand flew to her chest. "I'm going to cry. This is the sweetest thing ever."

She started hugging each person. "Thank you for coming, Mariana. I mean *Vee*." She hugged Tess. "Essie."

Camilla quickly wrote CeeCee on a nametag and stuck it to her shirt.

"And Grant! Is 'Tee' really a name?"

"It's a nickname. Because I'm so bad at golf."

Elle laughed and moved to Everett. "A-r-e?"

"Hey, don't knock it. And it's pronounced *R*. I'd like to say it's my middle name, but really, it's the middle of my first name."

Then she went to the phone her mom held and said, "Levi! You're here, too!"

"Happy birthday, sis. Since my middle name is just an initial—thanks, Mom—you can call me W."

"Oh, I love you all. Mom, I mean *Kay*, did you plan this?"

"The party? Yes. But the name tags are all Declan's doing."

Elle turned and looked at him with such love in her eyes that it was hard to take it all in. But he kept his happy face on and smiled back at her. Elle reached out and hooked her arm in Camilla's. "Declan, I'd like you to meet my best friend, Camilla Sanchez. Cam, this is Declan Davenport."

The corners of Camilla's mouth turned up. "Oh, so you're the guy who is 'amazing in every way' and makes Elle unable to focus."

Declan chuckled. Unable to focus? He'd take it. He reached out to shake Camilla's hand. "And you're the friend who will stand by her side through thick and thin."

"That's me."

Elle's mom turned on the music. As the sun started to set, everyone danced, chatted, ate the refreshments, and made Elle feel loved. Declan got it—she was an easy person to love. He especially enjoyed seeing her interact with her parents and Camilla since he hadn't seen it before.

Once it was fully dark, Declan got a campfire going right on the shore and helped set camp chairs all around it.

Then they all raised their beverages to Elle in her official "Cheers to twenty-nine years" toast.

Since everyone had work the next day, the guests eventually got up, gave Elle their final Happy Birthday wishes, and helped Tina and Duane haul everything back to the vehicles.

And then it was just Declan and Elle left. Not quite alone—there were still a few people not from Elle's party walking along the shoreline—but they were mostly by themselves. While Elle was facing the lake, he stepped up behind her, wrapping his arms around her and pulling her close. She leaned her head back against his chest. They watched the water in silence for a while, feeling the gentle breeze blow across the water and gazing at the moon's reflection glittering back at them.

Elle turned in his arms so she was facing him and stared into his eyes. "This was the best birthday. Thank you for your part in it, *Jay*."

Declan chuckled. He'd forgotten he was still wearing his name tag. "Anything for someone as incredible as you."

She smiled and gave him a sweet and much too quick kiss before she pulled back and bit her lip. After a moment's hesitation, she asked, "Is everything okay? I get the sense that something is bothering you."

She was a little too perceptive. That, or he hadn't been as good at hiding his emotions as he wanted to think. "Everything is good. Happy Birthday, Elle." He wasn't about to burden her with his fears and doubts on her birthday.

She nodded, and in the glow of the moonlight, gave him a bright smile. "Congratulations again on that partnership for your kids' science camp. I am dying to hear more about it."

He smiled widely too. Imposter syndrome or not, he was thrilled that the deal had gone through and that he'd get to go nationwide with the camp. Elle had shown a lot of enthusiasm when he'd texted her about it earlier, and she still seemed happy about it now. She was thrilled about *his* success—on *her* birthday.

He reached out and brushed his fingertips along her temple, tucking the hair behind her ear that the breeze had blown into her face. "Do you have any idea how perfect you are?" He was definitely nowhere near good enough for her. She deserved the best, and he wasn't.

He held her close and traced his fingertips along her jaw and down her neck as she played with the hair at the nape of his neck. He didn't know how many more times he'd get to experience a moment this perfect, so he tried to take in each tiny detail with every sense he had, memorizing how it felt to be there with the woman who had managed to capture his entire heart.

Chapter Twenty

ELLE

lle had spent the last forty-eight hours with several of her coworkers and fifty student ambassadors at the usual lodge. There was a reason the Welcome Center brought students there—it was located far enough from town to pull the kids away from their normal lives, yet close enough that getting them there wasn't difficult.

They'd spent the time training the new group of students who would be giving campus tours, helping with recruitment efforts, and leading team-building exercises as soon as classes started. As she walked into the great room where all the ambassadors were seated in every possible space, listening to music and chatting as they waited for her closing speech, the song *A Dad and his Daughter* came on and she flinched.

Normally, she was fine when she heard her dad's music. He had some songs that could get stuck in someone's head, and she'd long ago disassociated herself from them. But she couldn't manage that with *A Dad and his Daughter*. She'd spent far too much time as a kid watching the music video and dreaming of him acknowledging her as his daughter and actively being her dad. She'd also spent far too many emotions, all of them exquisitely painful once that dream was stomped on, to ever truly distance herself from it.

"Music off," she called to the smart device as she made her way through the mass of limbs on the floor to an open space at the front and tried to shake off the emotions the song had thrown at her.

With the music off, all eyes went to her, and she smiled at them. "You have spent the past two days and nights together, hopefully bonding with each other and getting excited about your roles this coming school year as ambassadors."

Based on the cheers, hugging, and fist-bumping, they had. She felt that strong bond with them too. As she spoke, the emotions from the song faded away and she could focus on these kids. A few students in this group had been at the State Leadership Academy she'd run last summer. A handful of others had been ambassadors last year, returning for their second year. Most were new faces who would just be starting college in a week. And she loved being up in front of them with all their attention on her as they ate up everything she said.

"Our theme this retreat has been about breaking barriers. The things that stand as obstacles in our way and keep us from really connecting with others, taking risks, and trying new things."

She knew she had given them great advice during the entire retreat and had them participate in activities to practice what she'd been preaching.

But was she taking her own advice?

About halfway through her closing speech that wrapped up all they'd done over the past forty-eight hours, it occurred to her that she knew the reason she craved getting up in front of crowds—it gave her validation that she was a person worthy of listening to. Maybe the reason she'd been so shy as a kid was her worry that what she had to say didn't matter and people didn't care about her enough to care about her words.

And she probably never would've had that epiphany if she hadn't just heard her trigger song from her dad. Maybe her childhood belief that no one cared about what she had to say was because her dad had never cared.

Her voice started to wobble as her throat grew tight. She stopped talking for a moment to smile at the kids, trying to calm the emotions so they wouldn't be able to tell she'd just figured out something that felt so huge. "Now are you all ready to break down those barriers stopping you from accomplishing your goals and have a great start to the fall semester?"

They all let out a huge cheer, and she called out, "Let's do this!"

They were so pumped up that she knew their freshman—or sophomore—year would start with a bang. Summer could feel it too, based on the grin and thumbs-up she gave Elle from the back of the room.

Elle then took that excitement and directed it toward getting the cabin cleaned and all their gear packed and lined up in the foyer.

As they worked, the student who had attached their phone to the Bluetooth speakers started playing music again. And of course, the song *A Dad and his Daughter* started playing where it had left off.

"This song again?" Elle said to a group of girls who were working nearby, trying to make her voice less annoyed than she felt. "Why is it getting played so much lately? This song came out forever ago!" And, recent epiphany or not, every single time she heard it—which was a lot lately—those familiar pains of being unwanted and unworthy hit her hard. She might have figured out some things, but it didn't make the pain of her dad's rejection any less.

One of the girls, Becca, said, "It's because they did a remake of the music video for its twentieth anniversary. I heard that the first one was made with an actor as his daughter, but this one is with his actual daughter. It is *so* sweet. Have you seen it?"

Elle's world stopped. Through the ringing in her ears, all she could hear was the same line repeating over and over *This one is with his actual daughter*. The familiar pain she'd first felt at age nine came rushing back.

She was shaking her head when another girl, Kailey, said, "Wouldn't it be so cool to have him as your dad?"

Elle couldn't respond. She couldn't let these students see on her face what her answer to that would be. Her dad had a daughter? It was too much to even comprehend. How had she missed that bit of news? She didn't go online searching for news on her dad anymore, but those kinds of things always found a way to her. Why hadn't this? She swallowed. "How old is his daughter?"

"Eight," Yuri said. "Apparently, he didn't even know about her until recently. But as soon as he found out, he became the best dad ever."

"I saw a picture on Insta of him taking her to Disneyland," Becca said.

Another girl, Bryn, said, "I heard they're going to make a movie out of their story."

Yuri shook her head. "I heard they decided to do a reality TV series instead."

"Either way," Kailey said, "I would watch."

"Excuse me," Elle said, and headed downstairs to check on the cleaning efforts down there, but her legs were shaky and her vision blurred. She stopped halfway down the stairs and just leaned against the wall, unable to go any further. Her dad found out about a daughter he didn't know he had and then instantly became the World's Greatest Dad to her? That was what she'd spent her childhood dreaming of. Yet he couldn't so much as acknowledge her existence. Why? What was different about Elle?

She still hadn't moved when her phone rang. A glance at her screen told her it was Lindee, her editor at Aquamoose Rising, LBSU's magazine. She swallowed and told herself that these emotions were stupid and she didn't have to have them if she didn't want them, then answered the call.

"Hi, Elle! I just wanted to let you know that I read your article about your interview with Declan Davenport, and I think it's excellent."

"Yeah?"

"You really did well."

There was a pause, and Elle could practically feel the "but" coming. So she nudged her by asking, "But?"

"When things are well-written, it's much easier to notice when something is missing or just isn't as right as it could be. I feel like everything you put here left us with a burning question that we want an answer to—*Why?* What drove Declan to get to where he is now? Because plenty of people *want* to do this, but it takes someone incredibly driven to pull it off. There's always something behind that drive."

Elle's eyebrows drew together. "I thought I answered that—he does it in memory of his mom because she had such a strong belief that he could do it."

"That might be a big drive of his *now*. But he had to have spent his life aiming toward this for it to happen. What was his drive when he was younger?"

Elle didn't reply. Mostly because she didn't know the answer

"This is a great article as it is now," Lindee said. "And I'm willing to print it without any changes at all. If you want it to be phenomenal, though, dig a little deeper. Find out the base of that drive."

Elle said she'd see what she could do and get back to her.

The students grabbed their bags and headed back to campus in their carpools. Every year, there were always things that got missed in the cleaning process or items that got left behind, and final things on the cabin list that had to be closed down after everyone else left, so Elle and a couple of her coworkers always stayed behind to finish things up.

And just like they had planned, Declan showed up as she was close to finishing and met her in the kitchen. "You are such a sight for sore eyes," she said as she left the list on the counter and pulled him close, planting a kiss on his lips.

"Three days is far too long to go without seeing you," he said.

"Agreed. Let's never do that again. And I am almost ready to leave." She went back to the list to see what else they needed to do. She and Declan were going to head to Sioux Falls to get dinner and then watch an outdoor movie in his backyard with his team. She couldn't quite focus on the list though. Instead, she glanced at him. "Why don't you ever talk about your childhood?"

"I've told you a lot about my childhood. About my mom, about how poor we were..."

"True. But not about where you grew up. What your home was like. Elementary school. Things like that. Whenever I ask, you change the subject."

He leaned his hip against the counter and folded his arms. "Why does it matter?"

It wasn't just his arms. Everything from his posture to his expression suddenly seemed so closed off. Part of her brain was working on why that was, making it difficult for the other part to figure out how to say what she wanted to say. "It partially matters because my editor says my article about you would be better if I wrote about what motivated you as a child to aim toward where you are right now —"

"You know my motivation."

"—but it also matters because I want to know everything about you. There's this big part of you that shaped the man you are today and you always hold back from telling me anything about it."

He took a frustrated breath and looked out the window toward the open field bordering a small wood. Then he met her eyes again. "Rock Falls, Minnesota. In a home surrounded by trees. Woods, really. River Valley Elementary." His words were clipped. They came out not exactly angry and not exactly annoyed, but somewhere in between.

Elle turned back to her list, unsure if she wanted to just retreat from the conversation or be annoyed. Maybe she wanted both. Maybe she had no idea what she wanted in her current state. "Fine. Never mind. Forget I asked." She rubbed her forehead and then picked up her pen. It was such a mistake to bring it up. She should've just left it alone. Lindee said the article Elle wrote was still good without it, and she already knew how to deal with the disappointment that came from someone not wanting to open up in a relationship. It was okay. She wasn't exactly used to opening up fully in her relationships either.

Declan stepped right up behind her and wrapped his arms around her waist. "I am sorry, Elle. I didn't mean to be snippy. It's just something I don't like talking about."

She got that. She really, really did. But it was also a huge chunk of his life. And it didn't seem like something he didn't want to discuss *in general*, but rather something he didn't want to share with *her*, specifically.

Why was that? Did he not trust her? Or did he only share it with a select few and she didn't rank high enough? Or did he think they weren't going to keep dating, so he wasn't willing to share? Did he see that there was something defective about her?

She had ended plenty of relationships over the years when the doubts and fears settled in. But she'd never given herself so fully to a relationship, so all her doubts and fears felt stronger than ever.

She knew all the feelings about her dad were probably mixed up in the emotions swirling around inside her. But she also knew that her inner tornado was mostly worry about being enough for Declan, so she needed to take action. He might not be to the point of realizing that she wasn't good enough for him yet, but he would figure it out before long. And then he would reject her just like her father did.

And the longer they waited to bring this to its inevitable end, the more painful it would be. The pen in her hand started shaking, so she set it down, ignoring the unshed tears making her vision blurry. Then she turned to face Declan.

"I don't think we should see each other anymore."

His eyebrows drew together and his eyes widened.

"What? Why?" The look of shock and hurt on his face was almost more than she could bear to see.

Because I'm not worthy of the love of a man as incredible as you. "Because I think that, deep down at the core, there's something wrong that will never be right."

He studied her for a long moment, his face crumpling before he fought to control his expression. She hated seeing the sadness on his face. She wanted to reach out with her fingers and smooth the hurt, wrap her arms around him, tell him everything would be all right. But it would be worse for both of them if she waited longer.

Her own heart felt like it was shattering into tiny pieces even as she frantically tried to build a protective wall around it. She tried to steel herself for the loneliness and pain that would come from being in a world without Declan, but the task seemed too uncomprehendingly huge.

Then he gave a single nod and said, "Okay."

That was it. *Okay.* She felt the buzz of a text from the phone in her pocket, but she ignored it. After all they'd been through, she thought there would be more than the word "Okay," but maybe he'd realized that she was right.

Summer walked into the kitchen, looking down at the phone in her hand. "Did you see the text? Pavani had her baby! They barely had time to get to the hospital before—" Then she must've looked up at Elle and Declan, the tears now falling freely down Elle's face, because she said, "Oh."

The news was too much. Elle's emotions were already full to the top, and she didn't have the mental space for Summer's news. She swiped at her tears. "I've, um... I've got to go."

Declan nodded and looked to the side, like he was trying to hide the devastation on his face. She looked down at the floor before turning to walk out of the kitchen, leaving him behind.

Chapter Twenty-One

DECLAN

Declan sat slumped on his couch, phone in hand, watching the video that he and Elle had made together on repeat. It had only been forty-seven days—less than seven weeks—since they'd made that video. Yet so much had changed in that amount of time that it felt like a lifetime ago.

There had been so much optimism and promise on their faces that day. But also, clear back then, he hadn't believed anything could happen with Elle. Then it had . . . and, he was surprised to realize, he'd started to believe that things would work out. He didn't know why. Deep down, he knew the issue that had stopped him from dating long before Elle came along hadn't gone away.

Elle knew it too. She had sensed that there was something wrong with him. *Something wrong that will never be right*. Even thinking about her words made the pain hit him just as hard as a couple of hours ago when she said them.

But still, he'd felt himself change over the past seven weeks. And she had given him so much hope.

He paused the video right as Elle jumped into his arms. He wanted to reach out and touch her cheeks. To feel the way her smile made them rise. That smile was so open, almost a laugh, and was filled with joy and surprise. From the moment he'd first seen the video, he'd understood Jen's happiness at capturing it on film. Elle's expression said she'd just been swept off her feet and was elated about that. His expression said the same.

And that had been before their dinner and talking on the couch. Before they'd been up in the middle of the night, eating dessert, connecting with each other. Or all the dates since then where they had both shared so much, made each other laugh, shared their dreams for the future, and made one another feel like they could do anything.

His partnership with Kids Camp Nation to take his science camp nationwide likely wouldn't have happened if Elle hadn't made him feel so confident. She really did bring out all the best emotions in him.

And when she'd said she wanted to end things, he'd just said, "Okay."

Okay.

Like it was fine. Like it hadn't just crushed his world.

A knock sounded at his door and he sat up straight. He wasn't expecting anyone, was he? Honestly, he couldn't even say what day of the week it was and had no idea about the time. He walked to the door, straightening his shirt, and opened it.

His entire team—Mato, Halona, Jen, and Sam were all standing on his porch, expectant looks on their faces.

He ran his hands through his hair. "Movie night. I completely forgot."

Jen eyed him up and down. "You look like crap."

"Thank you."

She walked past him into his foyer as everyone else followed, then she turned back to him. "No, seriously, you look terrible. What happened to you?"

Mato seemed to instantly know. A pained expression crossed his face. He shook his head and looked down, putting his hands in his pockets.

Then Halona said, "Oh, no," and Jen gasped.

Sam looked back and forth between them all. "What? He didn't even say anything! How do you guys know what happened? *Tell me.*"

Mato met Declan's eyes for a moment, then he turned to Sam. "He and Elle broke up."

"Wait, really?" Sam asked. "I thought you two were great together."

Declan turned and walked to his living room. No sense in everyone standing around in the foyer. "I thought we were too." He sat back down on the couch. "But I wasn't good enough for her."

Jen sat in the armchair across from him. "No way that was the reason."

"She said that deep down at the core, there's something wrong that will never be right."

Mato met his eyes as he sat down with the others and gave him a look he couldn't quite interpret. Maybe it was just Mato letting him know that he felt bad for Declan.

"She said that about *you*?" Halona asked. "For real?"

Declan nodded. "That's why I don't date. Because she's right."

"Okay, that's seriously messed up," Jen said. "Have you spoken with a therapist about this? No, seriously. There is not something wrong with you. I can't imagine anything that you, Declan Davenport, could have in your past to justify that."

Declan ran his hands over his face. "What if it's not something in my past, but just part of who I am?"

"And who are you, Declan?" Mato asked. "Because from where we're standing, you are someone who is hardworking and full of integrity. Who has a great sense of humor and looks out for others."

"Brilliant," Halona added. "Loyal."

Jen nodded. "Cares for people. Charismatic."

"Kind. Fun." Sam said.

Declan appreciated all the compliments, but he had a

hard time letting those compliments in. Just like Elle, they didn't know the whole story. Even Mato didn't know anywhere near the whole story. "Thank you."

"So," Sam said, "what are you going to do?"

"What do you mean, *do*?"

"You know, in the movies, the couple breaks up and the guy goes and fights for the girl. So what are you going to do?"

"I'm not going to do anything. Elle deserves more than me, and I'm not going to try to make her settle for less."

Halona shook her head. "It's not about one person being better or more worthwhile in the relationship than the other."

"Yes, it is."

"No. In every relationship, there's always one person who, on paper, is better than the other. That isn't the point at all. The point is that both of you *are better* because of the other person. *Both of you.* That's what makes a relationship work. Are you better because of her?"

"Yes. Without a doubt. But, she's not better because of me."

"Do you know that?" Mato asked. "Or are you just assuming? Because you're not in a position to be objective right now. Maybe you should let her decide that."

"I am pretty sure that breaking up with me was her way of deciding exactly that."

"It definitely could be," Halona said.

Jen leaned forward in her seat. "But I don't think it was."

Declan breathed in deeply and met Jen's eyes for a long moment. "You don't?"

She shook her head.

He looked around at the others for confirmation of what Jen said before looking back at Jen. "How do you know?"

"None of us knew Elle before you two met," Halona said, "so we can't speak to you making her better than she was without you. But all of us have spent enough time with the two of you to know that what you have together is genuine. Real. And sometimes 'real' gets scary because it makes you confront some of the things you've been burying."

He could attest to that.

"She might even have her own buried issues she's dealing with," Jen said.

"Do you want my advice?" Mato asked. "Figure out what you've been burying and unbury it."

Chapter Twenty-Two

ELLE

*E*lle was not the kind of girl to drown herself in a pint of ice cream while dealing with emotions that felt overwhelming and big and sad and big and devastating and *big*. Apparently, she was the kind of girl who wandered around the condo she was so proud of buying herself, going from room to room, thinking about how very alone she was.

And wondering if that was what she'd always be: alone.

Except it was worse than that because her home now reminded her too much of Declan. Like the time he sat in the living room chair and grabbed the book off her coffee table and started reading it to her in that gloriously deep voice of his.

Like all the times she opened her front door and felt

happiness wash over her as she saw his smiling face with those adorable dimples.

Making cookies with him in the kitchen, kissing in front of the oven as they cooked.

Being snuggled up next to him on that couch, sometimes watching a movie, sometimes watching each other, sometimes not watching anything at all, and just kissing each other breathless.

Even the memory of Mato standing by her kitchen table, asking her to sign an NDA, made her miss Declan.

Last night, after getting home, she'd even gone outside to her little square of garden and dug in the dirt, pulling out the little weeds that had started to grow and the grass that had spilled over its border. She didn't have anything to plant, but somehow just having her hands in the soil made her feel connected to him.

Everything reminded her of him. Everything made her miss him. Was this where she'd gotten in life? She was twenty-nine years old. Yes, she had her own place, but was she destined to forever be alone?

She needed her best friend. She pulled out her phone and texted Camilla. *Declan and I broke up last night.*

She'd barely counted to five after tapping send before her phone lit up with Camilla's face. She answered the call and told Camilla everything.

"So," Camilla said, "if I'm hearing this right, you broke up with Declan because you're afraid."

She hadn't said it in those words, but now that she thought about it, it felt like Camilla had pinpointed it exactly. "If I fully share my heart, he'll know that I'm not. . ." She wanted to say *worthy of love*, but instead, she said "lovable." It was still one of the most vulnerable things she'd said to anyone in a long time.

And she could see the irony in breaking up with Declan right after asking him to share something he didn't want to share when the reality was that she didn't share everything with anyone. Not since sending her dad that letter when she was nine and telling Hannah Hales about it at eleven. She hadn't ended her relationship with Declan because he wouldn't share—she'd ended it because of her own fears of opening up and being rejected.

She knew if she wanted a relationship to be successful, she'd have to open her heart. All of it. But she also knew what kind of pain that could cause. She could imagine how much worse it would be with someone she loved as much as she loved Declan.

"What about you are you afraid that he will find out if you fully share your heart?"

"Nothing specific. Just about me in general, I guess."

"Well, if it's just that, I can assure you that you have nothing to worry about. All of you is lovable."

That was easy to say. Less easy to believe.

"Oh, I wish I could hop on a plane and come be with you!" Camilla said. "There's no way I can take off work again so soon though. Do you know what? I'm texting your mom to tell her to go to your place."

"No, you are not."

"Yes, I am. We need reinforcements."

"She and Duane are currently on the other side of the state seeing a bunch of presidents' faces carved into the mountain."

"Then I'm adding her to this call."

Elle sighed. When Camilla made a decision, it was difficult to talk her out of it. "You're not adding my mom to this call while she's on vacation."

"What? If you're saying anything to me right now, I can't hear you because I'm typing a number on my phone so it's not up to my ear."

And suddenly her mom was on the call too.

"Thanks for joining us while you're on vacation," Camilla said. "Do you have a moment? Elle broke up with Declan because she doesn't think she's worthy of love."

Elle hadn't even said those words to Camilla, and yet she'd still gotten the message. And wow, it sounded so much worse hearing it out loud. "That's an exaggeration," Elle said, but her voice came out all shaky and scratchy, making it sound like the lie that it was.

"Oh, Elle belle. I know you better than anyone and I love you like crazy, so we know that's not true."

Her mom might know Elle better than anyone, but that didn't mean she knew everything about her. Besides, she was the one person who was obligated to love Elle, no matter what. Although her dad was under that same obligation . . . .

"Why would you even think that, sweetheart?"

She felt a story rising inside, the one she'd kept hidden for a full decade before telling Declan. Either telling him made this easier, or she felt so vulnerable right now that things were just spilling out. "Camilla," Elle said, "remember when we went to Minneapolis for our graduation trip?"

"Yeah."

"My dad was in concert there at the same time. I emailed him and asked if I could meet him in person. He never even responded."

"Elle, that doesn't mean—" her mom began.

"Did you know he found out that he had a daughter not long ago and now she's the apple of his eye?"

Camilla scoffed. "And you think that is evidence that Declan won't stay in love with you? Or that you're not worthy of his love?"

"Not evidence, exactly. Just precedence."

"That is not the same thing," her mom said. "Your dad hadn't known about you and hadn't planned for you. His absence is his loss. A pretty sizeable loss too. Declan has been *choosing* to be with you from the start. From the moment you met, he was a goner for you."

And she was a goner for him. The truth was, she *had*

opened her heart more to him than she had to anyone else in her entire life. He had truly seen more of her mind and soul than anyone else, and he'd loved her anyway. "That's why this is so painful. But it would be so much worse if we dated for even longer before—"

"Before he broke up with you?" her mom asked.

She couldn't answer. Her mom and Camilla were quiet for a beat too.

Camilla said, "We need more reinforcements. I'm texting Summer."

"You don't even have Summer's phone number."

"It's my job as the best friend to have the phone number of an in-town backup."

Then her mom said, "Remember back before I met Duane, when you first started college, and you had me go to all that therapy? Let me tell you something I learned. Sometimes we hold onto negative feelings from the past because those feelings are familiar to us. They're all comfy, like an old couch. We know how to live with them, so they become something we rely on. Like a crutch.

"Those feelings served their purpose back then, but Elle, they're not serving their purpose now. Now they're just holding you back. It's time to let go of that and let in all the good you have in your life."

Maybe her mom was right. It did feel like she was holding on tight to all the emotions surrounding her dad. The ones she'd had as a kid, the ones she'd had as a new graduate, and the ones that overcame her every time she heard *A Dad and his Daughter* or saw a news article about him. Almost like she was clutching the feelings to her so tightly that her arms and hands had seized in that position and she didn't know if it was possible to let go.

A knock sounded at her door. She wasn't expecting anyone, which meant it was probably a salesman. "Sorry, I've got to go—someone is knocking."

"It's Summer," Camilla said.

"You texted her like one minute ago."

"She was already on her way."

Elle shook her head, said goodbye, then hung up the phone and opened the door to see Summer standing there, wearing a cute tee in her signature yellow color. "That shirt is way too happy for today."

"I know."

"Listen, I don't need you to tell me I shouldn't be sad or afraid, or that I'm great, or that Declan and I together are great."

Summer smiled. "Well good, because I'm not here to tell you any of that. I'm here to take you to see Pavani's baby."

Elle stood a little taller. "We can go see him?"

"Yep! Now go wash those mascara tracks off your face and brush your hair. You look awful."

Chapter Twenty-Three

DECLAN

Declan leaned against one of the cabinets in his dad's woodworking shed, arms folded, watching his dad build a display case for Ian's first medal and all the ones that would follow now that he'd discovered a love of track and field. His brothers were both away at a Cub Scout day camp, which would normally make Declan miss them, but he was glad to be one-on-one with his dad. Especially because they were talking about Declan's mom.

His dad lifted a piece of wood he'd just cut with the table saw, running his fingertips along the edge to inspect the cut. "So you know how your mom always got you boys helping to cook when you were just little?"

Declan nodded and smiled, looking down at the ground. Those were some of his favorite memories.

"Ian couldn't have been more than two, and she had him standing on a step stool so he could reach the counter, helping her make—I don't even remember. A cake or bread or something like that. And his little plastic dinosaurs were on the counter, of course, watching over them. Then Hayden woke up from his nap and your mom went to get him out of his crib and change his diaper.

"Now somehow, in the middle of all this, Ian snuck back into the kitchen and with those two-year-old arms of his, managed to get the bin of flour from the counter to the floor where he proceeded to use it as a playground for his dinosaurs.

"I walked in from the grocery store maybe one second after your mom walked into the kitchen, Hayden in her arms, and saw Ian in the flour. He was covered from head to toe in it, looking up at her with a flour-covered dinosaur in each hand. And do you know what your mom did?"

Declan smiled, knowing exactly what she'd done.

"She handed Hayden off to me, pulled out her cell phone, and got a picture of Ian."

Declan still had the picture on his phone of Hayden looking like a ghost that his mom had texted him.

"And then she got right down on the floor with him, played for a minute, and asked if he had any suggestions on how they could clean it all up." Declan's dad shook his head. "Your mom was one of a kind. She knew just how to let you boys make mistakes, learn what you needed to learn from them, and then find a way to fix it."

Conversations like this with his dad were one of Declan's favorite things. But it also made him miss his mom exquisitely. "I wish I would've lived at home my first year of college and, I don't know, gone to the University of Sioux Falls or maybe USD instead of LBSU. I would've liked to have been here when Hayden was a baby."

Dad shook his head. "I think you were right where you needed to be."

It wasn't just that Declan had wanted to be there while his brothers were babies and toddlers. He'd wanted to be there to experience living with both a mom and a dad for longer. They'd only been married for two years when Declan moved a forty-five-minute drive north to start college. At least he hadn't moved farther than that.

He'd also wanted to experience seeing how happy it made his mom to have Gary in her life. He knew his mom wanted that same happiness for Declan—a partner who was well-suited to him, who he could love and protect and spend his life with. A partnership where they could help each other grow in ways that would be impossible on their own. And a woman to have kids with, because as afraid as he was of being a dad, he *did* want his own kids. He wanted to show them the kind of love his mother showed him.

His dad glued along the cut side of one of the boards,

got it perfectly positioned against the side of another, and then used a brad nailer to sink a couple of finishing nails into it. Then he set the nailer down, still looking at the partially finished case, and said, "So, do you want to tell me what happened between you and Elle and why you're not fighting for her?"

Declan stared down at the wood project too. That was exactly what he'd wanted to talk about, so he needed to get over his reluctance and just say it. Finally, he looked up. "Do you remember Abby?"

"Your college girlfriend? Yeah, I remember her. You never really told us much about your breakup."

It wasn't the easiest thing to talk about. "I found out that she was cheating on me."

"No."

Declan nodded. "With one of my friends, Logan. He wasn't a close friend—he was in the group just outside of that. The kind you get together with occasionally and see around everywhere. One night, Abby asked me to go to a party at one of the off-campus residences. I told her I had too much homework and couldn't go.

"Then sometime that evening, I decided that I studied way too much and didn't spend nearly enough time being a social college student, so I decided to go and surprise her at the party."

He cleared his throat, trying to dislodge the emotion at the memory. "I walked in, and Abby and Logan were sitting on a couch, kissing. She must've sensed me walk in because she pulled away and met my gaze pretty quickly. I couldn't tell whether the look on her face was worry that I'd seen or relief that I finally knew. Logan just had a smug expression, like he had come out conqueror."

In a quiet voice, his dad asked, "Then what happened?"

"Abby told me that she'd realized she and Logan had a thing, and what I saw wasn't the first time they'd kissed. Logan stood up, came right up to me, and said, 'We've done a lot more than kiss. Your girl here is quite the pleaser.'" Declan shook his head. "The anger built up in me so quickly that I didn't have time to think before I punched him."

His dad looked at him for a long moment before he said, "That isn't like you."

"The moment I punched him, I was horrified. It made me wonder if I was more like my bio dad than I wanted to admit. I mean, I do have his genes. And I came to the conclusion that people like me shouldn't be in relationships."

"Do you believe that?"

Declan lifted a shoulder in a partial shrug. "I thought that I'd gotten more okay with being in a relationship, at least with Elle. Maybe because everything was more incredible than I thought it could be. But, yeah. The part of me that worries is always there. And then we were in a conversation about having kids not long ago, and I just kept thinking, what kind of dad would I be? And if Elle knew what my bio dad was really like, how could she ever love a guy with some of those same genes?"

His dad just looked at him, studying him, with so much care and concern in his eyes that Declan wondered how different his life would be if Gary had been in it from the start. But he was glad he had him in his life now. "And you think she sensed your biological dad's genes in you and that's why she broke up with you?"

"Maybe."

"Or do you think all of your thoughts and worries about all that maybe made you pull away and it was the distance that made her end things?"

"I don't know. But either way, I'm not sure I can be who I need to be for her."

His dad was quiet for several long moments as he just looked down at the project he'd been working on, the woodworking shed just as silent, the smell of freshly cut wood surrounding them.

Then he leaned back against the same counter that Declan still leaned on, his hands also resting on the countertop, and said, "I can honestly say I've never seen you do anything that made me think to myself, 'Oh, that must've come from his biological dad.' I never met your dad, of course, and your mom didn't talk about him much. She worked hard to overcome her trauma from that. It was in her past, and she didn't like to live in the past. But I *do* know you and I *do* know your mom, and I can tell you that there's a lot more of your mom in you."

He knew there was. That didn't stop him from worrying.

"You know that my sister, your aunt Karly, has two biological kids and two that are adopted."

Declan nodded.

"She told me once that having both is like an experiment in nature versus nurture since it makes it easier to see what came from genes and what comes from parenting. And she'd be the first to tell you—as I'm sure most adoptive parents would—that most kids come with a whole lot of nature in them."

A weight dropped in Declan's stomach.

His dad shrugged without taking his hands off the counter. And then he said, "We all have a whole lot of nature in us. I mean, isn't the whole purpose of life to work on the parts of our nature that we don't like and make them better? We're all born with a set of challenges, internal and external, and we're given our entire lifetime to work on overcoming them.

"And *nurture* doesn't only come from your parents; it also comes from *you*." He turned and tapped a finger right over Declan's heart. "You nurture the parts you want to improve and work hard on them. Just like your mom did. Just like we're all trying to do. I don't think I've ever seen anyone work harder to turn the nature parts into what he wants them to be than you."

Declan didn't know what to say. Everything was swirling around in his brain so much that he didn't think he could form words if he had to.

"I know how aware of that you are and how hard you work to constantly make yourself a better person. Your mom was always improving herself at something or the other. I think that's a big part of why she was such an incredible person. And I know that she taught you the same thing. You grew up learning how to overcome weaknesses from the start. It's so ingrained in you that I would say it's a bigger part of your DNA now than anything your bio dad ever contributed."

"You think so?"

"Yep, and I've got my good buddy, Ralph Waldo Emerson, backing me up," he said as he motioned to the framed quotes on the walls. "'The only person you are destined to become is the person *you decide* to be.' I'm pretty sure you decided a long time ago who you wanted to be."

The emotions built up thick in Declan's throat and he tried to swallow them down.

"It's important to understand your past so you can work through it. It's also important not to live in your past. You've worked hard to get to where you are—I think it's time to let go of the past and let yourself live in the present." His dad smiled and shook his head. "I'll tell you what. Instead of going to my main guy, Ralph Waldo Emerson, for another load of wisdom in a short quote, I'll go to one in your field—Albert Einstein. He said, 'Learn from yesterday, live for today, hope for tomorrow.'"

Declan's mom had spent much of her life teaching him how to learn from yesterday. Elle had given him hope for tomorrow. It was time he lived for today.

As he left his dad's house, he sent a text to his team.

DECLAN: Sam, remember when you asked me what I'm going to DO? I have an answer. I realize I've spent my life fighting to become who I want to be. Now I'm going to go fight for Elle.

As the texts from Sam, Jen, Halona, and Mato started pouring in, filled with excited emojis and animated gifs, Declan smiled and slid his phone back into his pocket. He had work to do.

Chapter Twenty-Four

ELLE

Summer didn't ask Elle any questions during their drive to the hospital, which was perfect since Elle needed time to process her emotions. They even made their way through the hospital to Pavani's room without Summer bringing up the breakup.

Pavani was lying in her hospital bed, wearing a gown, looking tired but happy.

"How are you?" Elle asked as she leaned in to hug her friend.

"I am good! Things progressed rapidly." Pavani chuckled quietly. "Which was nice, except for the fact that I very nearly had him in the hallway before making it to the delivery room."

Elle sat down in a side chair. Summer took a seat

beside her and said, "It sounds like the little guy has his momma's drive to get things done quickly."

Pavani smiled. "I wish he understood that being speedy doesn't always make things faster—he'll have to stay in the NICU for a few days. Zane is there with him now—I just needed to rest."

"But he's doing well?" Elle asked.

"Zane or the baby?" Pavani chuckled softly again. "Zane's a little frazzled still, but he's floating along on cloud nine. Baby Ajay—" Pavani wiped a tear that had escaped at saying her new son's name. "He's such a strong kid already. Stronger than me. I don't know how I'm going to be able to handle being released when he has to stay behind. Oh, but he is just so precious! I want to hold him and love him and never let go. It was worth every moment of every struggle to get him here."

Both Elle and Summer reached forward and squeezed Pavani's hand.

After a few minutes of chatting, Elle and Summer left so Pavani could sleep and headed to the NICU. When they got to the window, they could see Zane sitting in a rocking chair, holding the newborn baby against his chest, rocking back and forth.

"He looks so happy," Elle said.

Summer nodded. Zane glanced up and noticed them. He lifted Ajay up a bit like he wanted to show him off, grinning so wide that the sight made Elle's injured heart hurt a little less.

As they both watched, Elle cleared her throat. "I like being up in front of groups, talking to them."

Summer studied Elle for a moment, probably trying to figure out what made Elle change the subject so abruptly. Then she looked back into the NICU. "I know."

"Do you know why?"

Summer shook her head.

"During my closing speech at the retreat, I had an epiphany about it."

"Yeah?" Summer glanced at Elle before returning her gaze to Zane and the baby.

"Yeah. It makes me feel like I'm someone worth listening to." She shook her head. "I think nine-year-old Elle has been bringing up old emotions because my dad's song *A Dad and his Daughter* has been playing pretty much nonstop lately.

"And if that wasn't a big enough whammy, since then I've realized that I use talking to a crowd as a way of covering up my insecurities rather than dealing with those emotions." She swallowed hard, hoping to keep the emotions at bay. "I also think it might have been a factor in me breaking up with Declan."

"Just a factor?" Summer asked with no judgment. It was simply a question.

Elle shrugged. "Maybe it was the entire reason. Hard to say."

Summer was quiet for a long moment, then she nodded toward the baby. "He really is precious, isn't he? He is worth everything to them. You can hear it in Pavani's voice and see it on Zane's face."

"He really is."

"What do you think he's done to earn that?"

Elle's eyebrows drew together as she looked at Summer, confused.

"You know," Summer prompted. "His worth. What did he do to get it? What impressive things?"

"Summer! He has worth from simply being alive. He came with his own worth."

Summer smiled at Elle. "And so did you. From every moment I've spent with both you and Declan, it's obvious he sees that worth."

A single sob caught in Elle's throat as emotions built up in her, threatening to spill out. "But what if he doesn't want to stay?"

Summer turned back to look through the window at baby Ajay. "That's a risk in every relationship. Does someone fully seeing your worth mean that everything will work out? Not always. But even if it doesn't, your worth won't change. What you miss out on by backing away is the chance at something glorious."

Elle knew her relationship with Declan had the potential to be glorious. That might have been what scared her the most. "I know. I just feel like I've been holding on so tight to the insecurities that came because of my dad. But I've had them all of my life, so I don't know how to let go."

Summer turned to face Elle. "I've heard you mention nine-year-old Elle a lot over the years. I think she might be the key to everything."

Elle cocked her head.

"I think you should tell nine-year-old Elle that you're sorry she had to go through all she did. That it was tough, and she had to be tough to deal with it. Then thank her for having your back, tell her how grateful you are for all she's done, and say that everything is okay now and she doesn't need to protect you anymore. She can just be nine-year-old Elle. Twenty-nine-year-old Elle has got it from here."

This time a sob did escape. Elle wrapped her arms around her friend and they held each other tightly as Elle's tears started to flow.

Maybe she could let go of past hurts. She, Elle Markle, had worth—regardless of what happened in her life. And Declan had seemed determined to remind her of that every day. She could let go of the fears she'd been holding onto for so long not only because she deserved it, but also because *he* was worth holding onto.

Elle didn't pull back from the hug for a long time. When she finally did, Summer put her hands on Elle's shoulders and said, "You have a lot of people who love you a lot."

Elle nodded and wiped a tear from her cheek.

"And I think that maybe the one who loves you most is Declan."

Chapter Twenty-Five

DECLAN

Declan glanced over at Elle as he sped down the state highway past the flat, open fields. The past few days of not seeing her had felt like a lifetime. Although it wasn't a quick drive from Lake Baldwin to Rock Falls, they had only talked about surface-level topics. There seemed to be an unspoken agreement that anything deeper needed to happen afterward. He was just grateful that when he'd texted Elle about taking this drive, she'd been willing to spend her afternoon headed to a secret destination.

As soon as the *Welcome to Rock Falls, MN* sign came into view, Elle sat a little taller. She didn't say anything though, so Declan kept driving through the town that he'd grown up in. Rock Falls was small enough for everyone to feel like they knew each other but big enough that it wasn't actually the truth.

When they reached the edge of town and he kept driving, he could almost feel the confusion in Elle. It mixed with his own feelings of being back here. It wasn't his first time driving these roads since moving to Sioux Falls back in high school, but the emotions never went away—the good and the bad. A mile further, he turned onto a gravel road leading into the woods he loved that had unquestionably shaped who he was.

Halona and Mato had been right that night when Elle had broken up with him. Genuine relationships got scary because they made you confront what you'd been burying. And it was time for him to unbury it.

The road narrowed to the width of a single vehicle, trees lining both sides, the pale dirt and equally pale rocks crunching under his tires as he drove. The vegetation encroached on the edges of the path even more than the last time he'd been here.

Then he turned off the quasi-road onto a rough pathway between the trees that he guessed only animals used now, the car bouncing as it went over the uneven ground. Elle held onto the handle at her door as leaves from a low-hanging tree branch brushed the windshield. The last time a vehicle drove along this path was probably a year ago when he had last visited.

Finally, he turned off the path and onto a flat area

filled with grasses and weeds right in front of a small, run-down shack. It was always strange seeing this place, even more weathered than it once was, with adult eyes and height. Nothing felt the same, yet everything did. It took him right back to his childhood.

He got out of the car, walked around to the other side, opened Elle's door, and held out a hand to her. "You wanted to know more about where I grew up."

She put her hand in his, as he pulled her to her feet. "It was here?"

He nodded, then shut Elle's door as she slowly walked toward the shack he'd called home for eight years. He put his hands in his pockets and walked alongside her.

"Does anyone live here now?"

He shook his head. "It was abandoned long before we moved in, and I'm pretty sure it's been abandoned ever since."

"You were homeless?"

"What? No. I never once felt homeless. This was my home and I loved it. Come here. I want to show you."

He led her to the back side of the shack and pushed the door open. The hinges had long ago rusted and made plenty of screeching and creaking noises. He turned on his phone's flashlight and shone it around. The light was hazy from all the dust motes and the air had a definite rotting wood smell, but it still brought back happy memories of the place.

"I know it's hard to imagine now, but we kept this place very clean. My bed was over there and my mom's was there. We had a small table and a couple of chairs right here, and those cabinets used to be filled with all of our stuff. We used that fireplace all winter long." He took in a long breath. "I swear I can still hear the crackle of the fire."

Elle was quiet for a moment as she took it all in. Then she asked, "Is that how you cooked your food?"

He knew she must have a million questions. "Sometimes. But mostly we used a barbeque we kept just outside the back door. We didn't have running water or electricity, so we used ice and coolers. There's also a well with a pump a couple dozen feet away."

As they walked around, stopping whenever Elle did, he said, "I told you once that my mom worked as a maid for a wealthy family and I got ready for school in their pool house. That was where we both showered and did laundry. They were the only people who knew where we lived."

"No one else?"

He shook his head. "When I was in elementary school and a friend asked if I could play after school, I always told them that my mom worked and didn't want me to have people over while she was gone, so we always played at their house."

"How long did you live here?"

"From when I was four until I was twelve. Don't feel bad for me though. I knew my mom was saving all the money she could, and she made sure that we ate healthily and I had decent, clean clothes for school." He turned and led her back out the door into the woods and motioned at everything surrounding them. "And I got to grow up here. I was actually sad to leave and move into a regular house."

"You came from a background like this and worked to get to where you are now? Declan, that's inspiring. Why did you not want to tell me about this?"

If he just needed to "unbury" the part about living in a shack in the woods, he probably would have before now. That part of his history wasn't something he told people, but he would've told Elle. And a big part of him wanted to stop at that.

But Elle was not just anyone, and he wanted to show that he could open his entire heart to her. He couldn't do that while keeping hidden a big part of who he'd been and how he'd become the man he was now.

So he led her to the two tree stumps he and his mom had used whenever they ate a meal outside, and they both sat down. Talking about all this wasn't easy. But he told himself again that he could do it.

"I was twelve when I found out the real reason we lived here. Yes, we were poor. But," he took a slow, deep breath, "we were also in hiding from my biological dad. He was... not a good person. He'd been abusive and controlling and told my mom that if she ever left, he would hunt her down. She managed to escape with me anyway and moved us here, to a random state where she had no ties, and found us a place to live where we'd never be discovered."

His eyes were on the ground in front of him, but he heard Elle's gasp. "Oh, that sounds so scary. And stressful."

"I'm sure it was for my mom. But it wasn't for me—I never felt any of that growing up. I loved it here." He motioned at their surroundings, which filled him with imagination and excitement even so many years later. "I had the whole forest as my backyard. Whenever I wasn't in school, I was out here, exploring. I'd get down in the dirt and study the bugs, the way the plants poked their way up through the dirt, all of it. I'd spend hours investigating things, lost in my thoughts, trying to figure everything out."

She shifted on the log, her knees turned more toward him now. "You said you found out the reason when you were twelve. What had changed?"

Her voice was soft, and he found himself *wanting* to tell her everything. Something he'd never experienced before. "My mom found out that my bio dad had just been sentenced to life in prison—another woman had suffered the fate that he'd threatened my mom with."

He heard Elle suck in a breath and her hand immediately found his. He watched for a long while as her thumb skimmed along the back of his hand, making small circles, the touch giving him immeasurable comfort.

"My mom didn't exactly make a big salary here, but she squirreled away all that she could. Without the threat of my bio dad finding us anymore, we could finally move into a real place." He chuckled and shook his head. "That was a hard move for me. I mean, it was great to have indoor plumbing, electricity, and a real kitchen, but that didn't quite feel like it was worth leaving the woods."

Elle seemed to understand that he didn't want pity. He wanted her to know everything and understand where he came from, but he didn't want it to feel dark and heavy. He wouldn't trade his childhood experiences for anything. She nudged her shoulder into his. "Oh, come on. You were heading into your teenage years. You can't tell me that you weren't thrilled to be getting a fridge."

He laughed. "Okay, you're right. And being able to have friends over was a huge plus, too."

"And not having to trudge through snow past your knees when you had to go to the bathroom in the middle of winter?"

"Another definite huge plus. Having a house came with a lot of benefits that I was completely grateful for. But that didn't mean it was easy to leave my woods."

She looked around at everything that had surrounded him as a child. "I can see why." Then she met his eyes again. "How did you find out about your dad?"

"From my mom. I don't know if she would've chosen to tell me at twelve, though. I had just gotten back to her work after school that day and she was on the phone in the pool house. I caught most of the call where she'd gotten the news about my bio dad before she noticed that I was there. I heard enough to be filled with questions, and I think she knew that I needed the answers to most of them.

"You know, it was funny—we were the most in danger when I was in elementary school, yet I was blissfully unaware and afraid of nothing. We became safest at the time of that phone call but finding it all out made me more afraid.

"I started spending a lot of time worrying about being helpless and incapable if we were ever in danger or if my dad ever escaped or was released. I focused on getting stronger and smarter. I think I figured that if I got to be smart enough, I'd be able to keep me and my mom safe. And later, when she married Gary and after Ian and Hayden were born, I wondered if I could keep them safe. Especially when I was away at school and wasn't physically there to protect them."

He'd never voiced his thoughts and emotions so succinctly, especially with the perspective that time and life experience brought. It felt freeing to share it with her.

"That's a huge load to carry."

"It was. But it also gave me a greater appreciation for

my mom's strength and for Gary's willingness to do anything for us. That lifted a lot of the weight."

Elle met his gaze and studied him. Then she said, "I'm sorry for pushing you to tell me more at the retreat cabin. You really didn't have to tell me all this."

"I know. But I don't want to hide anything from you." He wanted to reach out and place a hand against her cheek. To skim his fingertips along the skin just in front of her. To wrap his arms around her.

Instead, he just gazed into her eyes. "You're so important to me. But I understand if knowing about my history and my biological dad makes you want nothing more to do with me." The words were hard to say, but he needed to say them. He would understand if she wanted to turn and walk away from him. But it didn't mean it wouldn't crush his whole world all over again.

Declan took in every part of Elle, from the way her eyelashes curled, to the shape of her cheekbones, to the shade of her lips, to the way a lock of her hair fell in a loose curl in front of her shoulder, to the hand that still held his. He tried to memorize every inch of her, knowing this could be their last day together if she ran from his revelations about his past, or it could be the beginning of something that would last forever if she didn't.

He looked into her eyes, but he didn't see fear, or revulsion, or worry. Just love. Hope. A promise.

"I'm glad you told me. It makes me realize that you're

even more extraordinary than I thought you were."

"I know you wanted things between us to end. But our relationship is essential to me, and I want to fight for it. It wouldn't be fair if I tried to convince you to give us another chance, though, if I didn't first open up about what shaped so much of who I am. You've been willing to share so much about your life—you deserve the same courtesy you showed me."

Elle grimaced. "I didn't share everything."

"No?"

She tucked a lock of her hair behind her ear, looking a bit scared. Hesitant. She blew out a long breath. "Well, you've gotten most of the story. I just haven't shared how much things with my own dad affected me. I don't think I really knew before this week. But," she glanced upward and shrugged, "I think I might have some abandonment issues. Which is stupid! Because my dad didn't abandon us—he wasn't there in the first place."

Declan took both her hands in his and looked deeply into her eyes. He wanted to make sure she really heard what he was going to say. "Elle, it isn't stupid. It's still abandonment, and all your feelings about your dad—recently and throughout your life—are valid. It's okay to feel them."

She chuckled, shaking her head as she looked down. But when her eyes met his again, he could see that tears were welling up. "Thank you," she whispered.

Declan stood and pulled her to her feet. For a long, dazzling moment, he just gazed into those beautiful brown eyes of hers with the golden facets. He remembered looking into those eyes on the day they'd met, thinking about how they could be so expressive yet only show a glimpse of what went on behind them.

Over the last seven weeks, he'd gotten to see much more of what lay behind them. So much of her heart and mind. Yet he could stare into those eyes forever and never tire of discovering more about her. The more he got to know Elle, the more alluring those eyes became, grabbing his focus entirely, rendering him powerless to let go.

He reached out and lightly skimmed two fingertips along her cheekbone, just below those captivating eyes of hers. "Before I met you, my life was pretty good. I had a job that I loved and was successful at, a team of talented people who had become my best friends, a family I adored, and a home that I enjoyed."

Elle studied his eyes, and he wondered what was going through her mind, her heart.

"But then I met you and I've been completely entranced. The more time I've spent with you, the more I've discovered how smart, and kind, and talented, and hard-working you are. You bring out the best in me and open a part of me that I thought would forever be dormant. I wake up every morning happier than I've ever been, and I know it's because my last thought before I go to bed and my first thought when I wake up in the morning is about you. I figure I must be spending all night dreaming about you, too, because I wake up with that happiness in me before I've even had my first thought.

"When I question myself and my abilities, I know you believe in me, and that gives me incredible strength. You've made me more capable of love than I've ever been, like my heart has expanded just by knowing you.

"For as good as I thought my life was before I met you, I've realized that with you, it's phenomenal. Beyond compare." He tried to swallow down the emotions in his throat. "Now that I've found out how extraordinary and how full life can be *with* you, I can't go back." He let out a breath, shaking his head as he looked at the ground. Then he met her eyes again. "'Good' is no longer enough once you've experienced 'incredible.' Elle, if you'll have me, I will spend my life making sure you never feel abandoned. I will cherish you and love you for as long as I live."

A tear that had been building up in Elle's eyes spilled onto her cheek, he reached out and brushed it away with a knuckle.

She studied him for another moment, her eyes searching his. He held in a breath, unable to release it as he studied her face, too, trying to decipher everything behind those eyes.

Then she reached up and, hands on either side of his face, pulled his lips to hers.

Chapter Twenty-Six

ELLE

lle let out a small moan as Declan's lips moved against hers, his arms firmly around her waist, her body pressed up against him. This whole trip—seeing where Declan grew up, learning about his past, hearing him open up about things she knew he didn't share with many people—was exactly what she needed without even knowing she'd needed it. She'd never felt so close to another person before.

And getting so close to Declan, experiencing him being so open and vulnerable, made her love for him even stronger. It made her want to face everything in her future with him by her side. Because she knew now that together, they could face anything.

He smiled into the kiss and she felt the breath of a

chuckle against her lips. She pulled back just a tiny bit while still holding onto him. "What?"

In that gloriously deep voice of his, he said, "I take it this means you *do* want our relationship to continue?"

She chuckled softly too, then planted another kiss on his lips. "Very much. Forever and always."

He pulled back a little more, allowing her to soak in the way he had been looking at her all afternoon—his head cocked just slightly, the corners of his mouth pulled up just enough to show a hint of those dimples, his expression warm, like he did, in fact, cherish every single bit of her and always would.

It was somehow both overpowering and soul-healing to have the force of those eyes looking at her like she was his everything. They had been her Kryptonite from day one, and she knew that wasn't going to change.

"Come with me," he said as he slipped his hand over hers. "I want to show you more of this place."

She could easily see why he'd loved growing up here as they walked through the woods so he could show her the paths, plants, animals, bugs, and soil that had captured his imagination as a kid. The place smelled so clean and fresh and crisp. It had obviously planted a seed of curiosity that sprouted into a desire to become a scientist and share his passion with everyone.

As they walked along the creek he used to play in, she thought about how everything he had accomplished so far would've been impressive even if he'd had everything handed to him. But it was even more impressive knowing where he'd come from. And maybe he wouldn't be where he was now if he hadn't gone through everything he had.

Somehow, though, that thought felt like she was robbing Declan of the credit. It took someone truly incredible to go through what he had and turn it into a life so beautiful.

She stopped by the edge of the creek and turned toward him. "I was just thinking—we have very different fathers, yet we've both been worried about how much our dads influence us. To the point that it nearly cost us each other."

"Yeah." Declan shook his head. "I don't ever want it to affect me ever again."

"Me neither. I mean, most of the time, it doesn't affect me at all. Then something will happen that makes those old emotions blindside me."

"Okay, let's make a deal. If either of us notices those old feelings rearing their heads, we immediately go to the other person. We help each other through them right from the start, so they can never take hold again."

A smile spread across Elle's face and she held out her hand. "Deal." She liked that he knew everything, understanding her so well. She had no doubt he'd have her back through anything.

Declan grabbed her hand to shake it, but instead

pulled her closer and sealed the deal with a kiss. Which was so much better than a handshake.

Afterward, they watched the water as it meandered its way down the creek. Declan broke the silence to say, "I bought this property just over a year ago."

Elle looked up at him in surprise. "You did?"

He nodded. "Just over fifteen acres of these woods. I was thinking about how this place was the beginning of everything. Eventually, I started dreaming about building a cabin here. A place to get away."

"One with indoor plumbing?"

He chuckled. "One with indoor plumbing. And electricity and a fridge. Maybe even turn it into a place where I can host events like a science camp. This place changed my life. I want others to experience it too."

Elle looked out at the woods before turning back to Declan. "Will you ever tell the world about growing up here?"

"Like in my videos?" He shook his head and used the toe of his shoe to move some of the dead leaves around by his feet. "That's not really the subject of them."

She tried to guess what lay behind the hesitation. "You don't have to share the entire story—just the parts you're comfortable with. But you never need to feel ashamed about growing up here. Not only is this place fuel for the imagination, but you could inspire other kids who are struggling with their own obstacles."

He had a smile on his face and a lightness in his eyes that hadn't been there moments before.

She tapped her fingers on his chest, right over his heart. "And if you've had thoughts of this being a location for a science camp, I'm willing to bet that you've had thoughts about sharing some of your story before."

He pulled his head back in surprise. "Huh. I hadn't even realized that." He paused. "Maybe I can share." Then he said "Huh" again. "Maybe I actually *want* to share."

Elle could tell the idea had grabbed hold of him pretty strongly. By the way the smile continued to spread across his face, carrying a sense of wonder with it, she could also tell that whatever ideas now ran through his head about how he would share felt freeing to him. Like he was finally letting go of a secret that he hadn't realized had been holding him down.

Smiling so wide that his dimples were on full display, he wrapped his arms around her and spun her in a circle, almost like he wanted to share the feeling of freedom with her. She soaked it in. She wanted to feel all of it with him.

After he set her back on her feet, he said, "So what do you think of this place? Do you think we can turn it into something even greater than it is?"

She didn't miss his use of the word *we*. "I think that together, we can do all kinds of great things." She gave him a kiss. "Maybe we can even use it as a venue for an ambassador retreat. Or a team retreat."

He pulled back and gazed at her with a face full of wonder. She decided it was one of her favorite looks on him. "I love you, Elle Markle."

"And I love you, Declan Davenport."

"You're right," he said and kissed her again. "We are going to do great things together."

Epilogue

EVERETT

Everett loaded the final case of water onto the cart. The last two student ambassadors pushed it through the Welcome Center lobby and headed toward the quad where they'd join the other forty-eight ambassadors getting LBSU's (hopefully) future students checked in. Whenever he and his coworkers spent a Saturday at work, it was for an event, so there was usually an excitement that ran through them. Today, though, was excitement on steroids.

His boss, Tess, strode into the room. Of everyone on their team, she was usually the most restrained. But today she looked more excited than he'd ever seen her. "I can't believe how many students are already out there!" She motioned to Elle and Declan, who were loading the last of the LBSU giveaway swag into a tote. "Who knew that you two dating would bring this many prospective students to an event?"

Elle cleared her throat. "Not *dating*—we're engaged."

Summer gasped, dropped her stack of LBSU t-shirts onto the counter, and said, "You made it official?" She hurried over to inspect the ring on Elle's outstretched hand.

"We did." Elle looked at Declan and the two of them smiled at each other like the lovesick fools they were. And to be honest, Everett was a bit jealous of them.

Everett gave Declan a hug, clapping him on the back. "Congratulations, man. I'm so happy for you." Then he gave Elle a tight hug, lifting her feet off the ground. "You too. Congrats."

After Deja, Brock, and Tess all gave their congratulations, Deja said, "Well, now tell us the story already!"

"It happened last night," Elle said as she slipped her hand into Declan's. "That day when we had the interview and I first met Declan, his assistant ordered dinner for us from the most amazing restaurant—Bartolini's—and set it up all fancy on Declan's dining room table, like a date. Candlelight and everything."

Declan chuckled as he rubbed his forehead. "Yeah, that wasn't awkward at all. But for as awkward as a date-like setting was for a professional interview, I knew right then I wanted to take her to Bartolini's for real someday."

Elle looked at Declan in surprise. "You knew *that night*?"

He smiled and leaned over to whisper something in Elle's ear that made her grin and blush. That made Everett chuckle.

Elle cleared her throat. "Anyway, we ordered the same Tuscan chicken we had that night, with the same chocolate vanilla berry panna cotta tart for dessert.

"Oh, that sounds divine," Deja said.

"Trust me, it was," Elle said. "The next time you're in Sioux Falls, you should definitely stop and get some."

Declan smirked. "Fair warning, though—it acts like a truth serum."

Everett's eyebrow raised.

"Which worked out perfectly," Elle said, "because then we went to Falls Park. We walked around and enjoyed the falls for a while, telling each other all the reasons why we fell in love. Then Declan said he had arranged for us to go up to the viewing tower just after they closed, so we were there all by ourselves. The view of the falls at night with all the lights shining on them was *incredible*."

"I mostly had my eyes on Elle. My view was pretty incredible too."

Elle's smile widened. Then she said, "My view when Declan got down on one knee was even better."

And then everyone said *Aww* at the same time and Elle and Declan were both grinning at each other like they were disgustingly in love and didn't care that everyone knew it.

"I am just thrilled for you both," Tess said. "And not only because today we have tripled our previous record for the number of prospective students attending a True Aquamoose Days event."

"Well," Everett said, "when you promise teens they can be in a video that's going up on Declan Davenport's Instagram and TikTok accounts, that tends to attract the masses."

"Seriously, Declan," Tess said, "We really appreciate all of this. I have a feeling we won't be struggling to get our enrollment numbers this year."

"I am glad I can help. I owe a lot to this school." Declan looked at Elle with the most smitten look on his face. "And I owe a lot to the Welcome Center, specifically."

Elle smiled back with her own smitten expression and kissed Declan.

They all turned to look as Pavani and her husband, Zane, walked into the offices pushing a baby stroller. Everett grinned at them. "Does this mean you're ready to come back to work?"

Pavani shook her head, chuckling. "Nope, not for a

few more weeks, so don't get yourself too ready to hand the tour scheduling back to me. I just didn't want to miss this event."

Almost as if pulled by an invisible force, Everett found himself at the baby stroller, looking in at baby Ajay's cute little face and reaching out to let Ajay's cute little hand wrap around his finger. "Oh, look at you, champ." He made a few faces at the tyke and some baby babbling sounds that he should probably be embarrassed that all his coworkers heard him say.

But he couldn't help it. The little guy was just so... adorable. He looked up at Pavani and Zane. "Can I hold him?"

"Of course," Pavani said. She moved the baby's blanket to the side, unbuckled him, slid her hands underneath to pick him up, and placed him in Everett's arms.

The little dude fit in one arm, no problem. Which left Everett's other hand free to offer a finger for Ajay to grab hold of again. "This little man is growing like a weed! How old is he now?"

"Six weeks," Zane said. "Yesterday was his original due date."

"Well, Happy sorta Birthday yesterday, Ajay." The little guy's face looked so sweet and peaceful. Then he scrunched it up and wiggled, stretching his arms and torso, and suddenly that face looked more like a miniature version of an old man's. Everett could swear it made him happy right to his core.

Not taking his eyes off the baby, he asked, "Are you two just loving this?"

"Every minute of it," Pavani said.

He shook his head. "I wish I could get a little one of my own." He smiled down at the kid. "You know, without the 'find a wife first' part."

"You'll find her," Summer said.

He looked up from the baby for the first time. "I don't know. I've been dating for a long time and I have yet to find her."

Brock clapped him on the back. "Well, if you'd stop dating girls who are completely wrong for you, that might help."

"Speaking of which," Elle said, "are you and Madelyn still dating?"

Ajay's squirming and face-scrunching turned into some serious grunts from the kiddo, and Everett felt the rumbling of a diaper being filled.

"I think that's my cue to relieve you," Zane said as he reached out and took the baby from Everett's arm.

Everett missed holding the kid pretty much instantly. He stuck his hands in his pockets. "No. We broke up two days ago."

"I figured as much," Brock said. "I mean, the woman went by the nickname *Mad*, after all."

"Ha ha. You're so funny."

Declan clapped him on the back too. "Don't you worry, Mr. Sunshine. We all have faith you'll find the right one."

"Come on," Tess said. "We better go corral the masses and get this party started."

Everett had heard how many students had signed up and knew that many were bringing a parent or guardian too. The crowd would be three times bigger than that one record-breaking event a couple of years ago. But it still shocked him to see the mass of people gathered on the quad.

His team had worked together to get the student ambassadors trained for this event specifically, and they were all at their assigned spots, doing exactly what they were supposed to be doing. So Summer, Elle, and Declan went to the front of the crowd to take their places on the portable stage. He, Tess, Brock, and Deja took their places at the edges of the crowd where they would use their phones to shoot footage from different angles. Declan's media manager, Jen, was already on the stage, getting cameras and audio ready for the filming.

Summer stepped up to the mike, welcomed everyone, and gave a quick rundown of the schedule before introducing Declan. She handed the mike off to him.

Once the crowd stopped cheering, Declan said, "I

want to tell you a story about the first time I met Elle, here, who works in the Welcome Center. If you come back for another tour or to find out more about the school, she'll help you with that.

"How many of you read the article in last month's *Aquamoose Rising* about me?"

Most of the crowd responded with shouts or cheers. The guy had a seriously deep voice, and this crowd was eating it up.

"Oh, wow," Declan said. "That's... a lot of you. Well, the first time I met Elle was when she showed up at my house for that interview. Before that point, I'd had zero interest in dating and even less interest in getting personal with the interviewer. But then Elle walked into the room where I film my YouTube videos. From that very first *glance*..." Declan paused for a moment as rumblings went through the crowd at hearing the word, "I knew my life was about to be forever changed."

Hearing Declan talk about Elle made Everett start thinking about how to find "the one." He was tired of dating women that he knew from the very first date weren't a good fit yet continuing to date them anyway.

"Okay," Declan said, "by your reaction when I said the word *glance*, I can tell that some of you have already figured out what we're going to do. This trend is called *Your Glance Makes My Heart Jump*. Now, it's usually done with one or two people. Maybe a handful. We are going to try it with over one thousand." The crowd cheered, definitely excited. "This is my social media manager, Jen, and she'll explain what we're going to do."

Everett watched the crowd of hundreds of thrilled high school students and their parents with a smile on his face. He had the best job ever.

Declan handed the mike to Jen and she began, "The song is *Jump for You* and has a repeating eight beats. For the first three beats, glance at the person to your left. Then glance at the person to your right for three beats. The beat drops on the seventh beat. When it does, you crouch down like this, then you immediately jump up. High as you can. Put your arms in the air when you do, if you'd like. Then you repeat. Got it? Great! Let's get the music started!"

Everett started the video recording on his phone and began filming the crowd, moving along the outside so he could get as many students in the frame as he could. It was pretty cool to see so many people all doing the same thing simultaneously and jumping into the air together. Pretty epic, actually.

While looking through the small screen on his phone, his attention landed on a woman who made him look up to find her in the crowd. She wasn't old enough to be a parent, but she was older than the bulk of the students. His job in the Welcome Center included working with non-traditional students—the ones who *weren't* freshly out of high school—so he could easily recognize one when he saw her.

And this one was beautiful. She had blonde hair that fell in shiny curls and wore a brilliant smile that was so genuine, he swore he could feel its warmth even as far away as he was. He was immediately captivated. He had to talk to her—find out more about her.

The crowd shifted just then and he lost sight of the woman. He kept moving along the edge of the crowd, catching glimpses of her now and then between the bodies blocking his view. Every once in a while, he'd get a good view of her for several beats.

As the last notes of the song played, Everett let his finger hover over his phone's "stop recording" button. He wanted to make a beeline for her and at least ask her name before the crowd began the next activity.

But when he stopped recording and looked up again, he couldn't find her. He made his way along the edge to where he'd last seen her as Summer stepped back up to the microphone, thanked everyone, and told them when the video would be posted on Declan's social media. Soon everyone took a seat on the grass and the concrete risers surrounding the trees.

With everyone seated, Everett hoped it would be easier for him to spot the woman. For some reason, he just had to find her. He scanned the sea of people with growing desperation before feeling his hope drain away.

No matter how carefully he looked, he couldn't see that blonde hair or brilliant smile anywhere.

Look for Everett and Cora's story in *It Started with a Dream*. Sign up for Meg's newsletter at megeaston.com so you won't miss its release announcement!

USA Today Bestselling Author
MEG EASTON
It Started
with a Dream

More small-town romance from Meg Easton

Coming Home to the Top of Main Street

Second Chance on the Corner of Main Street

Christmas at the End of Main Street

More than Friends in the Middle of Main Street

Love Again at the Heart of Main Street

More than Enemies on the Bridge of Main Street

More small-town romance from Meg Easton

Listen to the audiobooks on YouTube

Meg Easton is the *USA Today* bestselling author of contemporary romances and romantic comedies with fun, memorable, swoon-worthy characters, and settings you'll want to pack up and move to. She lives at the foot of a mountain with her name on it (or at least one letter of her name) in Utah. She loves gardening, bike riding, baking, swimming before the sun rises, and spending time with her husband and three kids.

She can be found online at www.megeaston.com

Sign up to receive her newsletter and stay up to date with new releases, get exclusive bonus content, and more.

If you liked this book please leave a review. Your review can help other readers find books they might fall in love with.

youtube.com/@megeastonauthor
bookbub.com/authors/meg-easton
instagram.com/megeaston_author
facebook.com/MegEastonBooks
tiktok.com/@megeaston_author